QUANTUM SPACEWALKER SERIES, BOOK 3

QUANTUM SPACEWALKER

QUINN'S QUEST

GRACE S. GROSE

OTHER BOOKS BY GRACE S. GROSE

Quantum Spacewalker Series

Quantum Spacewalker: Jarl's Journey

Quantum Spacewalker: Aneera's Assignment

Published by Author Academy Elite
PO Box 43, Powell, OH 43035
www.AuthorAcademyElite.com

Identifiers:
Paperback ISBN: 979-8-88583-108-6
Hardcover ISBN: 979-8-88583-109-3
Ebook ISBN: 979-8-88583-110-9

Available in paperback, hardback, e-book, and audiobook.

Library of Congress Control Number:
2022915532

For the One who holds Eternity

and

*For my mom, Marilyn Stokes, who has been
steadfastly encouraging and
supportive throughout this journey*

TABLE OF CONTENTS

Part 2: Adventure Finding

Part 3: Adventure Living

        Check out Quantum Spacewalker: Jarl's Journey
        Check out Quantum Spacewalker: Aneera's Assignment

PROLOGUE

Light beckoned me from the open door, penetrating the darkness encompassing me. I rushed—or was pulled—toward it.

When I reached the doorway, I hesitated.

What exactly will I find in there?

My indecision became like an ant crawling along my hairline. It was soon ticklishly unbearable.

I took a deep breath, raised my right foot, and half-lunged into the light.

The room was round, no bigger than the kitchen at Granny's farm in Wales. Pearly white light undulated on the surface of the walls. As soon as I stepped across the threshold into the room, the door snapped shut, melding seamlessly into the pearly walls.

A podium that came up to the middle of my chest stood in the exact center of the room. It sparkled like it was cut from a diamond, although I couldn't imagine one diamond large enough to chisel out this entire podium.

A book sat on the podium, opened to the last few pages. I walked up to it. The open book had names in it. Hundreds of names were written in a perfectly legible hand over the two pages I could see. My eyes ran over the columns, stopping at a name that lit up in gold and floated up in front of my eyes.

"Quinn Edward Evans."

My name?

I reached out to touch the book. As soon as my finger caressed the page where my name was highlighted, the book exploded into innumerable golden shards. They pierced me like fiery shrapnel.

I glanced down at my torso, expecting to see blood leaking from all the holes poked in my flesh. Instead, I saw light glowing from the wounds where I had been punctured.

The pieces of the book still floating in the air turned needle-sharp ends in my direction, like I was their homing beacon.

Fear arose in me, but it was shattered by the pain of millions of fine golden needles penetrating my body.

The last thing I heard was my own voice screaming.

PART 1
ADVENTURE LACKING

CHAPTER 1

My name is Quinn. On the last, best day of my childhood, my dad caught me in a hug and told me not to worry—he and my mum would be back in three days to pick up my sister and me from Aunt Jenny's. The sun still shone brightly that day. I remember the sky was endless blue.

The darkness came the next day, and never really left until the day he walked into my life.

How he arrived is still a mystery to me. I had walked to the stream at the edge of Granny's pasture. I didn't want anyone to see me cry. Eighteen-year-old boys can be proud like that.

I was leaving for London the next day—leaving my Granny's farm in Wales where I had lived the last ten years after my parents were killed in the car wreck that ended my childhood.

Starting a new job far from home might have been the right thing to do, but I had never been so scared in my entire life.

Quinn means "wise counsel" or "intelligent." I certainly didn't feel either wise or intelligent at this moment. Instead, those things were what I needed.

"Dad, I miss you so much. I wish you were here," I whispered into the wind, tears still flowing from my eyes.

A rustle behind me told me I wasn't alone. I spun to see a middle-aged man with a shepherd's staff walk into my little clearing. He was greying at the temples and had a lean, powerful build. His eyes arrested me. They were thunder-cloud grey with hints of lightning.

I didn't recognize him, and I thought I knew all the farmers and shepherds in the area. I was embarrassed to be caught with my blotchy, red, tear-stained face.

"Ho there, lad," the Shepherd said. "Are you all right?"

Normally, I wouldn't spill my troubles out to a complete stranger. But this wasn't a normal day.

"No, I'm not all right." I swiped a sleeve over my face. "I'm supposed to be a man. I'm supposed to be *brave* when I step into a completely unknown situation tomorrow." I sucked in a shuddering breath, fighting fresh tears. "I'm not brave. I don't want to leave my granny and sister to go work in London. Except they need the money I'll be sending in order to survive." I gulped, trying to force the lump in my throat down.

I wish I had someone to hug me and tell me this will work out. That I will make a go of this new life.

No sooner had I thought this than the Shepherd dropped his staff and pulled me into a hug.

The surprise stopped my tears. In a few moments, comfort and peace melted into my bones. Strength took root in me and began to blossom.

When the Shepherd stepped back, he held me by the shoulders and said, "Quinn, you are braver than you think. You won't be alone in London. The best lies ahead of you."

Watching the shifting light in his thundercloud eyes mesmerized me. He sounded confident.

"Who are you? How do you know?" This encounter was unlike any I had ever had.

He smiled. "I'm only a shepherd in search of a lost sheep. Keep your hope in the guidance of the greatest Shepherd of all. You won't go astray." He picked up his staff and walked out of the clearing.

I stood quietly for a few minutes. Then, a thought occurred to me. I ran after the man.

"Hey! Hey, Shepherd. How did you know my name?"

But he was gone.

CHAPTER 2

"You're not from around here, boy," the barrel-chested beast of a man said to me.

The extension cord hung loosely in my hand. My welding visor was pushed up, and I was heading over to my work area to plug in my new lamp.

The man moved to block my path. I had seen him with two other cronies when I began work at the machine shop three weeks ago, but I didn't have any dealings with him.

Until now.

His two henchmen moved to his left and right side. The three of them effectively cut off any way around them.

Uh oh. This could get ugly.

One of the cronies said, "Your accent gives you away, Welsh boy. We don't like your kind around here."

Oh brother. The bullies have left the schoolyard and moved uptown.

I slowly tied a knot in my extension cord, turning it into a thick, yellow-wire lasso, all the while keeping an eye on the men. I planted my left leg about three feet behind my right and loosened my grip on the rest of the cord.

The three men watched me curiously but quickly got

bored. I anticipated the leader when he lunged toward me.

I whipped the lasso over his head and, with a jerk, plowed him into the man on his right side. They crashed to the floor.

The third man started toward me. I pulled the cord taut as he tried to step over it, tripping him.

When he hit the floor, I moved. Using the rest of the extension cord, I quickly trussed up the men's arms and legs, leaving them in a cursing, thrashing pile on the floor.

"You boys are no match for Granny's big hog on the farm. That hog was tricky...." Before I could continue, the shop floor manager walked up.

"Briggs," he said to the large man on the ground. "I've been watching you for a while now. You and your toadies are the reason two of our best workers recently quit. The three of you, get to my office. Now."

He turned to me. "Evans, I'll talk to you later." He started toward his office, but stopped abruptly. "You'll probably have to untie them," he said, pointing at the man-pile. "I'll wait."

I released the men, careful not to meet their angry eyes. They grunted while they made their way to their feet. One of the henchmen had the beginnings of a black eye where Briggs had rammed his elbow into him as he fell.

"Come with me, men." The manager led the way as the three tormentors trudged behind him.

I wound up the extension cord and headed to my work station.

My work circumstances changed in the blink of an eye. Or, in this case, with the flick of an electrical extension cord lasso.

Briggs and his two fellow bullies were fired. That same day, I was promoted to shop floor manager's apprentice.

I shared the good news with Granny and Tessa during my nightly phone call.

"But you're all right, dear?" Granny's concerned voice made me smile.

"More than all right." I yawned and stretched before continuing. "I got a two pound an hour raise, which will help our situation. You can get the furnace fixed and be toasty warm this winter. That's my immediate goal."

"You're so good to us." Granny's appreciation was evident.

"But we miss you like crazy," Tessa added. I could picture her sitting in her usual perch on the couch near the phone extension in the living room. She probably had the phone cord intertwined in her fingers.

"I miss you, too." Homesickness hit me hard. "On a positive note, I found a small home church to start attending. One of the older ladies there has already taken me under her wing. She thinks I'm too skinny."

Granny's laugh vibrated across the phone wires. "You are too skinny, my boy. Let her help fatten you up a little."

"Well… her chocolate chip cookies are pretty tasty." My mouth watered, thinking about the plateful of cookies waiting for me in the kitchen. "In fact, I think I'll have a couple now. Adults can eat dessert before dinner, right?"

"You're *barely* an adult." Tessa loved to tease me.

"Right back at you, *baby* sister." I snorted back a laugh.

"Only by two whole minutes," Tessa shot back.

"Children, cease and desist!" Granny sighed, but I heard the amusement in her voice. "It's high time we all had our dinner. Goodnight, my sweet boy."

I smiled wistfully. "Goodnight, my two favorite ladies."

I hung up the phone and headed for the cookies.

CHAPTER 3

I laid the pastel chalks by my sketch pad, which sat next to the empty cookie plate. The Shepherd I had met a few weeks ago had been taking shape on the paper before me.

Searching my memory, I was satisfied that I had gotten his hair and facial features correct. What was bothering me were his eyes. I couldn't quite capture the right shade of grey, nor could I find a way to incorporate the streaks of light I had seen in his pupils.

Every time I reviewed our meeting in Granny's pasture, it seemed more unusual. I couldn't deny, however, the strength and hope that were alive and growing in me from that encounter.

I tossed a silent prayer toward heaven, asking for illumination.

—⁂—

3:00 a.m. I couldn't sleep. Again.

The bed in my tiny, rented London flat was comfortable enough, but my mind was whirring away. I couldn't relax.

A cup of tea would be just the ticket.

I got up, slid into my slippers, and then meandered to the kitchen. The electric kettle began sputtering away while I prepared my tea strainer and loose-leaf tea.

After I had stirred the sugar and milk into my tea, I went to sit at the table and review the Shepherd's picture.

Startled by what I saw, I set my mug down too hard, sloshing tea over the rim. I moved my sketch pad to safety, then raced to get a towel to mop up the quickly spreading liquid.

When the mess was cleaned up, I checked out the Shepherd's picture again. There were words written on the bottom of the page. Words that hadn't been there when I went to bed.

What the heck?

Underneath the Shepherd were the words, "Remember who you are," written in a firm, masculine hand. The words were in the perfect shade of thundercloud grey that I had been trying to achieve for the Shepherd's eyes.

A chill crawled up my spine. Was there someone else in my flat? The main door had hinges that squeaked. Surely I would have heard anyone trying to get in.

I did a cursory inspection of the flat. Nothing was out of place.

When I returned to stare at the picture, I would have sworn that the Shepherd was laughing. I imagined I saw his eyes flash with humor. He seemed to be sharing a fatherly joke.

I had no reason to feel reassured, yet somehow I did. Smiling, I finished my tea, went back to bed, and immediately fell into a peaceful sleep.

—m—

Work was moving along nicely. My favorite projects involved laser metal-cutting machines. They were so precise they could get within a millionth of an inch on any pattern programmed into them. I had never been a huge technology fan, but the fun I had with these lasers started to change my mind.

As my skill grew to encompass these machines, the artistry that used to only show up in my sketches or attempts at sculpture flared to life. I began to train other machinists until we had a team of ten men who could program or cut any pattern given to them.

The shop floor manager noted my abilities in this area. The apprenticeship I was under shifted so that I became the "laser machine manager" of our team. Fortunately, our team was pulling in so much business for the company that this new title brought a hefty pay bump. This let me rent a nicer flat and save a little money while still funneling much of my pay to Granny and Tessa.

After a satisfying three years working in this job, I had put aside enough by my twenty-first birthday to buy a used motorbike. The years I had lived in London had transformed the city from an intimidating stranger into a familiar friend, but I longed to see more of the countryside. Having transportation would also open up the opportunity for me to be able to see Granny and Tessa more frequently.

Granny's age had crept up on her. She was vibrantly energetic into her early eighties, but had begun to slow down. Tessa was able to keep much of the farm going with occasional help from the neighbors, but it became obvious that she would have to cut back on the size of the gardens this year because Granny needed more time from her.

I wanted to spend my and Tessa's milestone twenty-first birthday back in Wales. After getting my motorbike license,

I practiced on some lightly-trafficked roads to build my confidence before I made the longer five-hour trip to our farm on Dinas Island.

I missed the rolling green of the sheep farms, and the fierce comradery among all of us there who worked hard to make a good life out of often difficult circumstances. It would be good to be home.

I planned to leave on Friday after work.

—⸎—

July was a good time for motorcycle travel. I was prepared for rain should it happen, but the weather forecast for this afternoon was sunny and pleasant.

I slid on my biker leathers and new jacket after work. I hoped I looked a little like James Dean. Or Granny's favorite—Elvis Presley in *Roustabout*. Grinning to myself at the thought, I shoved my clothes into one of the bike's saddlebags. I was itching to get on the road.

In the next few minutes, I headed out with only a slight squeal of tires. Worries flew off me the farther I got down the road until I thought I might float off the bike. It was good to feel so light.

Best purchase I've ever made.

The motorcycle ate up the miles and hours like a greedy puppy chomping and chewing through an enormous pile of food. It was grand, even though I had never attempted this long of a ride before. My hand pressing the throttle, as well as my backside, were getting a little sore.

I stopped at a service station an hour away from home to fuel up and get a bite to eat. Dusk was coming on fast, but the sunset was glorious. I took my fish and chips outside the station to watch while I ate.

A man was perched on a rock twenty feet away from my table. He was gazing at the sunset too. I noticed a shepherd's staff on the ground at his feet. Instantly, I knew it was my Shepherd. The one I had met in Granny's pasture.

When he eventually turned around in my direction, his grey eyes were ablaze with light. I couldn't tell if it was from the sunset's rays or something else. He was smiling as he said,

"Hello, Quinn."

CHAPTER 4

"Do you believe in time travel, Quinn?" the Shepherd asked.

"I've never thought about it." I crunched on a piece of my fish as I walked over to him. "Do you always begin conversations this way?"

Sunset rays flashed off the Shepherd's white teeth as he threw his head back and laughed.

I sat down on a rock not too far away and faced the Shepherd. "Now that you're here again, will you tell me who you are?"

"You know who I am. We've known each other since before the world was made." The Shepherd's pleasant expression gave no indication that he was, apparently, bonkers.

"And no, I'm not 'bonkers,' as you seem to currently be thinking," he added.

I stopped chewing and stared at him while I tried to process the fact that he had just read my mind. I choked down my half-chewed bite and asked, "Are *you* a time traveler?"

"I own time." His serene expression never changed.

How to respond to that?

"I'm afraid I don't understand." I was torn between my desire to know more and my desire to escape now while I still could.

"You will." The Shepherd fell silent as he resumed watching the final vestiges of the sunset.

We watched the sun disappear under the horizon. Twilight lingered. This was always my favorite time of day on the farm because it usually meant the chores were all completed and dinner awaited me.

Tonight, my fish and chips grew cold in my hands. I waited for the Shepherd to speak again. Eventually, he stood and picked up his staff, giving every indication that he was going to leave.

"So, that's it?" I tried to think of what to say to stall him. "You're not going to explain your comments any further?"

"You need to be getting home. You don't want them to worry about you." He walked over to me and put a hand on my shoulder. "Remember who you are, Quinn." With that, he walked around the corner of the petrol station and out of sight.

I sat on the rock as the night got darker. I didn't try to follow him. I was sure there wasn't any point and I suspected I would be running into him again sometime.

Mulling over his words, I finished my cold, formerly appetizing food. Didn't want to waste what I had paid good money for.

Fed and fueled up, I hit the highway again.

I was the only one on the road as I got closer to the farm. Not surprising. The farming community didn't keep late hours unless there was a party to be had.

Driving up the road to the house, I saw that the lights for the porch and kitchen were still on. I knew that I would be met with hugs and some sort of freshly baked treat. My heart lifted in anticipation.

Tessa met me at the door after I parked my bike and got my gear out of the saddlebags. She was smiling, but I saw worry lines around her eyes.

After a hug, she said, "Granny went to bed early. She said she would see you at breakfast."

I followed Tessa into the kitchen, where the aroma of recently baked brownies hung heavy in the air. Wasting no time, I set my things down and started in on the chocolaty bites, washing them down with cold, frothy milk.

When I had finished my third brownie, I asked Tessa, "How are you two doing? I can tell you're worried about something. Let's hear it."

Tessa sighed. "Granny's energy has been failing. She has been sleeping a lot for the last month." The corners of her mouth twitched, trying to hold back her emotion. "I have a feeling she might be leaving soon. She keeps talking about the 'home country.'"

I knew what that meant. The "home country" referenced heaven in our area of Wales.

"What can I do to help?" I covered Tessa's hand with my own, noticing how rough her hand had gotten from the extra work she had been doing.

She sniffled once but then drew on her resolve. I often marvelled at her strength.

"You're already doing what you can. Your generosity has made this old place the most comfortable it's ever been. I just don't want you to be surprised when you see how frail Granny has become."

I squeezed her hand as I nodded. We knew this time

was inevitable, but neither of us wanted it to come. Regardless, it wouldn't be put off forever.

"Maybe I should take a couple of weeks off work and help you out around here? I have holiday time accrued."

Tessa raised hopeful eyes to mine. "If you think you can swing it, we would both love for you to be here."

"It's decided, then." I raised my glass and polished off the milk. "I'll ask for time off on Monday morning."

CHAPTER 5

Granny sat outside in a chair in the late morning sun, watching as I completed the drip irrigation system in the garden closest to the house. When I was done, I walked over to her and sank down to sit on the warm earth beside her chair.

She reached over and tousled my hair affectionately, much as she had done ever since I was five years old.

"I'm proud of you, Quinn. You've become the kind of man I know your dad and mum hoped you would be." Her eyes grew distant, like she was peering into somewhere I couldn't see. "You should know...." She paused, silent for several moments before beginning again. "I suspect you *do* know that I'll be joining them soon."

My heart twisted painfully. Not trusting myself to speak, I nodded. In the week I had been home, it had been easy to see Granny's strength was nearly gone.

"Don't be sad for me, boy." She gave me a curiously carefree smile. "I'll be where I long to be. I'm glad for the time we've had together. Raising you and Tessa brought me more joy than I anticipated." She laughed softly. "I saw a bumper sticker a few years back that said, 'If I'd have known how much fun grandkids are, I would have had them first.'"

I laughed along with her.

"Not that you two didn't keep me on my toes." Her smile became wistful. "Still, I wouldn't have traded any of it. It's only a shame that you couldn't have known your grandfather better. He died far too young."

Thinking of my grandfather, who had died when I was three, brought an image of the Shepherd to mind.

"Granny, do you know of a new shepherd in the area who always carries a staff, has salt and pepper hair, and striking grey eyes?"

She turned to me sharply and stared, several emotions flitting across her face. She resumed looking forward again before saying, "Aye, I know him." A pause, and then she continued, "He's not new. He's much, much older than you might think and has been around these parts for ages."

"Can you tell me about him?" I searched her face, trying to draw out every clue I could find.

"Why don't you first tell me how the two of you met." Her keen eyes pierced mine.

My face flushed. Describing that meeting at the edge of her pasture would lay bare many of my eighteen-year-old insecurities. However, I didn't know if I'd have this opportunity again. So, I told her about meeting the Shepherd before going to London, and how I had been having a hard time leaving. I explained how he had helped, comforted, and even encouraged me.

I went on to describe the unusual writing on my sketch and how, when I had seen the Shepherd again recently on my trip home, he had said the same thing that was on my sketch—"Remember who you are."

"And that is exactly what you must do, my boy," Granny said, a hint of a twinkle in her eye.

"I know who I am," I protested. "We can trace our lineage back for hundreds of years on both sides of the family. Our bloodline has seen kings, leaders, warriors, murderers, a few statesmen, and many ordinary people. I'm born and bred a Welshman, and proud of it!"

"That you are." She smiled at my passionate outburst. "That you are. But, there is a great deal more to you than that. What you've described is your physical heritage. It's important. However, it isn't who you are at your core, in your essence."

"Who am I, then?" This conversation wasn't going as I had anticipated.

"That, my boy, is what you need to remember." Granny chuckled. "You'll discover who the Shepherd is in the process."

CHAPTER 6

"Nanobots?" I wondered why Trent had brought this up. "Why would we want to do anything with them?"

"It's the wave of the future." Trent made vigorous wave-like motions with his hand. "Or one of them anyway. The ones I'm talking about *eat* metal. In patterns. Which means… if this works, we won't have to spend so much time programming the laser cutters. This could triple our output."

"Or make us irrelevant." That wasn't a good thought.

"C'mon, Quinn. I don't see any downsides to this. Right now, that is." Trent was puncturing the air with his ballpoint pen, emphasizing his statement.

I regarded Trent with raised eyebrows. "I was recently reading about 'inhaled nanobots' that can carry digitized messages or pictures. They—whoever 'they' are—could make you a spy or something like that without you being aware. Cut me some slack if I find the whole field of nanotechnology a little disturbing. You telling me about nanobots that eat metal isn't helping."

"I never took you for someone stuck in the past." Trent huffed, then grinned. "I'll convert you to a technology lover yet."

"Now, be fair. I love *certain* types of technology. Lasers I can totally understand and embrace. Freaky little machine-eating-things, not so much." I grimaced.

Trent laughed out loud, then slapped my back. "Fine, then. Let's go cozy up to some lasers. We have a full roster of orders today."

—ɯ—

The beautiful, clean edges the laser cut on the metal insert I was working on gave me a sense of deep gratification. This was the last piece of our one thousand piece order. We had finished a day ahead of time. I knew that would earn us kudos with the boss.

Fingering the insert after it had cooled down, I couldn't imagine how a mini-machine could eat metal in such a clean way. I wasn't sure Trent knew what he was talking about.

I was being pulled toward new technology at a rate that was—figuratively—wearing the soles off my shoes as I dug my heels in to slow things down. So many people, like Trent, were rushing toward the latest advance. The line from *Jurassic Park*—"Just because you can do something doesn't mean you should"—had been on a loop in my brain for several months now.

Maybe I watched too many movies like *The Terminator* or *The Matrix*. I wasn't automatically of the opinion that all technology was good technology. In those movies, it eventually enslaved or killed you.

Although, I had to concede that I appreciated the technology that was making Granny's life easier. We had rented a hospital bed for her room at the farm. As feeble as Granny had become, she still loved playing with the buttons that made the bed go up and down. She had learned her limits when she nearly folded herself in half. She and Tessa had been laughing so hard that it took several minutes to unbend Granny and the bed. There was no lasting damage, and Granny chuckled about it for days afterward.

Hospital bed antics aside, I felt the acceleration of the world's knowledge and technology in the very fibers of my being. I didn't welcome it.

—ꝏ—

On Friday morning, I got the call I had been dreading.

"Come home, Quinn" Tessa tried to hide the tears in her voice. "Granny is leaving."

I raced to my flat, threw my things together, and headed home. It had been eight months since I took my vacation to help at the farm. Granny's decline had been more noticeable every time I had been home after that. She knew it, and we knew it. We made sure everything we wanted to say to each other was said.

March rain pelted my face and body. I was forced to drive much more slowly than I wanted to. At least it wasn't hailing. Our weather this time of year could be dismal.

Tessa met me on the porch after I had put my motorbike in the barn. We hugged for a long time. Her cheeks were wan, her eyes red-rimmed.

Siobhan, our neighbor, had been helping out with cooking and farm chores while Tessa tended to Granny. She opened the screen door and ushered us inside.

A steaming bowl of cawl[1] and fresh buns were waiting for me at the table. None of us spoke. Sorrow was heavy in

---

[1] Cawl – Welsh stew

the air.

"Do I have time to eat," I asked, splintering the silence, "or should I go see Granny right away?"

"She's sleeping right now." Tessa's voice was a wisp of what it normally was, and her shoulders were slumped.

"I'll take the food to Granny's room." I picked up the bowl of savory stew and several buttered buns before I went into the room.

Granny's chest continued to rise faintly as she lay in the bed. Her breathing was raspy.

After I set the food down on her bedside table, I took one of Granny's hands in mine. It was cool to the touch and almost birdlike in its fragility.

Leaning over, I whispered in her ear, "I'm here, Granny."

She didn't stir.

Tessa sat down a little ways away. I began to eat my stew. Strange how the food could taste so good while my emotions were such a mess.

"I knew this morning." Tessa's voice made me jump. "I just knew."

I nodded slightly as I slowly chewed. Seconds stretched into minutes.

I heard someone come into the room when I was down to my final few bites. I turned to see the Shepherd walk through the bedroom door. I was too surprised to say anything.

Tessa gazed in his direction, but didn't seem to see him.

I watched as he walked to the other side of Granny's bed. He reached out his hand and said, "Time to go, Auron."

He lifted his head and caught my eye. He winked, looked at Tessa, then said, "The two of you will be fine."

Granny gasped, then let her last breath out slowly. I saw her sit up, although her old, tired body still lay in the bed.

She smiled at us, blew Tessa and me a kiss, and took the Shepherd's hand.

CHAPTER 7

Tears ran down Tessa's face. Granny's body had a smile on her lips and a peaceful expression. I told Tessa what I had seen.

"You saw her leave? She went with this Shepherd you keep seeing?" Tessa blew her nose, then started mopping up her tears.

"Yes. She blew us a kiss when she left. She was positively girlish, like in the picture of her and Grandpa on their first date." I walked over to the dresser, picked up the picture I was referring to, and handed it to Tessa.

"This was one of her favorite photos." Fresh tears swamped Tessa. "I'm really happy for Granny." A few sobs interrupted her. "But I'm going to miss her so much. What am I supposed to do now? What are *we* going to do?"

I put an arm around Tessa's shoulders. "We get through the next few days. Don't think about anything beyond that."

We had a traditional wake. The coffin was set in the living room, with numerous pictures from Granny's life surrounding it.

Granny had been loved and respected in the community. Neighbors brought piles of food. A couple of friends directed traffic at the house and logistics for people coming by to pay their respects. I was glad others took care of these details.

Cassandra, from two farms over, played the telyn[2] in the background as people came and went. Her harp music was what Granny had loved best. The music stirred up such deep feelings, I had to leave for a while.

Escaping the house, I went to the barn. I sat on a hay bale, numb, listening to the gentle sounds of our cow a few stalls away.

I felt him before I saw him.

"You do keep popping up." I didn't turn my head to him.

"Auron mentioned that you probably suppressed the memory because it was around the time of your parents' deaths. I know you did, but it's been making its way back to the surface." This comment didn't seem to fit what was happening with Granny's death.

I finally glanced over at the Shepherd. His hair was neatly combed and he was wearing a tasteful suit, appropriate for the occasion.

"Are you an angel?" I didn't have the energy to play games tonight, nor did I care which memory he meant.

"No."

"You can't be who I think you might be." Suspicion had been growing in my mind. I twirled a piece of hay between my fingers, then lapsed into silence.

---

[2] Telyn – Welsh harp

"Why not?" I heard amusement in his voice.

"Because... because you wouldn't do things like this. Would you?" Nothing was making much sense to me right now.

"How do you know what lengths a father would go to for one of his children?" He paused just long enough for me to give him my full attention. "And you are my child, Quinn. One with an extremely important purpose. You're one of my Golden Ones."

I shook my head in despair. "I have no idea what you mean."

He placed a hand on my head. Peace flowed over me. "That will change soon enough. Remember that this is who you are. For now, know that you're loved. You and Tessa will make it through this. You have much awaiting you on the other side of this grief."

He squeezed my shoulder and left.

We buried Granny the next day. The drizzly weather and the sounds of weeping surrounding me put me into a funk. I imagined myself underwater, swimming in my pain, while the rest of normal life flowed unhindered overhead. Tessa's haggard expression, I suspected, was mirrored in my own face.

Granny loved God with an intensity that surpassed even her love for Tessa and me. She often spoke of her conversations with the Father, Jesus, and the Spirit. Her delight in the personalities of each member of the Godhead spurred me on. I wanted to know them the way she did.

I remembered walking into the kitchen one afternoon after school. Granny sat at the kitchen table, arms raised in worship, tears of joy flowing from her closed eyes. Right then, a sun ray burst through the clouds, came through the kitchen window, and landed on Granny's face.

The sunlight sparkled brilliantly off her face and clothing. I noticed that the table and floor were also sparkling.

What's going on here?

Quietly, trying not to break the moment, I inched forward to see what was causing all this sparkling. The closer I got to Granny, I could see fine golden flakes covering her hair, skin, clothes, and the surrounding furniture. It gave the impression of a golden glitter explosion.

I stared, working to process what I was seeing.

Granny opened her eyes, smiled at me, and then nodded at someone sitting at the kitchen table with her. A someone I couldn't see.

She made no mention of it as she said, "I baked a fresh apple cake. Go help yourself to a slice, and bring me one, too."

When I brought the cake over, along with two cups of tea, I saw Granny clearing the golden flakes from the table and pushing them into a pile.

"Guess I'll put these with the other ones." She got up and went into her bedroom. She came back with a small, square box. Opening it, she swept the small mound of golden dust into it with her hand. I noticed that the box was almost three-quarters full.

"Does this happen often?" I pointed at the flakes still on her clothing and the floor.

"Often enough. It usually occurs when I'm having a chat with the Father." She bent her head to take a sip of tea, then laughed when gold dust from her hair fell into her teacup.

"Why have we never noticed it before?" I stared at the golden flakes scattered around Granny's chair on the floor.

She chuckled. "It gets cleaned up before you come in the house."

"Is it real gold?" My thoughts sprang to our empty bank account. I was beginning to learn about our woeful financial situation.

"I'm not sure. I've never checked." She glanced over at me with a thoughtful expression. "You can check when I'm gone. For now, it's a sweet reminder to me of my times in prayer."

Was this the memory the Shepherd said I had suppressed? Doesn't seem right, though. It happened several years after my parents died.

However, now I was curious. Where was Granny's gold dust box? I wanted to get it checked out immediately.

This could be the answer to keeping the farm going. Or give us options for a different life.

I got up and exited the barn. My steps quickened as I walked back to the farmhouse.

CHAPTER 8

Tessa found me rummaging through Granny's nightstand.

"Everyone has taken off until dinner later tonight. What are you trying to find?" She surveyed all the items I had placed on the bed from the nightstand drawer.

"Granny's gold dust box."

Tessa looked at me like I was loopy.

"You didn't know about her gold dust box?" I asked as I pulled out a nail clipper set and set it on the bed.

Tessa shook her head.

"Did you ever see Granny appear… shiny?" I could see Tessa mull the question over.

"I suppose," she said. "There were a couple of times she seemed to be glowing or something after she had been praying."

"But you didn't see gold dust?" Granny's nightstand drawer was now emptied out.

No little square box.

"A few times I saw little glittery things on the bed or a chair. There was never a lot of it. I assumed it was glitter from those cards Siobhan's kids used to make for Granny." Tessa picked up a packet of cards tied with a red ribbon off the bed. "Here they are. Do you remember them? See, there's still glitter all over them."

"Yes, but that is green, pink, and purple glitter. What I'm talking about is only gold colored." I cast my eyes around the room, wondering where Granny would hide her box. "Didn't Granny have a place she stashed her journals?"

"I think they're at the back of her wardrobe." Tessa pointed to the large wooden closet standing against the far wall.

I walked over and opened the doors. Seeing all of Granny's clothes and catching a whiff of the vanilla-scented sachets she kept with them brought a fresh wave of grief. I tumbled under the waves for a few moments before I remembered what I was after.

Carefully moving the clothes aside, I checked the floor at the back of the wardrobe. An old wooden crate on the right side held neatly stacked books. I recognized the leather pattern from one of Granny's most recent journals on top.

"Found the journals." I pulled the crate forward, then set it on the floor under the ceiling light where we could go through it.

"I've never explored her journal box before." Tessa knelt beside the box and picked up the journal on top. She lovingly caressed it.

We unpacked sixty years' worth of journals. No luck.

I glanced back into the wardrobe and noticed the edge of a small box tucked into the back corner behind where the journal box had been.

"This is it!" I grabbed it and held the little square box up in triumph. It was heavy for its size. I sat beside Tessa on the floor.

"Well, open it then." Tessa's curiosity shone in her eyes. "How did you know about this box anyway?"

I slowly worked the snug lid off the box. It was full of gold flecks and flakes. Granny must have done plenty of praying since the time I found her in the kitchen after school.

Tessa touched the dust with her fingertip. Bits of gold stuck to her skin. She moved her finger under the light, watching the gold flecks sparkle.

"Do you recall that place in Swansea that bought Mum and Dad's wedding rings when we needed to sell them?" That had been a hard day.

Tessa frowned at me, troubled. It was still a sore spot that we had needed to sell our parents' rings in order to pay bills.

"We should go there tomorrow and get this dust appraised. It's not quite two hours one way." I would be happy to have the question about the gold dust settled by an expert.

"So, are you going to tell me how you knew about this box or not?" My lovely dark-haired sister, with her furrowed brow and quizzical expression, reminded me strongly of our mother right now. They both liked to get to the bottom of any mystery that presented itself.

I explained what I had seen when I walked in on Granny praying a few years ago.

"If this *is* actual gold," Tessa said, "then it's heavenly gold. Do we have any business trying to sell it?"

"It might be our only legacy, other than the farm. And the farm is in rough shape. If this dust is worth something, we might be able to keep the farm. If you want to keep it, that is. Granny's small pension will be gone now that she has passed away, and we never did sell enough produce, sheep, and wool to pay all our expenses here." It was a longer speech than I had intended to make, but Tessa got the point.

Her eyes welled up. "I can't bear the thought of leaving the farm right now. It's too soon. All my memories are here. I might be willing to let it go later, but not yet."

"Then come with me to Swansea tomorrow." I got up from the floor, holding the little box in my hands.

Tessa gave a quick nod and began putting the journals back in the crate.

—⟋⟍—

Mr. Penoyre met us as we entered his Coins & Precious Metals shop. His kindly gaze held recognition as we greeted him.

"Ah, the Evans twins. What brings you to my humble establishment?" He smiled as he shook my hand.

Humble didn't seem to be the proper description for his immaculate store, full of displays that glittered with precious metals, jewelry, and coins.

"Hello, sir." I waded through a brief flashback from our previous visit when I was a teenager. "We have something we'd like you to take a look at." I handed him a small baggie of the gold flakes.

He held the bag up to the light and shook it gently, watching the flakes move and settle.

"Hmm…." Mr. Penoyre was intrigued. Tessa and I followed him as he moved to a back desk with a microscope and other appraisal tools on it.

Mr. Penoyre shook a few flakes into his hand and placed them inside a black box-like machine that had a screen on the front of it attached to a keyboard.

"What is that?" Tessa pointed to the machine.

"It's an X-RF machine." He closed the door and hit a switch. "This is an X-ray process for precious metals. The sample has X-rays applied to it, then it will emit an energy level light specific to the sample's atomic structure. It is highly accurate and will not destroy your sample, as other methods would."

We heard a quiet whirring as the machine began working. Mr. Penoyre attended to the display. His eyes widened. He raised his head to us in surprise.

"Where did you get this?" His sharp tone sliced through the quiet shop.

We returned his shocked gaze silently.

He shut off the machine, opened the lid, and poured the rest of the baggie's contents onto the area used to test the metal. He started the machine again.

I observed the X-RF's display. Its gold purity level was maxed out.

Mr. Penoyre turned off the machine, then retrieved our sample and put it back in the baggie. He hit a few keys to print out the results.

He handed the page with his findings to us. The column for gold purity was at one hundred percent. No other metals were present in the report.

"It's pure gold." He wiped the slight sheen of sweat off his forehead with a handkerchief pulled from his jacket's breast pocket. "Gold this pure doesn't exist on this planet."

CHAPTER 9

"You won't tell me where you got this?" Mr. Penoyre glanced back and forth between Tessa and me.

"We don't think you'd believe us." I put the sample back in my coat pocket.

Mr. Penoyre had treated us kindly during the emotional time when we sold our parents' wedding rings. I was sure he had been more than generous with us.

"You might be surprised at what I would believe." He walked over to the shop door and flipped the "Open" sign to "Closed." After he locked the door, he motioned to us. "Come back here. I'll make us tea and you can explain the source of your gold to me."

Tessa and I followed him a trifle nervously. We seated ourselves in his tiny kitchen at the far back of the shop. Mr. Penoyre put the electric kettle on and pulled out a tin of shortbread.

"My weakness." He bit into a shortbread cookie and sighed happily. When our tea had been served and we had made our way through half the tin of shortbread, he said, "All right, out with your story."

I moved gingerly into the tale. "Our granny—you knew

her, I believe—spent a lot of time in prayer."

Mr. Penoyre inclined his head in understanding.

"I have no explanation for this, but occasionally during praying and worshipping God, these golden flakes would appear." I cleared my throat, then took a sip of tea.

The jeweler started chuckling, and then he laughed loudly. "I knew it! Your granny Auron was one of the Golden Ones."

Time seemed to stop for a moment. I thought of what the Shepherd had recently said to me.

How does this man know about the Golden Ones?

"Would you explain what you mean by 'Golden Ones'?" My heart sped up, waiting for his reply.

"I've only met two others in my forty years of being in this business. They came in with a small handful of the same kind of gold flakes you have. We didn't have such a sophisticated testing machine then. I used the older 'fire assay' testing process, which is more time-intensive and involves melting the sample down. The results, as closely as possible to tell, were identical to yours."

"Did their gold flakes appear the same way?" Tessa held a half-eaten cookie in her hand, listening in rapt fascination.

"I could only get one of them to tell me how the flakes appeared. It was similar to your story. After I tested his sample, I never saw him again." Mr. Penoyre shrugged. "I was always curious about those situations. And now, here you are."

"Was there any other reason you referred to the other two people as 'Golden Ones'?" I wanted to know if he understood more than he was saying.

"No reason. The one fellow described being covered in golden flakes or dust, like your Granny."

On to the business at hand.

"We also have a more practical reason for being here." I was embarrassed to reveal our need for funds yet again.

The jeweler quickly grasped the situation.

"Gold this pure is almost impossible to put a price on." He wiped crumbs from his jacket, pausing to give me a moment. "However, if you choose to sell what you have, I can assure you an excellent price for it."

"Okay." I stood up to go get the box out of our rickety old pickup outside. "Is it all right if I go and get the rest of the gold so that you can give us a quote?"

"Certainly." Mr. Penoyre nodded. "Bring it on in." He smiled as I walked out to retrieve our future, blessing God and Granny as I went.

"Well, that ought to keep us going for quite a while." Tessa leaned back on the truck seat as we began our journey home after depositing our newly acquired funds in the bank.

"Yes, it should." I was deep in thought.

Tessa stared at me. I felt her eyes on me, willing me to tell her what I was thinking. That's the thing with twins—it's hard to keep any secrets.

"My flat in London is too small to have you come stay with me." I wasn't sure how to say this. Her "uh-huh" encouraged me to keep going. "Do you want me to check into getting a larger place? Or do you want to stay at the farm for the present, like you said yesterday?"

She took several minutes to mull the questions over.

"I need to tend to business at the farm. There are so many details that have to be dealt with now. I'll keep you up to date...." She trailed off, tears flowing again.

"You can hire Timmy to help you. I'm sure Dane would

help out as well." I was thinking of other people who could help when Tessa gurgled out a disgusted sound.

"Oh, these tears!" She swiped at them with her sleeve.

"There are tissues in the glove box."

"Thanks." She opened the glove box and grabbed a tissue packet. "Yes, I'm sure Dane would love to help, but I don't know if I want to encourage him."

"He's a pretty good guy." Dane wasn't the sharpest tool in the shed, but he had a good heart and was a hard worker. And he had been after Tessa to marry him since she was sixteen.

"That's the problem." Tessa sniffled into a tissue. "He is a good guy. Too good, and rather boring. I don't think he's the one for me."

I glanced at her with a grin. "You want a bad boy, do you?"

She laughed wetly, then started coughing from trying to speak, cry and breathe at the same time. "No," she finally said. "Just someone with a sense of fun who doesn't mind an adventure now and then. And who loves Jesus."

"Oh, he should be easy to find. There are dozens of *those* guys around." I was going to say more, but Tessa punched my shoulder. "Ow!"

"You worry about your own love life, Mr. Matchmaker." She looked a bit like a sad, brave, adorable little girl with her puffy eyes and lopsided smile.

"Okay. Don't let those potential heartthrobs see you after you've been crying, though. You're quite the sight…."

She raised a fist to whack my arm again, glaring at me.

Well, there went the adorable, brave little girl.

"Don't beat the driver." I cringed away from her into the car door. "It's distracting."

She lowered her fist reluctantly. "I'll wait until we get

home. Or you can do penance by taking me out to dinner."

"Done." I directed the truck to The Grill House. A good steak would do us a world of good.

CHAPTER 10

"He doesn't have any idea what it means yet," Tauren said. The glittering, statuesque angel spoke to the Council of 13.

"We have to make contact—insinuate ourselves into his awareness. He needs to become attuned to our voices." Jaburn raised a regal hand to each Council member for emphasis.

"You know we are the true Golden Ones." Chorne's nearly indiscernible smirk betrayed his emotions. "If he is a 'Golden One' too, it's only right that he makes our acquaintance."

Shevril stood up at the head of the table, commanding all the angels' attention. "His memory has not surfaced. We have nothing to be concerned about until—or if—it does. Observe from a distance. Do not interact."

With this command, the Council of 13 disbanded.

—ɯ—

Back in London, life and work found a new rhythm. I went to the farm at least once a month to check on Tessa. The ten-hour round-trip on my motorbike had grown familiar.

We had gotten fancy new cell phones and video-called every day, but it was harder for Tessa to hide how she was really doing when I was right in front of her.

We both took Granny's death hard, but I wasn't surrounded by memories every day at my job in the machine shop. Tessa was struggling to know how to move forward.

A year and a half plodded by. We reduced the garden sizes and number of sheep; kept only a few chickens and one cow. We rented out our two best pastures to our neighbors for their sheep to graze. Finally, we purged the house and barn and sold what we couldn't use.

All the activity helped us move through the larger part of our grief. When we were nearly finished cleaning the farm, I noticed an undercurrent of desperation in Tessa.

"Dane came over for dinner last night." Tessa wouldn't meet my eyes as we came inside after putting the chickens to bed. It was a Saturday night in August, and the weather was fine. The cool summer air blew in from the open kitchen window.

I looked at Tessa. Carefully looked at her. She was lean and tough from the work she had done over the past eighteen months. The shadows under her eyes had lessened, but her eyes shifting around the room reminded me a little of a trapped animal. Her hands moved restlessly, never settling on anything for long.

"Tessa." I stood in front of her. "Look at me."

She stopped fidgeting, then took a deep breath before she raised her eyes to mine.

"What are you doing?" I tried using my own "twin radar." "Have you changed your mind about Dane?"

I saw a flicker of panic in her gaze before she shuttered her expression. "Yes. Maybe. I don't exactly know." The fidgeting resumed. She moved to the stove to put the kettle on. When it was heating, she leaned back against the kitchen counter and faced me.

"I'm so lonely without Granny here." She picked at a spot on the counter top, then clasped her hands behind her back to still them. "I feel... lost. Maybe life with Dane would give me some direction. It would be good to have a family of my own...."

Lord, help! What to say?

"Marrying someone because you can't see any better options right now sounds like a recipe for disaster. You think you feel stuck now? Jumping into that kind of relationship is diving from the frying pan into the fire." I walked across the kitchen and took her shoulders. "Don't you remember what Granny told you about the potatoes?"

She stared at me blankly. "Potatoes?"

"You know, when you were digging potatoes. The bit about you having a 'big life inside you'. Do you think she was wrong?" I watched as she remembered. She smiled faintly.

"Oh, right. 'Don't settle for small potatoes.'"

I stepped back. "You might not want to hear it, but—for you—Dane is 'small potatoes.'"

She sighed, then massaged her temple with her right hand. "Unfortunately, I think you're right. But where does that leave me?"

"Right in the middle of having to trust God."

She twisted her lips ruefully before pulling the whistling kettle off the stove and making two cups of tea. Then, she set the soup on to warm and cut thick slices of the fresh, crusty bread that Siobhan had brought over that morning.

We took the tea and bread to the table. I was hungry, so I took a piece of bread, slathered it with butter, and took a huge bite.

"Okay." Tessa picked up the heel of bread, which had always been her favorite part, and buttered it. "Dane is off the table, at least for tonight. We'll see how I do tomorrow."

I started praying for divine intervention.

—⁂—

The old adage, "Be careful what you pray for—you just might get it," slammed into Tessa and me in a big way.

Divine intervention took the form of Granny visiting Tessa in a dream and telling her that she was going to become a Quantum Spacewalker.

Dane was off the table permanently.

Tessa became immersed in her Quantum Spacewalker training for six months. Two angels were instructing her. I was only able to learn bits and pieces of what this was all about as she attempted to describe it to me in our video calls.

Tonight, however, Tessa appeared in my tiny living room.

Guess I'm going to get a firsthand spacewalking demonstration.

I dropped the book I was reading onto the floor, nearly tipping my tea over. Once I was over my initial shock, I said, "Practicing your spacewalking, I see."

Tessa laughed. "I know you're not as calm as you're trying to appear." Still giggling, she came to sit by me on the couch.

"You're right. But, this is definitely better than video calling." I poked her to make sure I wasn't seeing things.

Grinning, she bounced up and went to get a drink, then started opening cabinet doors. "I'm craving crisps. I thought overflowing mounds of crisps were standard single-guy fare."

"Bottom cabinet on your right."

She pulled out a bag of salt and vinegar crisps and sat down in my lone armchair. After crunching on a few of them, she said, "I sold the animals to Siobhan's family. I'll be closing up the farmhouse."

"Because…?"

"I'm moving into hard-core spacewalking." She gestured excitedly with a crisp. "Remember how I told you that Jesus is the Word who upholds the Universe at the smallest, most basic level of existence? Beyond what any scientist has even come close to touching on?"[3]

"Sort of."

"Well, because those of us who belong to Jesus are one with his Spirit,[4] we can travel instantaneously on those pathways…." She crunched a crisp loudly.

"Hold on." I waved my hand to stop her. "Isn't everyone who belongs to Jesus in the same position? Why aren't we all blipping around the quantum realm?"

"Well, a lot of people have and currently are." Tessa frowned. "Remember the story of Phillip in Acts 8? Almost all those who spacewalk are taken places by the Spirit. I'll be able to direct myself through the quantum realm because of my assignment."

"What actually is your assignment?" I was anticipating finally learning about this new job of hers.

"Quantum spacewalking delivery girl, at your service. Tips are accepted…." She held her hand out, giggling.

I dug around in my pocket. "Here's two pence. That's all you're getting from me until you explain further."

---

[3] Hebrews 1:1-3
[4] 2 John 17

She snorted disdainfully at the two pence coin and flipped it back to me. "I'll be traveling to other planets—can you believe it? Other planets! I'll collect things to bring back to Earth to help those who follow Jesus, because we will be moving into the end of this age soon."

"I'm sure of that." I nodded vigorously.

The ramifications hit us both at once. Tessa's smile died. So did mine.

When did my insides become hollow?

"I guess video calling is out." I didn't seem to be able to catch my breath.

"I guess so."

I watched my sister, loving her more fiercely than I ever had before. I stood up, pulled her to her feet, and hugged her. Crisps scattered across the floor.

"Be careful out there." My eyes were stinging.

"I'll pop in from time to time. You be careful here." She hugged me tighter.

"When are you leaving?" I let her go and brushed my hand over my eyes, wiping the wetness onto my jeans.

"In two days."

I tried not to act like I'd been punched in the gut. "Well, then. Let's order from my favorite fish and chips place, and you can fill me in on all this training you've done."

Tears brightened Tessa's eyes, but she smiled in agreement. I picked up my phone and started dialing while she picked the crisps off the floor.

CHAPTER 11

My home church group was a lifeline for me after Tessa began quantum spacewalking. I had never anticipated how hard Tessa's absence would be. I felt like I'd lost a limb or a vital organ.

The group encouraged me, even though I couldn't explain about Tessa's new job. They were an understanding lot, but I wasn't sure they would actually believe me, so I kept quiet on the details. They only knew that Tessa had accepted a job that included a lot of travel.

I needed their company, and they cajoled me into trying things I never would have otherwise, like cricket. It took a little time to get the rules down, but soon I was swinging a cricket bat well enough to help our team to victory a few times.

Jared, a good friend, also had a thing for darts. He kept forcing me to go to a pub not far from his home to play. After about the fifth time playing, when I beat him soundly, I decided darts weren't so bad after all. I'm sure all that hand-eye coordination I earned lassoing Granny's hog was coming in handy now. I'm not so sure Jared was impressed.

These people blessed my life and I was trying to bless

theirs. Their laughter eased the tension between my shoulder blades. And in my heart.

Changes crept into my workplace. A robotics line was installed for orders in excess of five thousand pieces. Our profit margins had grown to allow for these robots without any human workers having to be made redundant.

Trent, my future-loving co-worker, was ecstatic when we were able to start small experiments with metal-eating nanobots. Sure enough, these teensy biotic bugs were voracious metal shapers. They were slow "chewers" at present, so we couldn't use them on large-scale projects, but they were shockingly precise. Trent kept calling them the "wave of the future." If they began working at a faster rate, he might be right.

These changes, and other future-bearing waves, beat down on me relentlessly. World events—pestilences that infected our daily lives with fear and death, famines, shortages, violence, wars—were all spreading. Artificial intelligence was finding its way into everyday algorithms. The web spinning around us that would eventually funnel nearly everyone into a one-world government was drawing tighter. That knowledge drained me like a perpetual low-grade fever.

Whenever my thoughts turned toward my own future, I hit a blank wall. I certainly wouldn't mind getting married, having a couple of munchkins, or buying a place of my own. I was at a point now where I could take an "adult" step or two. Yet, I couldn't see it. I couldn't envision the ideal woman, the "proper" brick house, the family dog, the kids—any of it.

Then, I remembered.

—m—

"Quinn. Wake up, Quinn."

I rolled onto my back. My blanket was wrapped around me like a burrito, and I had to wriggle my arms free so that I could prop myself up. I was an active sleeper at eight years of age.

Blearily peering around my tiny, darkened bedroom, I saw no one.

"Who's there?" My heart was pounding.

No answer.

Was I only dreaming someone called me?

Suddenly, the far bedroom wall split in two. Light poured in as the wall moved left and right like the drapes in the living room when Granny opened them in the morning.

I was terrified.

"Don't be afraid, Quinn. Come here," a melodic voice said.

I couldn't move. I didn't want to move. Instead of getting up, I burrowed under my blanket and pulled it over my head.

It's bad enough that Mum and Dad were killed in that car accident. Now, I'm seeing things.

"You don't need to be afraid, Quinn." The voice sounded reassuring, but I didn't believe it.

Easy for you to say.

I burrowed deeper under the covers. "Granny, I need you!" I tried to shout. My voice came out as a squeak.

"All right, I'll come to you," the thing said.

A light came into my room. Even under the covers, with my eyes squeezed shut, I could tell it was getting brighter and brighter.

It stopped by my head. I could feel it—whatever *it* was—waiting.

After a long five or so minutes, I figured the bright thing wasn't going away. It hadn't attacked me or said anything else. I decided I would have to talk to it.

"What do you want?" I whispered.

"To show you something," the light outside my covers said.

The voice was warm and sweet, like molten honey.

Well, if I'm going to die, at least I'll be with Mum and Dad again.

I cautiously peered through a small opening in the covers. I don't know what I expected. I certainly would never have imagined what I saw.

A thick, golden book hovered open in front of me. It was thicker than three old encyclopedias stacked together. It was even thicker than Granny's ancient Bible that she got from her great-great-great Grandpa.

A talking book?

I sat up, staring at the book, the blanket still wrapped around my head.

"What are you?" I wanted to touch the book, but something warned me not to.

"The Book of Life."

Vaguely, I recalled a teacher at church talking about a Book of Life somewhere in the Bible.

"From the Bible?" I was astonished. "Why are you here?"

"Because," the Book said, "you're one of the Father's Golden Ones. He has chosen you to rescue me."

"Why do you need to be rescued?" I continued staring in wide-eyed wonder. "Am I supposed to come get you right now?"

"Perilous times will come. When the future meets the

time before time began, you will be called for your final mission. When all hope appears lost, the true Golden Ones arise." The Book began to fade.

"Wait. What do I do? How am I supposed to rescue you?"

The Book disappeared, saying nothing more.

I woke up with a start, wrapped in my blanket like a burrito.

The memories resurfaced in a rush. I had told Granny at breakfast the next day about my weird nighttime vision or dream. She gave the matter some thought before answering. "If that's the job you have to do, my boy, I'm sure you'll do it well."

I had asked her to show me what the Bible said about the Book of Life. There were several passages, but the one that grabbed my attention was Revelation 20:15 which said, "And if anyone's name was not written in the Book of Life, he was thrown into the lake of fire."[5]

This was an immensely significant book. People's destinies were recorded in it. I'm sure my fear over the whole incident made me suppress the memory.

I couldn't comprehend why such an important book would need to be rescued.

And why I was supposedly the one to do the rescuing.

---

[5] Psalm 69:28, Philippians 4:3, Revelation 3:5, 4:3, 13:8, 20:12, 20:15, 21:27.

CHAPTER 12

"Shevril is a fool!" Disdain dripped from every word Draven said. "The boy has remembered. The enemy is in open pursuit. We have to intervene." Golden light flew in jagged rays from him as he whirled to face Tauren.

Tauren, glittering as light sparkled off the jewels embedded in his skin, ignored Draven's outburst. His eyes held a faraway expression. Finally, he blinked and gave his attention to his agitated companion. Slowly, Tauren nodded. "I believe you're right. He needs to believe he can trust us. Then, if by chance, he ever does discover where the cursed book resides, we can follow him and apprehend it."

"What will it take to convince Shevril?" Draven's beautiful, flawless face almost creased into a frown.

"The weight of the rest of the Council. Come, let's go talk with the others. Present the evidence that the boy's memory has returned."

The two angels left to find their fellow Council members.

I was aware of a change in my neighborhood. Disquiet simmered in my bones, although I couldn't put my finger on *why* right away.

Nothing seemed that different on the outside. Occasionally, I saw a few strangers down at my favorite fish and chips shop. One day I noticed a man in dress slacks and a jacket walking the ugliest dog I had ever seen. It had mottled skin, a disproportionately long nose, and wicked-looking jagged teeth. When it passed by, it sniffed the air and turned toward me, whining. The man followed the dog's gaze and stopped to examine me with a hard, unblinking stare.

A shiver ran up my spine when I saw the dog's eyes. A nearly-human, unfriendly intelligence glowered back at me. I knew then that my time in the city was almost over.

Turning away, I hurried home without looking back.

When I got inside my flat, I grabbed the TV remote to check the news. I rarely did this because most of it was so blatantly false or twisted to fit an agenda that I couldn't stomach it. After seeing that disconcerting dog-thing, I wanted to see if there were any reports concerning that type of creature.

I had to wait until the newscast's end, but my patience paid off. The dog-things were part of "compliance task forces." The task forces were scouring neighborhoods, hunting for persons deemed a threat. From what I could discern, how they determined who *might* be a threat seemed to change every few minutes.

George Orwell's *1984* and the movie *Minority Report* seemed to be merging into reality. I could almost feel eyes piercing me everywhere I went, trying to get into my head and read my thoughts.

I'm getting a little paranoid.

The only things holding me in the city were the relationships I had built within my home church group. These people had become like family in Tessa's absence. However, seeing part of a "compliance task force" scouting around my area ramped up the urgency to get out of London.

—ɯ—

Tired from work and the additional burden of stress from thinking about scary-looking freaky dogs, I dozed off on the couch after my quick dinner on Friday night.

I woke up to variations of shimmering light playing over my eyelids. I noticed the changes in brightness even though my eyes were closed.

Struggling, I managed to open my eyes a crack. I couldn't move. I was enveloped in warm lassitude. Trying to move my head was impossible.

What's happening here?

I couldn't move a finger. I was paralyzed. I should have been concerned, but I couldn't seem to work up the energy.

"Greetings, Golden One."

My eyes could still move around. Glancing toward the shimmering light, I could make out a vague form but I couldn't see any definite features.

Unable to speak, I thought toward the intruder, asking, "Who are you?"

A chuckle emanated from the being. "Very good. You already understand telepathy. Learning how to live as we do will come easily for you."

The weight holding me down increased.

Why is it so hard to move?

The thought I directed to myself was answered by my visitor.

"Your energy signature is out of sync with your true self.

I will help you align yourself with the truth." The shimmering light moved closer to me.

A loud banging on the door startled me. I still could barely move but managed to turn my head a few inches toward the door.

Apparently, the knocking bothered my visitor as well. The shimmering light vanished as my buddy, Roderick, came through the door lugging six board games.

"Get up, sleepy head!" Roderick—affectionately known as Roddy—shouted in my direction. "Where are the snacks?"

I had completely forgotten about game night. Three other friends trailed into the apartment, lugging a small cooler of drinks and assorted tasty tidbits.

Now that my shining visitor was gone, I could move.

I got up to put the kettle on, pushing the strange incident back in my mind until I found time to deal with it.

CHAPTER 13

Our game night both made and destroyed several hopeful world conquerors. I ended the night as the supreme benevolent ruler of Catan, having overtaken and settled the entire continent with my many roads, armies, and cities. Jared ruled the world of Risk. Tony was the real estate magnate of the new, improved global Monopoly. Ben and Roddy were unfortunate peasants, conquered and poor. They made up for it by eating the lions' share of the snacks.

I noticed that there seemed to be a theme of ruling over the masses.

While munching on the snacks the two "peasants" were kind enough to leave for us in the wee hours of the morning, I brought up the ugly dog-thing I had seen. The gregarious mood instantly changed.

Roddy wore a sober expression. "They're trying to find people who don't align with their agenda. I heard that they scooped up a few followers of Jesus in Chatham and took them to an undisclosed location." We grew quiet.

The same kind of shiver I had when seeing the too-intelligent eyes of the ugly dog-thing swept over me again.

"I think I'll be leaving soon and going back to our farm."

I glanced down as I tossed some nuts into my mouth. That bomb dropped and exploded, creating groans of, "Oh man, is that necessary?" and "Don't let those ugly things chase you off."

Meeting several pairs of concerned eyes, I swallowed my mouthful, then washed it down with a swig of orange pop. "It feels like it's time to go. I don't know that I can explain it logically. A red alert began flashing inside when I saw that dog creature."

A couple of sighs escaped from the guys.

"My family has been wondering what we should do as well. My wife wants us to relocate to her parents' farm in Kent." Roddy rolled his eyes. "I've never much pictured myself as a farmer."

Tony, Jared, Ben, and I laughed. Roddy could have been the head of a biker gang with his shaved head, bulging tattoo-covered arms and trademark black leather. His love of motorcycles was what had connected him and me in the first place. He was a big, squishy softy inside with a generous heart. Once you got past his exterior, you discovered a deep thinker who would bend over backwards to help out. I had been grateful for his assistance many times.

"If you're considering leaving, I encourage you to go." I grew serious. "I think the cities will be progressively harder to live in."

"That's what Moira believes." Roddy gave a slightly bitter laugh. "I'm hoping we can negotiate less farming and more motorbike or small engine repair in Kent. And the kids would enjoy farm life."

"Well, you know what they say." Jared put on a knowing professor-ish air.

"Nope." Ben shook his head. "Which 'they' are you talking about?"

"Exactly," Tony said. "The big 'they' or the little 'they' or the overarching 'they'...."

"The 'they' that say 'All endings are really only new beginnings.'" Jared now adopted a thespian tone and extended his hand dramatically.

"Ah...the pithy philosopher 'they.'" Ben said, and then started pelting our budding dramatist with mixed nuts.

We all joined in while Jared lifted a couch pillow to shield his head and began returning fire with the nuts bombarding him.

It was a relief to sleep in the next morning. There were only a few pop cans and stray nuts on the floor when I stumbled out of bed. Surprisingly neat after a game night.

With all the distractions gone this morning, I thought back to the unusual shining presence in my living room. I didn't like how I had felt paralyzed and overpowered. Yet, I was intrigued. The presence had used the term "Golden One." Maybe I could finally gain new insight into what that actually meant.

If only I could make contact with the shimmering light creature again.

CHAPTER 14

Our home group spoke in hushed voices.

"There are two of them now," Roddy said.

Brian, our group leader for the evening, spoke up. "This is getting creepy. Jane saw the dog-things and their handlers outside the schoolyard this morning. She said two of her classmates were apprehended. No one knew where they went."

"Brian and I are thinking of pulling Jane out of school. She would probably learn much better at home. There have been so many school interruptions and closures that she barely learned anything last year. I've had to tutor her to catch up." Heather, Brian's wife, shook her head sadly.

"I saw a dog-thing in my neighborhood two nights ago. If Roddy saw another one, I'd say they're getting uncomfortably close." I rubbed a hand over my eyes. "I'll be heading back to our farm pretty soon. After praying through your options, you should take whatever precautions you think necessary."

"Don't you think it's better to stick together?" Heather was almost on the verge of tears. "You'll be by yourself on the farm, Quinn."

"That's true." I leaned my head back, closing my eyes. I wasn't sure why my eyes were so tired. Perhaps a combination of late nights and concern over my next steps was getting to me. "I have good neighbors in Dinas Island. We've helped each other out since I was a kid."

"You still need to be careful." Brian usually erred on the cautious side. "If we're heading into the timeframe of 'brother betraying brother to death,'[6] then even good neighbors of the past might not be the same in the present."

"You're probably right, but I have a sense I need to go." I blew out a heavy sigh.

"We'll miss you." Moira, always gracious, extended an invitation. "If you ever need a place to stay, you can count on us—wherever we happen to be living."

Roddy agreed. "That's right. We can put you out in the barn with all the machine parts. You'd feel right at home."

Irony dripped from my voice. "Thanks for your generous offer. I'll keep it in mind."

Roddy sniggered, giving me a glimpse into what he had probably acted like in his younger years.

We shoved our concerns aside as Brian led us to delve into John 16:33, where Jesus said "In this world you will have trouble, but take heart—I have overcome the world."

I jumped into the timely message with eagerness.

"Is there anything we can do to convince you to stay?" The shop manager's dismay was obvious. "I'm sure I could negotiate a substantial raise and benefits package. It won't be

---

[6] Matthew 10:21

the same without you here."

"Thank you for the offer." I hated doing this. A good part of me didn't want to leave this job, along with my circle of friends and co-workers. "I'm sorry that I have to go. The years I've worked here have been excellent. I need to return to Wales to deal with our family's farm."

And avoid the net that is being used to scoop people who don't agree with mainstream propaganda.

The manager's shoulders slumped. "All right. I'll get the paperwork in order."

"May I suggest giving Trent my position? He's as good as I am on the laser machines and is more than willing to incorporate innovative technologies."

The manager's gaze was direct. "I didn't get all these grey hairs without learning something about human nature. Trent is highly skilled at his job, but he doesn't understand how to use diplomacy with people. Dealing with teammates is at least fifty percent of your job."

"That's true." I grimaced as I thought of Trent's "bull in a china shop" method of dealing with most interpersonal issues.

"Don't worry about it, Quinn. We'll have you train several people. It will probably take a team to replace you."

I left the manager's office both flattered and saddened.

Where would this life change take me?

I was packing my tenth box of the day.

How did I get this much stuff in only five years?

I had given much of my household items and furniture away and sold a few things. The farm had everything I needed, so I was only taking favorite or useful goods like my electric kettle. There was still a large mound to pack.

The light in my living room seemed to be getting brighter.

Strange. I thought it was overcast outside.

I looked up from my packing to check out the window of my flat.

Yup. It's cloudy.

The light increased. I directed my attention toward my bookshelf in the corner of the living room. A shimmering orb appeared, then stretched, elongating to become a humanoid form. All I could see was an outline in the brightness.

The uncomfortable heaviness I had experienced previously descended onto me again. I wanted to get up from my kneeling position, but it was like my legs were encased in concrete.

"Who are you?" I managed to squeeze the words past my nearly paralyzed lips.

"A fellow Golden One." The shining form once again spoke into my mind. "I'm here to acquaint you with the finer points of who you are."

"Who I am? What do you mean?" I thought toward the being as I fought to move my heavy legs into a sitting position. It took a while, but I eventually succeeded. I had previously made a mental list to ask this being if I ever saw it again. Unfortunately, my mind was as sluggish as my legs, and I couldn't think of a single point.

"We'll speak to you mainly in your dreams." The shining one assumed I would agree with this program. "Your logical mind doesn't get in the way as much. Your spirit can understand and absorb the information we give you."

"How will I recall what you tell me?" This plan made me uneasy.

"Keep a pen and notebook by your bed. Record what you dream the instant you wake up."

"That sounds simple enough." I couldn't find anything to dispute in my slow-as-cold-molasses mind, so I agreed to the idea.

"Your dreams will begin tonight." The shining one disappeared abruptly, leaving sparkles glittering in the air.

The heavy feeling left. Jumping to my feet, I went to see if any sparkles remained, similar to Granny's gold dust.

There were no sparkles left.

Only a sense of bone-chilling cold.

CHAPTER 15

My home church had a goodbye party for me. They made all my favorite dishes and plied me with extra goodies to take on my trip to the farm.

Jared took time off work to drive the rented moving van. He had the proper license to drive that size of vehicle and would stay with me for a few days at the farm to get everything in working order before driving the van back. I was amazed I now had enough that I actually needed a moving van to transport it.

With my motorbike stashed in the van, I rode up front with Jared. We talked about how the world had changed. Uncertainty, accompanied by fear, tried to permeate every aspect of our lives.

I wanted to tell Jared about the dreams I was having. There had only been three of them so far, but they were more like out-of-body experiences than regular dreams.

"Jared, have you ever had any dreams that felt so real that you think they may have happened?" My leg bounced nervously. I hoped he wouldn't find the question too odd.

"Yes, I have. Most of them happened when I was a part of the New Age movement, before I met Jesus. They were *wild*." Jared's eyes grew wide with emphasis. "I could have sworn I was literally out of my body and traveling in space."

This sounded familiar. "Did you… meet anyone in these dreams?" My encounters were so brief that I had not yet figured out who these shining beings were. They had a simultaneous allure and repulsion to me when I met them.

"I always traveled with my guide." Jared's expression grew guarded. "But they were only dreams. I stopped having them when I started to follow Jesus. I have had a couple of dreams of heaven since then, but I never had a guide in those dreams."

Jared glanced at me but quickly turned back to the road before he asked, "Have you been having unusual dreams, Quinn?"

Have I ever.

I cleared my throat. "Um… yes, but I had a couple of interesting encounters before having the dreams. This shiny figure showed up and told me I would begin to have these dreams. He told me to record what I saw. I've been doing that for the dreams I've had up to this point."

Jared regarded me quizzically for a moment. "Can you describe one of those dreams to me? Are the shiny figures in your dreams, too?"

"I saw a figure in one of my dreams. In the other two, I only sensed a presence. The figure that first came to me in my initial dream seemed like he pulled me out of my body with a jerk." Reliving that memory still filled me with awe and dread. "It was abrupt and like no other dream I've ever had."

"What do you remember about him?" Jared asked.

"Tall, shining, with features that seemed to fade in and out. He had a face that was as smooth as alabaster or porcelain." My face scrunched in concentration. "I think I might have seen wings. Maybe. I'm not certain."

"This sounds familiar." Jared's knowing gaze met mine. "I've had similar experiences."

"What did you do when you had them?"

He grinned. "Mostly enjoyed the ride." Then, Jared grew sober. "But I would caution you. These dreams stopped after I met Jesus. I never really knew why, but I'm sure there's a correlation."

Great. Something to add to my growing list of things to ponder.

—⟶⟶—

It was slightly surreal being back at the farm house without Granny or Tessa there. Life in Dinas Island had rolled forward at its normal somnolent rate. There had been a few deaths and births since I lived in London, but much was exactly the same as when I left.

Which was what I had been counting on.

Once Jared and I aired out the farmhouse and got the electricity and water turned on, he headed back to London. The silence closed in around me, threatening to overwhelm my senses as I watched him drive away.

I experienced the exact reverse problem when I moved to the city. The continual noise at all hours of the day and night had driven me slightly crazy for a few weeks. I was only able to sleep there by using earplugs for a while.

This must be what reverse culture shock is like.

I stood in the driveway for a long time, turning in slow circles, absorbing the feel of the breeze, the waving of the weeds in our overgrown gardens, the chirping of birds, and the pastoral sounds of distant sheep. Underlying it all was a sense of anticipation, as if something hidden was biding its time before springing forth.

Would I be able to handle what revealed itself?

CHAPTER 16

The creamy white envelope lay next to the buns Siobhan had dropped off yesterday. I was sure it hadn't been on the kitchen table the night before.

A ripple of apprehension flowed over me.

I picked up the envelope and saw my full name embossed across the front in gold, raised letters. The envelope and card I pulled out were made from thick, heavy cardstock. Whoever had put this together had spent a chunk of change to make it so fancy.

Reading the card left me confused.

Somebody spent a lot of money on this practical joke.

Suddenly, a light flashed ten feet in front of me. A seven-foot-tall man with shoulder length brown hair, a brilliant white robe with a royal blue sash, and smiling brown eyes stood in front of me.

The card in my hand fluttered to the floor as shock immobilized me.

"Hello, Quinn." The warmth in the being's voice melted some of my temporary inability to move. "I see you received our invitation."

"Uhhh…." My brain and mouth weren't connecting

properly.

The being scooped the card off the floor and handed it to me. I managed to pinch it between my thumb and forefinger.

"Don't be afraid, Quinn. My name is Harnel. I'm here to explain this invitation to you."

The proverbial cat had grabbed my tongue between razor-sharp claws. I couldn't speak, so I nodded mutely.

"Good. An invitation to become a Universe Healer is a prestigious honor. On top of that, your specific job on the Quadrant 4 Healing Team has a larger scope than any other Healer. It is eternal in nature...."

Croaking like a large bullfrog, I managed, "I don't know if I want to accept this invitation yet."

Harnel stopped, then said, "Feel free to ask me any questions you would like."

"Who are you?" I decided to rephrase my question. "Who and *what* are you?"

"I am a messenger from the Holy One. You would most commonly call me an angel." The kindness never left Harnel's gaze.

I remembered something I had heard in my church back in London recently. Brian had said to test any spirit you came across with I John 4:1-3. I decided to do that now. "Did Jesus come in the flesh?" As I asked this, I realized I had never posed this question to the being who had visited me in my dreams.

Harnel didn't miss a beat. "Of course he did. He is my Master and yours."

Good answer.

I pulled out a kitchen chair and collapsed into it. My knees were feeling a little wobbly. I carefully placed the embossed card on the table, face up.

Drawing in a deep breath, I nudged the card with a fingertip. "All right. Please explain this invitation to me."

"A Universe Healer does exactly as the title implies." Harnel indicated the card. "The Healing Teams will be distributed throughout the four Quadrants of the Universe after our Master returns to Earth. This invitation is for the Quadrant 4 Team."

"Mmmhmmm…." I murmured. "Why did I get picked to be on one of these teams?"

"I was not informed of the reason you were chosen, only that I would assist you as your trainer." Harnel moved around to the other side of the table, drew out a chair, and sat down facing me. The chair could barely hold him. "Would you like to go meet your teammates?"

"You keep assuming I'll say 'yes' to this invitation. What if I say 'no'?" The childish, petulant note in my voice irritated me. I was afraid Harnel would peg me as a spoiled brat.

"That is your prerogative." Harnel was quietly thoughtful. "But you would miss some of the most spectacular miracles any human has ever witnessed. Do you want to do that?"

Did I?

"Can I have some time to think about this?" I wasn't sure why I was holding back, but I couldn't bring myself to agree yet.

"Yes. I'll return tomorrow." Harnel got up from the table and walked out the kitchen door.

—ɯ—

That night, I had one of my new traveling dreams. I was jerked out of my body in the dream. When I opened my eyes, I was in space, standing on nothing that I could see, although what was under my feet felt solid.

When I turned to my right, a ball of iridescent light was speeding toward me. I wasn't afraid. I merely watched its approach with curiosity.

The ball hit me with force, then expanded around me. Shimmering colors surrounded my body until it seemed that I was floating in a glittering rainbow.

Three forms walked out of the light. I saw faces for the first time. Each being had long flowing hair floating around its features.

"Hello, Quinn," the three beings said in eerie harmony. Their voices echoed around me as I watched the colors swirl over and through them.

I wanted to ask them who they were, but I couldn't speak.

Strange that I am always immobilized in some way with these creatures.

As one, the beings became brilliantly golden. They shone so brightly that I had trouble looking at them.

"Come, Quinn," they all said. "It's time for you to learn about your inheritance."

Six hands grasped me and we began to fly.

CHAPTER 17

We sped along pathways of light. It reminded me of a London freeway. Other beings whipped by us, heading in different directions.

"Where are we going?" I thought at the being holding my right arm.

"To the Council," I heard in my mind.

This is a first.

Councils brought to mind stuffy politicians making decisions that may or may not be welcome by the people under them. I wondered what kind of council I would be facing.

"It's a council of your brethren. There is no need to fear," the being said, answering my barely framed mental question.

It wasn't unusual to be told not to be afraid by spiritual beings.[7] That's usually how they greeted people in the Bible whenever they popped up.

That didn't stop the flicker of fear that passed over my mind.

---

[7] Luke 1:30, Luke 8:50, Matthew 28:5 are good examples.

Beings perfect in beauty sat equally spaced around a long, golden table as I arrived with my companions. My arms were released, and I was left standing at the edge of the room as my three escorts joined the others at the table. I received no invitation to sit down.

Several of the beings had sparkling jewels embedded in their skin. Their hair was long, shining in the light. Yet, their eyes were dark—almost entirely black.

I observed them without forming any mental questions.

Suddenly, from a distance, I heard my name being called.

"Quinn, wake up!"

One of the beings at the table stood up. His eyes flashed angrily. I noticed his meticulously embroidered outer robe, covered with mysterious symbols and constellations.

My shoulder shook. The table and beings began to fade.

"Hold him," one of the beings at the table cried.

But it was too late.

I was awake.

"Harnel." I groaned, sleep clouding my brain. "Why are you yelling at me?"

"I received an urgent message to come speak to you. I did not delay." The angel shook my shoulder again more gently than the first time. "Are you truly awake now?"

"Unfortunately, yes." I grunted as I swung my legs over the side of the bed and sat up. "But, I'm a little disappoint- ed. I was about to discover what being a 'Golden One' is all about."

"A 'Golden One'?" Harnel said. "If you are one of the Holy One's Golden Ones, that is an easy question to answer."

I was instantly alert. "It is? Then what in the blasted heck does it mean?"

"No need to get testy. Have you never read that the Holy One knows who are His, and that in His house there are vessels of gold and silver for honorable use?"[8] Harnel raised an eyebrow questioningly.

"Yes, I'm sure I've read that before, but I never connected it to this term." I stood up, pulled my clothes on, and headed for the kitchen to get the kettle started.

"The water's already hot." Harnel followed me out. "I thought you would want your typical morning beverage."

I laughed. "This 'typical beverage' is none other than the elixir of life. I don't know how people exist without tea."

Harnel snorted derisively. "You have not yet tasted the true waters of life. When you do, this *tea* you love so much will fade into obscurity."

"Well, until then…." I picked up my perfectly-brewed, brimming mug. "I'll stick with this." Popping bread into the toaster after I had taken a long slurp of my elixir, I set the mug down and resumed our conversation.

"A 'Golden One' means a golden vessel to be used for an honorable purpose? Is that what you meant?" I faced the angel, determined to get a solid answer.

Harnel nodded. "A golden vessel has been purified. It can stand in the fire now with no impurities rising to the surface. And it has been prepared to contain the most

---

[8] 2 Timothy 2:19-21

precious of treasures." He came and stood a few inches away from me. With his seven foot stature, I had to lean back to see his face. "However, you will only discover this for yourself if you accept the invitation to become part of the Quadrant 4 Universe Healing Team."

"Hmmm…." I stepped back and took another sip of tea before taking the bread out of the toaster and buttering it. "All right, then. Count me in."

Harnel smiled. "You've made a wise choice, Quinn Evans. We'll meet your teammates after breakfast."

CHAPTER 18

While I ate breakfast, which included more toast, several eggs, and a couple of sausages, Harnel asked me how I had been about to discover what being a "Golden One" meant.

Laying my fork down, I gave as good an explanation as I was able. "I've been having unusual dreams. Shiny beings were taking me to a council meeting in this last one when you woke me up."

"Do you remember what they looked like or how many were there at the council?" Harnel's eyes were intense.

"These dreams fade quickly after I wake up. I usually try to write down what happens in them, but didn't do that this time. One of the beings had really smooth skin. They were all shiny." I shook my head. The dream had almost completely receded.

Harnel's thoughtful gaze revealed little. "I encourage you to be cautious if you interact with these beings in the future. They may not be who they make themselves out to be but, then again, I am not familiar with every angelic order that the Holy One commands."

"They said they were 'Golden Ones' and could tell me about my inheritance as a 'Golden One.'" Picking my fork back up, I stuffed a large bite of eggs into my mouth. "I wrote that down from a previous encounter."

"Well, remember what I said." Harnel smiled at me while I wiped my mouth and took my dishes to the sink. "Are you ready to go now?"

Not remotely.

"How does this work exactly?" Breakfast was over. No more stalling. Now was the moment of truth. I would be spacewalking to meet my teammates—like Tessa had been doing all over the Universe for the last couple of years.

"For now, you take my hand. I'll escort you to our team meeting. You'll learn to spacewalk through the quantum realm soon enough." Harnel smiled and wiggled his fingers in invitation.

It's Now or Never started playing in my mind.

Thanks for the encouragement, Elvis.

Pushing down the flutterings of fear in order to act quickly, my hand shot out to grasp Harnel's and we were off.

In less than a blink, we arrived. I was on my hands and knees, groaning. Our rapid entry and exit from the quantum pathway had done a number on me. I shakily tried to stand up but toppled over into the thick grass.

"Lay there for a bit." Harnel smiled down at me. "You'll recover quickly."

"Tell me this gets easier." I lay for a few moments, spread-eagled on my back with my arm covering my eyes.

Harnel laughed. "It does get easier with a little practice." He grabbed my hand and pulled me up. "Come on. We have to walk to that house over there." He pointed to an enormous house in the distance that seemed like it could have been plucked from an old English novel. It appeared to be several miles away.

"Why didn't you take us closer?" I knew I was whining. "My legs feel like limp spaghetti."

"Don't worry. We'll get there quickly." Harnel waited for me to follow him, then began walking toward the house.

An odd sensation came over me. When I began following Harnel, the scenery zipped by. It was like being on a turbo-charged moving sidewalk in an airport.

Time and movement were strange here. The trail I had been certain would take over an hour to cover took less than five minutes. I blinked in surprise as we faced the stairway up to the large double doors of the enormous house.

The doors opened and a tastefully-dressed woman in a cream-colored suit came out.

"Oh good, you've arrived. Welcome, Quinn. I'm Ms. Pranwick. Please follow me."

She led us into the cavernous entryway, her heels echoing on the polished tile floor.

"Your journey went well?" She observed me with an appraising eye. "You appear a little rumpled. Is that from the travel or is that your normal appearance?"

I tugged my shirt down over my faded jeans. "This is my normal *working* appearance." I glared at Harnel. "I wasn't given a dress code for this meeting."

Harnel chuckled. Ms. Pranwick relaxed slightly. "You'll do fine here, Quinn. The others arrived in their current attire as well."

We followed the businesslike woman through large hallways filled with ornate furniture, huge paintings and lamps that probably each cost more than I made in a year.

Voices floated out of a doorway on our left. Ms. Pranwick turned into the room. Once we had followed her inside, she inclined her head to an angel with brilliant blue eyes, then left.

"Welcome, Quinn and Harnel, to the first Quadrant 4 Universe Healing Team meeting." The blue-eyed angel directed me to a chair. I sat down, and Harnel stood behind me. "We're waiting for two more people before we begin."

Nine other beautiful high-backed chairs were set around a large, round table. Each person seated in them had a tall angel with a different colored sash over his white robe standing behind them, except for the two remaining empty chairs.

A green orb, the size of the globe in my high school library, glowed in the center of the table. It was pulsing with light. The swirling lights inside it were hypnotic.

My concentration was broken when a young woman came in pushing a cart laden with tea and goodies. Even though I had eaten breakfast recently, I was hungry now.

Quantum Spacewalking must create an appetite.

I piled a plate with sandwiches and pastries, then dove into it after the tea was served. My only complaint was the tiny, froofy tea cup that held only two mouthfuls of tea. I constantly asked for refills.

Our remaining two team members came in while we were eating. They claimed their seats, settled in, and had their tea. A servant entered and placed writing pads and heavy gold pens in front of each of us.

Once we were done, the angel with the brilliant blue eyes called us to attention.

"I am Reynel. It's time to get this meeting started."

CHAPTER 19

Our Quadrant 4 team was a hodgepodge of races and colors. My initial impression was that we were odd choices to form something as important as a Universe Healing Team.

Reynel nodded to a lithe, powerfully built man who appeared like he could have been the ballet-dancer, Baryshnikov's, younger brother. He had blond hair and icy blue eyes that held a spark of humor.

"Misha, would you like to begin?"

In English only slightly tinged with a Russian accent, Misha introduced himself. "My name is Michael Sergeyvich Petrov, Misha for short. I come from Eastern Russia. My father was one of those who found the mysterious manufactured nano-structures in the Ural Mountains in the early 1990's. He always believed they originated with fallen angels."

My curiosity was piqued, but Reynel nodded to the person sitting next to Misha.

"G'day, mates. Mrs. Samantha Ferndale, or Fernie to you lot. My husband and I had a small farm in Queensland until his death two years ago. I limped the place along for a while, but sold it a couple of months ago. Now I've got time to play grandma to my daughter's kids and to work with you fine people."

It was impossible to guess Fernie's age. Her sandy, close-cropped blond hair and leathery brown skin from the Australian sun made accurate estimates unlikely. She had a mischievous twinkle in her pale grey eyes. I thought she was probably a fun grandma to have around, not much different from how my granny had been.

The exotic woman sitting next to Fernie began to speak. I watched as flowing Spanish words visibly came from her lips and were sucked into the glowing green orb in the center of the large, round table. Her statements then exited in each of our native languages.

"My name is Gabriella." She rolled her "R's" dramatically. "I am a Spanish ancestral dancer from the region of Andalucia. It is my joy to express story forms in the movement of dance."

A diva of the first order.

Almost as if she heard my thoughts, she gave me a side-glance and winked.

Fiery embarrassment started at my neck and reached my ears in 1.2 seconds. Gabriella ducked her head to hide a smile.

An Indigenous man sat next to Gabriella. He was of moderate stature but was as rugged as if the pressure of an ancient glacier carved him out of stone.

"I am Tulok, an Inuit from Umiujag in Northern Canada. I come from a long line of those known as 'warriors of the stars.' My ancestors warred in illegitimate, evil ways. I am glad to be warring for the Holy One."

Tulok's angel, a tall swarthy being with black hair and eyes, dressed in a bright white robe with a sea-green sash, positively glowed with Tulok's words as he stood behind his chair. I wondered what heavenly battles he had seen Tulok fight.

A slightly built woman in a flowing dress and flowered headscarf spoke next in a rolling language I had never heard before. I couldn't begin to guess where she was from as her words spiraled into the green globe.

"My name is Baktygul." She radiated joy. "My husband, Nurbek, sits beside me. We are Kyrgyz, living on the steppes of the Tien Shan Mountains." Her dark eyes were filled with laughter and wisdom. Her voice imparted warmth and happiness. Somehow, I literally felt it on my skin.

Nurbek, dressed in plain working clothes—not unlike me—spoke next. "We raised six children in our yurt as we cared for our sheep in the shadow of the 'Celestial Mountains,' as the Tien Shan are called. It was a surprise and an honor to be invited to be a part of this Healing Team."

Reynel nodded at the quiet woman sitting next to me. I guessed she must work at a school or office. I could easily imagine that she and all types of books were familiar friends.

"My name is Dottie," the woman began with a twinge of a Western-style drawl. "I work at the library in Pinedale, Wyoming as an archivist. History is one of my passions."

I had a hard time imagining Dottie being passionate about anything. Nothing was out of place. Not a hair. Not a wrinkle anywhere on her person. I would have placed her in her mid-forties, but her composed appearance made it impossible to be sure.

My musings were interrupted when I felt Reynel's eyes on me. I introduced myself and told a little about Dinas Island and the farm, along with working in London. At 6'3", I was one of the taller team members. My Welsh accent, black hair, brown eyes, and pale skin pegged me easily as a British Islander before I stated it, but I enjoyed briefly describing who I was and what I did.

Reynel surprised me after I was done by making an announcement. "Quinn is part of our team and will be taking part in a portion of our Universe Healing. However, his purpose is unique. He needs your prayers and support."

Everyone stared at me. My "fight or flight" response was kicking into high gear until, finally, Reynel moved his laser-like gaze from me to the man on my left.

The man introduced himself in perfect, cultured French. The hypnotic dance of his words entering our glowing green translation orb mesmerized me. His voice was at complete odds with his appearance, which included colorful ribbons twisting through his shoulder-length dreadlocks and intricate tattoos snaking down his well-muscled, black right arm. He wasn't as tall as I was, but he definitely worked out.

"I am Roger. I've lived in Paris my whole life. I am a painter, sculptor, and poet. My parents immigrated from Eritrea to escape a repressive government regime. The freedom we found in France enabled us to live happy lives until recently, and our family enjoyed the chance to worship God without fear."

An artist! Maybe he can give me some sketching tips.

Our last teammate chuckled delightedly when her turn arrived. Her girth shook the table as she laughed so that it vibrated under my hand.

"I am Ji Woo. Most Korean people you have seen before are skinny twigs. Bah! Not my family. We are the best chefs in our village. Someday I will prepare a feast for you, and you will see that I speak the truth. My mother, however, gave me a strange name. It was not a family name from my ancestors. Instead, it means 'to comprehend the Universe.' Maybe she knew then what I am discovering now—or will discover as a Universe Healer."

With our introductions complete, our briefing began.

CHAPTER 20

Reynel called us to attention. All eyes fastened on him.

"Universe Healers, you are a prestigious group the likes of which has never been gathered before, nor will ever be again."

I had never felt *less* prestigious in my life.

Reynel continued. "You have each been uniquely qualified and chosen for this task by the Holy One. You may have qualms about your abilities, but trust the Holy One to direct you."

Murmurs from the group rose around the table.

Reynel lifted a hand to stifle any questions.

"Naturally, you want more details, which your training will provide. You will be called to the training at the end of the current age."

I suppose that removes all doubt of what timeframe we're in.

Our meeting concluded. I was approached by Fernie and Gabriella.

"Well, you've got a little Elvis thing going on here." Fernie gave me the once-over. "Or is it James Dean?"

"I prefer Elvis." I reddened at the older lady's comment. "He was my granny's favorite."

"But can you sing?" Fernie asked, grinning widely.

"Nothing you'd care to hear. My talents lie in other areas." I glanced between Fernie and Gabriella with a wry smile.

Gabriella lowered sultry eyes. "Eres un hombre muy guapo," she said, "pero tendremos que ver lo que realmente puedes lograr."

Our green translation globe had powered down, so I didn't know exactly what she said, but I gathered it was a compliment laced with a challenge. This thought was confirmed when Harnel chuckled behind me.

The two ladies walked away, and I whispered to Harnel. "What did she say?"

"She thinks you're handsome." Harnel paused for a long time.

"Is that all?" I glared up at him, eyes narrowed suspiciously.

"And she also wants to see what you can actually do." Harnel's amused gaze pricked my pride.

I tried not to huff when I said, "Well, I look forward to showing her sometime."

"Indeed." The angel extended his hand. "Are you ready to go home or would you like to visit further?"

"Home sounds good." I took his hand and we whisked our way back to the farmhouse.

—∞—

"I will call for you when it is time for your Universe Healing training to begin." Harnel had brought me back to the farmhouse kitchen and was preparing to leave.

"Is there anything I need to do between now and then? Surely there's something I can do to get ready." I was all out to sea considering my immediate future. Gripping the heavy gold pen from the meeting that was still in my hand, I was assured that my experience had been real, but that didn't help me know what to do next.

Am I going to have to wait several years before this training starts?

Harnel put a hand on my shoulder. "Don't be concerned, Quinn. You will have enough to keep you busy."

"Like what?" It was decidedly different to have him tower over me. I was used to towering over nearly everyone I knew.

Harnel smiled, then disappeared.

"Thanks a lot!" Yelling after the angel in the empty kitchen probably didn't help, except to make me feel better.

"You're welcome. What for?" Tessa's voice spoke from behind me.

Tessa had appeared in the kitchen doorway. I nearly jumped out of my skin.

"What is it with spacewalkers and angels popping in and out of places?" My heart pounded from the shock.

"Who were you just chopsing?"[9] Tessa asked. "Or were you arguing with yourself?"

"My blinkin' angel trainer. He drops me off after my first Universe Healing Team meeting, telling me he'll call me when the training is to start. That's it. No other information. I would have given him more of an earful if he'd stayed longer...."

Tessa interrupted my tirade. "You're a Universe Healer with an angelic trainer? What is that? When did this

---

[9] Chopsing – Welsh term for arguing or saying disrespectful comments to someone.

happen?"

I took a moment to appraise my sister. She was tan, glowing with health and something else I couldn't quite put my finger on. I shut up and pulled her into a hug.

"Good to see you, sis." My previous annoyance dissipated like morning mist when the sun hits it. "To what do I owe the honor of this visit?"

"We have to go. Soon. I'll explain while you pack." Her forehead had creased with concern. She turned away from me and quickly started pulling various things out of cabinets. Matches, paracord, candles, a knife, and other things began to pile up on the table.

"What am I packing for?" The pile on the kitchen table gave me the impression that we were going on an extended camping trip.

"Your backpack is what you need. You won't be coming back here." Tessa continued to add items to the stash.

"What? But I only moved back a few days ago." My heart plummeted at the thought of leaving the farm forever.

Tessa stopped to give me a long, penetrating stare. "Trust me on this, Quinn."

Her urgency was undeniable. And I did trust her.

I went to find my backpack.

CHAPTER 21

When we had finished stuffing my backpack with everything Tessa thought I needed and I hoisted it on, I caught a
flash of gold on her finger.

Catching her left hand, I pulled it up to check it out. A
plain gold band encircled her ring finger.

"What's this?" I couldn't keep the surprise out of my
voice.

Tessa smiled as she blushed. "I met someone."

"So it appears. Who? Where? When do I get to meet
him?" As I fired the questions at her, I heard several cars
drive up to the farmhouse. I checked out the window and
saw men with automatic rifles and the same type of wickedly
ugly dogs I had seen in London begin piling out of the
vehicles.

"Later. We need to go." Tessa grabbed my hand, then
picked up a jug she had brought with her. In a flash, the
farmhouse and its invaders disappeared.

—m—

The first things I noticed were sticky heat on my skin and

the sound of crickets singing loudly in the grass. Glancing up, I saw a hazy sun shining through leafy tree branches. This place was completely unfamiliar and not terribly comfortable compared to the cool weather I was used to.

We had arrived on a cement road in a small neighborhood. Well-kept houses with spacious yards lined both sides of the street.

A screen door banged on one of the houses. We saw several people come out and stand on the front porch. They observed us for a short while before one of the women started down the steps toward us, followed by a man and another woman. We waited for them to approach.

Tessa took the lead. "Is there anyone named 'Aneera' here?"

A petite, pretty woman with strawberry blond hair and green eyes stepped forward. "I'm Aneera."

Tessa set her jug down and grasped the woman's hand in hers, shaking it with gusto.

That's an unusually warm greeting for a stranger.

"I'm so pleased to meet you." Tessa was beaming. "I'm Tessa. This is my twin brother, Quinn. We were wondering if Quinn could stay here. His area of London or at our farm in Wales is no longer safe."

We were?

Aneera seemed slightly taken aback by Tessa's greeting but was happy to introduce the others with her. The woman and man were Loraine and her husband, Gary. Gary said they would need to check with the community leadership before offering me a place.

We made our way over to a large ranch house and waited while they sent for the community leaders. Tessa delivered her jug to Gary, telling him it was from the planet Maqualan and would stay eternally full of water. This caused quite a stir because the water reserves in the community were low. Gary immediately took the jug to begin filling up the storage tanks.

Mark, the de facto leader of the neighborhood, showed up with others named Dan, Katherine, and Delores. They asked Tessa and me a few questions, expressing gratitude for the water she brought. As soon as they agreed I could stay, Tessa left.

I was frustrated that I never got to ask Tessa about how she had been or the new guy in her life. I was also curious about the warm way she had greeted Aneera. While I might not like having to wait, I would have to bide my time on these questions.

After Tessa left, I turned back to the group to find Aneera staring at me. She quickly dropped her eyes.

I began to think this hot, humid new home with its loud crickets might not be so bad.

CHAPTER 22

Days passed quickly after my impromptu relocation. Dan gave me a spare bedroom in his house to use. It was simple and comfortable, and I was grateful.

I discovered this group of fifty or so people lived in a southeastern area of Texas. Never in my wildest imaginations would I have thought that I would live in Texas someday. To say I experienced culture shock was an understatement of epic proportions.

"You mean to tell me you've never had 'mushy peas'?" I was incredulous as I watched Stella, Dan's sister, chop up the skinned carcass of an armadillo for the evening's stew.

Stella giggled as she continued to expertly de-bone the animal. Her grey ponytail bobbed as she worked. "You mean to tell me you've never had armadillo stew before?" she tossed back at me, her head down as she cut the meat into bite-sized chunks.

"I don't think I even knew these odd mini-dinosaur-type creatures existed." The plating scales covering the armadillo had fascinated me when Dan brought it into the kitchen and handed it to Stella to prepare. "It looks like a Jurassic rat."

"They're delicious as long as they're cooked properly."

Stella scraped the meat off her cutting board into a large pot. "Otherwise they're as chewy as an old tire."

"Well, if I'm eating armadillo stew tonight, I had better make a side of mushy peas. At least then I'll know there's something I can actually swallow." I grinned mischievously at Stella. She grabbed a kitchen towel and popped my leg.

"Ow!" I scrambled out of her reach and bolted for the door.

"Serves you right, Quinn!" she called after me.

I laughed as I made a beeline for the neighborhood machine repair shed set up at Steve's house.

Up ahead, I saw Aneera in the road talking to a stranger. He was wearing a backpack and had a tall walking stick covered with green leaves and ripe almonds. I watched as she hugged him tightly.

Hmmm… Aneera's boyfriend perhaps?

My heart sank, giving me pause. I had only met the girl a few days before. My reaction, however, didn't stop me from intending to find out who this new guy was.

As I walked up, the sandy-haired fellow saw me. His eyes widened in shock.

"Qui… Quinn?" he stuttered before he moved a step toward me.

"Who are you?" I tried to tamp down the note of suspicious challenge in my voice.

"How do you know Quinn?" Aneera's head moved back and forth between us.

A huge smile covered the fellow's face. "This is perfect. I can tell you both at the same time."

"Tell us what?" Aneera and I said, our voices interlocking as one. I laughed. She blushed, which distracted me from the fellow in front of us.

This girl is far too pretty for her own good.

"Tessa and I are engaged!" Now the fellow's smile was almost blinding.

I froze. "What? Who *are* you?" I no longer tried to keep the suspicion out of my tone.

"This is my brother, Jarl." Aneera inclined her head toward him, affection in her eyes.

"Your brother?" I stared at him. Not as tall as me, sandy hair, trim build, good-looking enough, laughing eyes. I could see why Tessa might be interested.

Well, that explains a few things.

"C'mon." Jarl's good humor was catching. "I'm thirsty. Let's get a drink and I'll tell you all about it."

Prynk perused the members of the Council of 13. "You've lost him. He's been snatched away into enemy hands. Knowing where he is doesn't make a whit of difference if you can't access his mind and heart through his dreams."

Chorne's dark eyes flashed as he stood up. Light fizzed out of his skin in sparks that radiated different colors. "I warned you all. I always warn you. Why haven't you learned yet that I'm always right?"

Nipher, the tips of his fingers shifting into impossibly sharp lancets, scowled. "Mind your tone. Or I'll mind it for you."

Quovern cowered away as Nipher stood to move past him toward Chorne.

Shevril's beautiful face momentarily contorted in rage. "Sit down, you imbeciles! This is a setback, but it is not impossible to overcome. We don't know for certain that we can no longer access his dreams."

Reluctantly, Chorne and Nipher took their seats.

"I don't think we can access his dreams anymore. It's those almonds." Vander drummed his fingers on the golden table top. "They have shielded the enemy's forces across Earth. That cursed youngster, Jarl, has finished his almond deliveries. Even you have to admit, Shevril, that this has seriously hampered our efforts to track the enemy's operations. And we may lose the book when or if it's found if we can't discover a pathway back to Quinn."

Fraynt and Korfal shifted in their seats, both speaking at once. Draven silenced them by asking, "Are there any open ones in the community where Quinn lives?"

Racil's smile held a sinister edge. "We don't need to access Quinn's dreams any more. Instead, let's use the oldest play in the book. A woman. And I know which one."

Chloe's grease-stained fingers waved in my direction. "Hand me that wrench, Quinn."

I passed the adjustable crescent wrench over to her and she quickly extracted the bolt she was working on. Chloe was one of my new neighborhood's inhabitants. She was a wonder with machines. I had never met another woman with such an intuitive grasp of mechanical things. We often worked in the repair shop together.

The sensor she had been trying to reach was easy to pop out. She held it in triumph, a smile creasing her attractive, pixie-shaped face. Tawny, catlike eyes found mine, drawing an answering smile from me.

"That was a chore. I think we have a sensor like this one in our parts closet. If it fits, this will keep our tractor going a while longer." She got up to go to the cabinet against the back wall where the parts were stored.

Something struck me as I watched Chloe move across the shop. "You don't seem to have a blue field around you like everyone else." I checked more closely. "Did you eat one of the almonds Jarl brought a while ago to shield you from hybrids and other nasty entities?"

She laughed over her shoulder. "I didn't bother with one of those. Why would I when our whole community has a covering of protection from them?"

"It seems risky to me." I was troubled by her cavalier attitude.

"Well, maybe I like a risk or two." She gazed at me archly. When she saw my expression, she gave me a disarming grin. "Don't let it bother you, Quinn. We're perfectly safe here."

I allowed her confidence to sway me.

For the moment.

CHAPTER 23

I put my welding visor up. The repair on the broken trailer axle I was working on appeared perfect. I pulled my work light over to give it a thorough once over.

Yup. Right on the money.

Doing things correctly the first time is what we all strove for in the repair shop. Our solar-powered batteries usually charged quickly, but we didn't want to waste electricity. Not with a whole community needing power at various times during the day.

I heard the office door close. Chloe was headed out the rear door, but she saw me look over and crossed the concrete floor, dodging machine parts, to come to my work area.

Examining the weld on the axle, her face lit up. "This is great. We can get the trailer back in operation tomorrow."

Her happiness was beguiling. "Want to go for a walk and grab a drink?" Spending a little time with this attractive girl seemed like a good reward for work well done. I hoped she would agree.

"Sure. Come over to my place. It's only two houses over." Chloe led the way out of the shop.

The inside of her house was cool, which was a welcome

respite from the heat outside.

"I don't know how you all manage to seem so refreshed. This heat makes me feel like I've been stewing in tepid water all day." I wiped sweat from my eyes.

Chloe got two glasses out and filled them with her signature sweet-spicy lemonade. "The secret is in the pinch of cayenne pepper." She handed the glass to me. "Believe it or not, it helps cool the body down."

"You Texans are crazy. How could pepper possibly cool you down?" I sipped my drink with trepidation.

"You northerners are a wimpy lot." Her eyes met mine with a flirtatious challenge. Her hand brushed mine as she closed the cabinet door to the glasses.

The tingle from our shared contact added a different kind of warmth. I took a larger sip of the lemonade, hoping she was telling the truth about it cooling me down.

Aneera's face suddenly flashed in my mind.

Having two attractive single women in my vicinity was unusual. I hadn't dated much before because I had been wrapped up in work and family obligations. This was a new experience.

But I liked it.

—∿—

"Do you want to go on a picnic?" Chloe sidled up to me as I was tinkering on one of the chainsaws. "We won't be needing that chainsaw fixed for quite a while. The community's firewood stash is at a good level."

"Okay. A picnic sounds great." I went to wash the lubricating oil off my hands. "Where should we go?"

"I've got the perfect spot. I took a chance you'd say 'yes' so I already packed a lunch." She smiled hesitantly, showing a small crack in her normal confidence.

"Fine with me. You know the area better than I do." I moved aside so she could precede me out of the shop.

She picked up the picnic basket which had been resting under a tree. "Follow me." She started walking between the nearest houses and heading for the outskirts of the neighborhood.

We walked at a leisurely pace for half an hour under the shade of the trees. Up ahead, I noticed the faint blue line that demarcated where the neighborhood's shield of protection ended. When we got closer to it, I began to get nervous.

Jarl had told us about a few of the monstrous hybrids he had encountered in his spacewalking travels. He had seen giants, serpentine shape-shifters who could appear human, and werewolves. None of these were creatures I personally wanted to meet.

When I described the wickedly ugly dogs I had seen in London and at the farm to Jarl, he agreed that they were almost certainly a type of hybrid.

"That's what Buddy's almonds conceal us from." Jarl nodded at his leafy walking stick. "Who knew that Aaron's rod that budded[10] would have such an interesting use later in history?"

I remembered being dumbfounded. "Um… Buddy is Aaron's rod from the Bible? How is that possible?"

"It's a long story. I'll tell you one of these days."[11] Jarl had moved off to talk with Aneera then. I filed the discussion away for future reference.

---

[10] Numbers 17:1-13

[11] Quantum Spacewalker: Jarl's Journey, Chapters 43 and 44

Now that we were approaching this boundary, everything Jarl told me came back in force.

"Where is your picnic spot?" The boundary was drawing steadily closer.

"Right over there, in that group of trees by the creek. This has been my favorite spot for years." Chloe pointed to a lush green alcove only one hundred feet outside the boundary.

She noted my wrinkled brow. "Oh come on. It's right over there. You can't seriously be worried about us being outside of the boundary. I've never had any trouble when I'm there."

"Perhaps not. I wouldn't want this to be the first time." I considered her thoughtfully. "Especially since you haven't eaten an almond."

"We'll have the picnic on the side closest to the precious boundary so we can make a break for it if needed." She set her jaw stubbornly.

"Or we could just be prepared with the command Jarl taught us to deal with hybrids. You know, the 'In Jesus' name, I prophesy to your breath….'"

"I know what he said." She ended the conversation abruptly and stalked over to the picnic area. "Are you coming?" she tossed over her shoulder.

This picnic idea was becoming fraught with tension. I followed Chloe slowly, alert for anything suspicious as I made my way into the dense trees outside of the boundary.

CHAPTER 24

Hearing the creek trickling nearby and laying back on the blanket atop the springy grass while I digested the delicious lunch Chloe had brought, a sadly-sweet feeling crept over me. I closed my eyes and let out a deep sigh.

"Goodness. What was that for? You sound like the weight of the world settled on your shoulders." Chloe lay on her side, facing me with her head propped up in her hand.

"It's the Hiraeth. Don't you ever have that?" I closed my eyes again after glancing at her, letting the slight breeze ruffle my hair and blow away a fly that had been buzzing around.

"Maybe I have, if I knew what it was." She reached over and flicked away the fly that had landed on my nose.

"It's a Welsh term. You can find the Hiraeth in our stories and songs. Occasionally you'll find it in our paintings and poems. And, during times like today, it presents itself in the sound of a lazy creek and a light breeze." I wrinkled my nose as another insect flew past.

"Well, that explanation is entirely too poetic. I'm no closer to knowing what you're talking about." Chloe poured some more lemonade into her glass. I heard her swallowing small sips.

"It's a spiritual longing for a home we never knew, possibly an ancient place or a lost place to which we can't return. It's still part of us and calls us even now. Sometimes through a melody, sometimes through water trickling over rocks. It's everywhere and nowhere. My granny thought it was a longing for heaven. I've always suspected it's encoded in our DNA."

I opened my eyes to find Chloe's gaze on me, the dappled sunlight creating shifting shadows in her eyes. I thought I caught a hint of fleeting regret.

"I don't think the Hiraeth will ever leave until we're back with our Creator." I closed my eyes again, feeling Chloe's continued gaze as I drifted to sleep.

—✺—

Paralyzed again, I was halfway between sleeping and waking, lassitude making my limbs feel like they were filled with lead.

"This is perfect. You did well to get him beyond the boundary. Even so, his own protective field is difficult to penetrate." The voice speaking was familiar to me.

"Getting him here was a piece of cake." Chloe gave a low laugh. "Appeal to a man's appetite. Works every time."

"You will be well rewarded." A cold breeze blew across my face as the voice spoke. I wanted to turn my head, but was feeling too heavy to move.

"I'd kind of like to keep him. I've been enjoying his company." The wistful note in Chloe's voice held an undercurrent of something feline. Was that a purr?

"He will never be yours to keep." The voice took on a commanding tone. "His purpose rests in our realm."

A snarl came from Chloe's direction. Something soft and furry brushed my arm.

Sure wish I could open my eyes.

Sneering, the voice said, "Don't be foolish. There is no form you can morph into that would change this situation. Retract your little kitty claws and go back to the neighborhood."

A mountain lion roared. A wind like something leaping over me. A yowl of pain. A thud, followed by silence.

I had to move. I had to speak. But I could do neither.

The voice came from above me now. "Quinn, it's time for us to go on another trip."

This wasn't a dream, although the voice was from one of the beings in my traveling dreams. I could sense the bright light shining through my closed eyelids.

In my mind, I called out, "Jesus, help me!"

My lips became slightly mobile. I forced air up and out of my lungs. It was torturously difficult.

As a hand grasped my forearm, I was able to mutter a guttural, "Jesus."

The hand dropped away. I heard a fading cry of anger until, finally, I sensed that I was alone.

It was several minutes before I could move. The light breeze continued to play with my hair and the insects still buzzed around, but everything else was silent.

My eyes seemed to have a gummy residue keeping them shut. I pried them open with my right hand. With blurred vision, I sat up, feeling the blood drain from my head. It left me woozy.

There must have been some sort of drug in the food.

I scanned the picnic area slowly, trying to find Chloe. A large catlike figure lay crumpled at the base of a cottonwood tree by the creek. I crawled to it and turned it over.

Chloe's features were melded with the tawny fur of a human-sized mountain lion. Her lips were curled back in a snarl, and sharp claws were extended from her paw-like hands. It was obvious her neck had been broken by the unnatural angle of her head as it rested against the tree trunk.

Horrified, I backed away. I crawled to a smaller tree and pulled myself up. When I could walk, I hurried back to the neighborhood as quickly as I could.

CHAPTER 25

"Steve! Caleb!" I burst into the repair shop, hoping to find at least one of the men there.

Steve looked up from the mower engine he was repairing. "What happened to you, Quinn?" He rushed over to me.

"I need help. We were on a picnic, and she shifted, and there was this other being, but now she's dead, but it's not her. It's a mountain lion. I need an ATV...." My incoherent rambling wasn't helping, but I couldn't make the words work properly.

Caleb heard my crazed yelling and came out of the office. "Whoa, whoa. Slow down. Come into the office. We'll get you some water." Caleb led me to the office swivel chair and sat me down.

I saw my hands on the chair's armrests. They were trembling, but felt strangely detached, like they weren't actually my hands. A clammy bead of sweat trickled down my cheek. Caleb left to get water.

Keep it together. No going into shock.

Grabbing a greasy jacket off another chair, I put it over me and held it before lowering my head between my knees. I was still shaking, but no longer thought I would pass out.

Caleb came with a cup of water. He held it up for me to get a drink. Steve came in with a shop blanket, which he put over my shoulders, then told Caleb to go get Aneera.

Steve sat and turned his chair to face me. "Tell me what's going on, Quinn."

I closed my eyes and took several deep breaths. I still felt strangely detached from my body. "I was working on the chainsaw motor when Chloe came in and asked me if I wanted to go on a picnic. I was hungry and had the prospect of good company, so I agreed."

A few more deep breaths. "We went to Chloe's favorite picnic spot by a creek. I was a bit concerned because it was outside our neighborhood's protective boundary, but Chloe got testy when I brought it up, so I went ahead. The food was great. After we ate, I laid down and fell asleep."

Caleb came in with Aneera. She took my pulse, then felt my forehead. "We need to have you lie down, Quinn, and elevate your legs a bit, just until you warm up and your pulse slows down."

She turned to Caleb. "Help me make space on the carpet here." Caleb began shoving repair manuals and boxes out of the way.

"No!" I tried to stand but got lightheaded and sank back into the chair. "We have to go back to the picnic site."

Caleb put an arm around my waist to get me out of the chair, then helped me to the floor. Steve put two thick repair manuals under my feet to elevate them.

"Relax." Steve's voice was kind. "We'll go out to the picnic site. Aneera will stay with you until we get back."

Aneera knelt beside me and put the shop blanket over me again. "It's okay, Quinn. Those guys will be able to figure out what's going on." She picked up my left hand between her warm hands and rubbed it lightly.

"You're so beautiful." Looking at Aneera's lovely face, I heard my groggy voice say the words before I slipped away into darkness again.

—⁓—

I woke up to Aneera gazing at me contemplatively. Steve and Caleb were back and speaking quietly outside the office door.

My head was pounding like several rhinos were practicing their tap-dancing routine on it. I groaned at the piercing office lights slicing through my eyes and into my brain.

Aneera got up and switched the light off. "There. Is that better?"

I grunted my assent.

Steve and Caleb came into the office. I heard the creak of the office chair as Steve sat down. Opening my eyes a slit, I saw his beard and characteristic grubby cowboy hat outlined in the dim light.

"We found Chloe." Steve was upset. "We brought her and the picnic items back. I'm not sure what she put in the food, but it must have been potent. A coyote ate the rest of your lunch. We found it passed out a few feet away from the blanket."

"Poor coyote." I groaned again. "If he feels anything like I do right now, he'll be hating life for a while."

"We also saw what you meant about Chloe. She was still in mountain lion form." Caleb's voice was terse. "We had no idea she was a shape-shifter."

I struggled to sit up. Aneera helped with an arm behind my back.

"It makes sense now why she didn't want one of Buddy's

almonds or for me to finish saying the prophetic declaration from Jarl that kills hybrids." I put my elbows on my knees so I could rest my head in my hands. "I guess I should have asked more questions."

I could hear the distress in Steve's voice. "She's been in the community for years. I don't think anyone knew what she was." Steve got to his feet. "I'll go talk with Mark and Dan about this. Caleb can help you get to your room, Quinn."

Aneera and Caleb got on either side of me, lifted me up, and helped me back to my room at Dan's house.

CHAPTER 26

I was out until the next day. A knock on my door roused me from the complete blackness of my sleep.

Stella walked in with a breakfast tray, followed by Aneera.

"Hey there, Quinn. Figured you could use some sustenance after your adventure yesterday." Stella set the tray down on the desk by my bed.

"What adventure are you talking about?" I had a dull headache. Searching my memory drew a blank. "Did something weird happen with the chainsaw I was working on?"

Stella shot Aneera a concerned glance. Aneera said, "This isn't surprising." She drew up a chair beside the bed.

"How are you feeling right now?" Aneera felt my forehead, took my pulse, and then used a small flashlight to examine my eyes.

"Not too great, now that I'm half-blinded by that light." I knew Aneera was a medical person, but wasn't sure why she was here now.

"The good news is all your responses are normal this morning, unlike yesterday. The bad news is that you don't

QUANTUM SPACEWALKER: QUINN'S QUEST

seem to remember what happened." Aneera tucked the flashlight into her shirt pocket.

"I remember working on a chainsaw motor." I tried to push past the blank grey wall in my mind. "I feel like I went somewhere after that. Was it an ATV ride? Why? Did I hit my head?" I ran a hand through my hair. "I do have a slight headache." I felt my head for bumps or sore spots but didn't find any.

"You don't remember a picnic or Chloe shape-shifting into a mountain lion?" Aneera watched my face closely.

She couldn't have shocked me more if she had backhanded me out of the blue. I shook my head mutely.

"Quinn, you've been 'roofied.'" Aneera sat back in her chair, shaking her head.

"I was up on a roof? What for? Did I fall off?" This made no sense to me.

Stella chuckled nervously. Aneera smiled, then shook her head. "Chloe put a type of drug into your food yesterday. We found it in her bedroom. It's similar to Rohypnol, which allows a person to remain conscious but not be able to move. That's where the term 'roofied' comes from. After its effects have worn off, the person who was drugged can't remember what happened. It's been used many times for evil purposes."

My mind was spinning, but no words would come.

Aneera had a glint of admiration in her eyes. "You must be pretty tough, though. You were able to make it back to the repair shop under your own power and tell Steve a little of what happened before you blacked out again."

She slapped her knees lightly and stood up. "Tell you what. Eat some breakfast and get dressed. Then come downstairs and we can tell you what's going on." She nodded to Stella and they left the room.

—∿∿—

Since I was ravenously hungry, I dove into breakfast first. Stella could certainly make a top-notch omelet. Combined with the fresh bread and homemade jam, it was better than anything a restaurant could put out – not that I had been to a restaurant for a long time.

My mind was working overtime as I brushed my teeth, washed my face, and got dressed.

How could I not remember most of yesterday?

I noticed I was pale and my eyes were red-rimmed, which wasn't normal. Yet there was no way I could wrap my head around cute little Chloe luring me out for a picnic and drugging me. What reason could she have possibly had?

No answers presented themselves, so I went downstairs to see what I could discover.

—∿∿—

Dan's living room was full of people. Mark, Dan, Stella, Steve, Caleb, Aneera, and Delores sat around, sipping coffee and talking in hushed voices.

It reminded me of a wake.

"Who died?" I asked as I came into the room. I meant it as a joke, but no one laughed.

"Chloe." Steve looked at me, sadness filling his face.

"What? You're not serious! How?" The questions sputtered out of me awkwardly. "She died? I thought Aneera said she drugged me at a picnic for some reason."

"He doesn't remember." Aneera addressed the group. "That's how this drug works. It's insidious, really."

Steve sighed. "So that means that what he said yesterday

is the only information we're likely to get?"

Aneera nodded. "Pretty much."

"What did I say yesterday?" Stella handed me a cup of coffee and led me to a chair. "I've tried, but I only remember working on a chainsaw."

"You came into the repair shop yelling something about a picnic, a 'being' of some sort, Chloe being dead and being a mountain lion." Caleb turned to Steve for confirmation. "You were frantic, and you didn't make much sense."

"While Caleb went to get Aneera," Steve recounted, "you told me Chloe had invited you for a picnic to her favorite spot outside the protective boundary. You were concerned, but went anyway when she got 'testy.' The last thing you said before Aneera arrived was that the food was great and you laid down to take a nap."

None of this jogged my memory.

Mark stood up. "Come with me, Quinn."

"Where are we going?" I was thinking I had entered the *Twilight Zone* and might be trapped there forever.

"You need to see Chloe's body." Mark headed for the door.

"You're sure that's a good idea?" Aneera was on her feet, following Mark.

Mark nodded. "From what Steve and Caleb said, Quinn was in shock along with what the drug did to him. Maybe a few memories stuck because of that." He beckoned me with his hand. "C'mon, let's go."

Reluctantly, I got up and followed Mark and Aneera outside.

CHAPTER 27

"We won't be able to keep Chloe in our underground cool storage for long. She'll have to be buried soon." Mark led us to the large root cellar on his property. It was a concrete-lined bunker that doubled as food storage and tornado protection.

A single bulb lit up when Mark pulled its chain, causing shadows to gather eerily in the corners.

A form covered in a sheet was laid on a metal table. Mark walked up to it and pulled the sheet back. A face frozen in a snarl greeted me. It was part Chloe and part large cat.

A snarl echoed around me.

"Don't be foolish." I closed my eyes and repeated what I heard in my mind. "Put your kitty claws back in and return to the neighborhood." My head was starting to hurt again. "You can't keep him. He belongs in our realm."

I gasped, then wobbled. Mark put out a hand to steady me.

"I can't open my eyes. I can't see anything." Bile began to rise. I pushed it down, not wanting to lose my breakfast. "Wind rushed past me. Then I heard a cry of pain, and it was quiet." A strange detachment crept over me. "I couldn't move. I don't know how long I couldn't move. Something was coming for me. His voice was familiar…."

The blank grey wall slammed into place in my mind. "I can't remember anything else."

"Chloe set you up." Aneera's eyebrows came together in a frown. "She was going to deliver you to someone. Who?"

"And why?" Mark stared at me, tapping his chin thoughtfully.

I was perplexed. "I wish I knew."

Mark pulled the sheet back over Chloe and we walked up the steps and into the sunlight.

We buried Chloe quietly in the cemetery on the edge of our small neighborhood. We told the community members she had died in an accident. Only a few people came to the graveside. She didn't seem to have had many close friends. A few of us who knew what had actually transpired lingered after the ceremony to talk.

Steve was the most broken up over her death, but not for the reasons I expected.

"I worked with Chloe for five years. How could I have never even suspected she was a hybrid? If I was that fooled, are there others here in the neighborhood too?" Steve gestured at our tidy enclave. "Are there others here waiting for the right time to betray us?"

When he said this, a cloud blocked the sun, casting a pall over the area.

Dan addressed us sternly. "Stop this fear immediately!"

As our resident Bible and prophecy scholar, Dan was intensely knowledgeable. And he was serious at the moment. "We have what we need to make sure there are no more hybrids among us. Are there any others who haven't eaten one of Buddy's almonds for protection? If so, we will speak to them individually. Otherwise, we should use the prophetic declaration at our next group gathering."

Steve visibly relaxed. "That's a good idea. I can't stand the thought of suspecting people I work with all the time."

"Fear is one of the devil's most effective tools. When you first begin to feel it, turn immediately to what the Bible says. We have *not* been given a spirit of fear, but of love, power and a sound mind.[12] Kick fear to the curb."

"And then run over it with a tank." Caleb grinned as he clapped Steve on the shoulder. "Dad, you'll find that this will work out for the good of all of us here. It's too bad that Quinn had to be the one to ferret Chloe out, but it's alerted us to the steps we need to take."

"Good words, son." Steve inclined his head to Caleb. As the two men moved off with the rest of the small group, I was left standing with Aneera.

"Do you really think I'm beautiful?" Her green eyes met mine and she grinned impishly.

Nothing like being put on the spot.

"Um…well…." Heat flushed my face and kept getting hotter. "You are. Did I tell you that?"

"You did. It's a memory I don't want to have erased in that drug-addled brain of yours." She winked, then walked back toward Gary and Loraine's house, casting a grin toward me over her shoulder.

I watched her go, knowing that the trajectory of my life had just taken a decidedly interesting turn.

---

[12] 2 Timothy 1:7

CHAPTER 28

"You know, I really haven't had much adventure in my life, contrary to what you might suspect." I joined Aneera on the large porch at Gary and Loraine's.

Aneera closed her journal and set a heavy gold pen on top of it before giving me her attention.

I recognized the pen as identical to the one I had gotten at my Universe Healing Team meeting.

"Am I in there?" I pointed at her journal.

"Wouldn't you like to know?" Her raised eyebrows included a hint of mischief.

Yes, the chemistry is high today.

I pulled my gold pen from my back pocket and set it beside hers on the journal.

She started in surprise, then picked up both pens and examined them closely. "Where did you get this?"

"Quadrant 4 Universe Healing Team member, at your service." I gave a little bow before sliding into a chair across from her at the porch table. It was a risk to talk about the healing teams, but I hoped my hunch was correct.

"You could have told me. It would have been nice to have someone to talk with." Her reproachful expression made me want to defend myself.

Bingo. Hunch confirmed.

"I was still getting used to the idea. I had only just returned from my team meeting when Tessa showed up to bring me here. Besides, I wanted to get to know you better before broaching the subject." The excuses sounded lame to me.

"And you feel like you know me well enough now?" Her green eyes darkened a shade.

If that wasn't an opportunity, I didn't know what was. "Not nearly as well as I want to." I started to reach for her hand. "Aneera...."

The screen door banged open, causing us to jump. Emily, Gemma's three-year-old daughter, raced out with a scrawny kitten in her arms. Gemma and Emily also lived at Gary and Loraine's house.

"Aneera!" Emily shouted. "Momma got me a kitten. I'm going to name her Strawberry."

Aneera rescued the kitten from Emily's enthusiastic grasp, looking over at me with regret. I retracted my hand and sat back while we admired Strawberry.

Poof. That moment was decimated.

I fervently hoped there would be another one.

Jarl arrived a few days later. As a Quantum Spacewalker, he had been tasked with supplying all the groups who belonged to Jesus on Earth with manna and protective almonds.

I was familiar with manna now. It was actual manna from biblical times. It was *amazing*. It would transform into the exact food you told it to become. The Texas community had been getting low on food when Jarl provided the manna a couple of years ago. With it and their ongoing agricultural efforts, we were all well supplied.

The protective almonds he had delivered were also necessary. Our community hadn't had to deal with many hybrids, giants, or any external threat because of them, but the rest of the world had experienced infiltration and the subsequent terror these creatures brought.

Once Chloe had been discovered, there were no other hybrids found inside our group. I, for one, was extremely grateful.

Now that Jarl had completed his deliveries, he wanted to stay with us. Since he was Aneera's brother and Tessa's fiancé, I anticipated finding out what kind of guy he was.

—✦—

"Tell us again how multi-presence works." Loraine handed Jarl another drink, leaning in expectantly.

Suddenly, five Jarls faced us. They spread around the room, each speaking and moving independently of the others. It was like each one was a perfectly complete Jarl.

"Don't you think this would be a great idea for choirs?" one Jarl said.

"Absolutely," another Jarl agreed.

"So, sing something," a third Jarl said.

"As the song title goes, *One*...." the fourth Jarl said, preparing to belt it out.

Aneera swatted Jarl #4 and rolled her eyes. "Really? Please don't sing. While one might be the loneliest number, it doesn't answer Loraine's question."

"I'm hurt. I'm wounded...," Jarl #4 said.

"Ok, drama king," Jarl #5 said. "Stuff it. To answer your question, it's important to understand the character trait of

God called omnipresence."

"Omnipresence," the other Jarls echoed.

I couldn't decide if this was cool or creepy.

Jarl #5 continued. "In John 17, Jesus talks about us being one as he and Father are one. Every person who has accepted Jesus' payment for their sins[13] has his Spirit living inside him or her. We are practically and spiritually one. Since the Spirit is omnipresent – or everywhere – we can be as well. In theory, we can be everywhere the Spirit is. In practicality, most spacewalkers keep it to a few hundred or thousand places. Infinity is still hard for us humans to grasp."

Jarl #3 said, "You also need to be aware that what happens to one of us, happens to all. That's the only real limitation we face by living in a physical body and operating in multi-presence."

"Which means, if one of us is hurt, we all are." Jarl #2 pinched Jarl #1's arm.

"Ouch!" all the Jarls said.

"Precisely," Jarl #2 said.

Aneera glanced over at me and whispered, "Do you think we'll do this someday?"

"Without a doubt." I tried to imagine a dozen "me's" running around. Or Aneeras. It was a stretch.

Jarl re-integrated himself and said, "Who's up for popcorn and Pictionary?"

A chorus of agreement arose.

Since I was the resident popcorn maker, I got up and headed to the kitchen to work my culinary magic.

---

[13] John 3:16; Romans 3:23; Romans 6:23; Romans 8:11

CHAPTER 29

The bed sagged as someone sat down on the edge of it. I fought my way out of sleep and flipped the lamp on.

The Shepherd was smiling at me.

"Hi there," I mumbled, still groggy. "I haven't seen you in a while."

"They're on to you, Quinn."

"Who? What have I done now?" I sat up, watching light flash in the Shepherd's grey eyes.

"They're bastards, you know. In the truest sense of that word." The Shepherd spoke softly, as if I knew what he meant. "The best definitions describe a bastard as something spurious, irregular, inferior, or of questionable origin."[14]

"Why do I always feel like I'm dropped into a conversation I have no clue about whenever I see you?" I blinked the rest of the sleep from my eyes and stared at the man who was staring at me.

"We've been having this conversation for a long time." His eyes crinkled at the edges in amusement.

---

[14] Merriam-Webster dictionary definition for *bastard*

"Do I ever understand who these bastards are in those 'ongoing conversations'?"

The Shepherd laughed soundlessly. His merriment shook the bed.

"Do you remember who you are? Who I told you that you are?" He waited patiently for my response.

"I handle pop quizzes much better in daylight after I've had a stiff cup of tea." Mentally racing through my encounters with the Shepherd, I hit on the one I thought he meant.

"You said I was one of your 'Golden Ones.'"

"Good job!" The Shepherd whispered as he clapped me on the back. "Has anyone else used that term with you?"

Clarity came slowly. "Those beings. The ones from my dreams. They called themselves 'Golden Ones' and were going to teach me about what that meant. My 'inheritance' they called it. I thought you sent them."

"And did they teach you?" The Shepherd watched my face.

"They were starting to. I had several dreams where either one or a few of them took me places in the Universe. In the last dream I had, three of them were taking me to a council meeting." I paused to recollect.

"What happened?" His question prodded me forward.

"I never learned anything at the Council. Harnel woke me up."

He nodded. "Did you ever wonder why Harnel was sent to wake you up right then?"

I hadn't thought about that. "No. I was annoyed because I was on the verge of getting an answer when he woke me up."

"Didn't you get an answer?" For some reason, the Shepherd's gentle question stung me.

Harnel's answer after he woke me up leapt to mind.

"Oh, please." Racil rolled his eyes. "Cover yourself. This is embarrassing. Do you think I'm so foolish as to leave him unbranded? I'll grant you that I acted hastily in destroying the woman. I had a moment of anger when she thought to attack me."

In a flash, Shevril's golden appearance was restored. Projecting a dangerous calmness, he walked over to stand in front of Racil. "How did you brand him?"

"It's a shame that you have been far less interested in guiding the development of nano and quantum technologies than I have. If you had, I might be asking you this question instead." Racil smirked up at Shevril.

"Don't push me further, Racil. We've replaced members of this Council before when I reached the limits of my patience with them."

The tiniest flicker of fear shone in Racil's eyes before he answered. "This little branding gem has actually gone far beyond any current human or angelic technology. It is a marker one Planck length in size that is attached to our subject's DNA. It will remain attached even during his future travels through the quantum realm and will re-attach to a strong strand with any DNA degradation that might occur. It was a simple matter to include this in the drug Chloe gave him."

Racil closed his eyes briefly. A small device appeared before him on the Council table. He picked it up with a flourish and showed it to Shevril and the other council members. "This tracking device will show us where Quinn is located in any time, space or dimension. I told you we didn't need direct contact with him, contrary to what other Council members thought. Even though he is no longer open to contact with us, we will be able to track him anywhere he goes."

Flicking a finger over the device, Racil turned it on. After glancing at it a moment, he said, "Quinn is in the repair shop in his neighborhood right now."

"Are you certain this can track him inter-dimensionally?" Shevril almost seemed impressed.

"I'm sure." Racil inclined his head confidently.

"How do you know?" Jaburn asked from several seats away.

A malicious smirk settled on Racil's perfect lips. "Because I've used the same type of device to track all of you."

CHAPTER 31

The warnings were converging. Jarl had told us that a planet would arrive that would block the sun. This was what he was shown in a vision, and it was why he had been told to distribute Buddy's almonds for protection. He reminded us of this frequently at our community meals.

The planet would bring the "friends from the Universe." They would allegedly offer help for the woes facing the peoples of the Earth like famines, diseases, wars and natural disasters. They would depict themselves as those who had "seeded" or "planted" humans here untold millennia ago.

But it would all be a lie.

In truth, they would be the hybrid offspring of fallen, evil angels and human women. Any help they offered would be deceptive and designed to destroy or enslave.

Not long after Jarl reminded us again about this planet, Mark made an announcement at our Sunday afternoon potluck.

We had finished our worship service and the enormous meal afterward. Mark stood up and addressed the group. "I want you all to know that the leadership team has been getting a sense that we won't be able to stay here much longer."

This shockwave whipped through the group, causing murmurs to buzz.

"I know that's a bold statement, but I bet many of you have been feeling the same way." Mark grew quiet. As we all waited for more information, I gazed out over the group and saw nods of assent to what he had been saying.

Dan came to stand beside Mark. "We've been kept safe here during the first part of Daniel's 70th week or, as we know it, the last seven years of this current age.[16] But, things are going to be getting *really* crazy soon."

Jeremy, our resident tech guy with our only solar-powered satellite TV, called out, "You mean even crazier than all the global devastation we've already seen? What they estimate now is that over two billion people have died from all these horrible things."

"Not to mention those who have been caught and killed because they follow Jesus," Steve said. "Chop, chop." Steve made a gesture with his hand like the blade of a guillotine coming down on a person's neck.

I knew it was true and shuddered.

Katherine, one of the women who kept the animals, said, "What if we don't want to go? I've lived my entire life here." Her jaw was set stubbornly.

Dan nodded, acknowledging Katherine's comment. "We can't make you do anything. We all need to realize that global disasters are going to ramp up. We need to be prepared to move if that's what you each decide to do. The almond protection we've had probably will not extend to major natural disasters."

The group broke up into smaller groups to discuss this

---

[16] Daniel 9:24-27

turn of events.

I was depressed by the news. This community had become my family.

Where could we possibly go to be safe?

—⁓—

The planet arrived the next week.

The horizon was ashen and dark, and the moon was the color of blood as it hung in the early morning sky. A massive black shape hung between the Earth and the sun, blocking the sun's rays.

It was the first time I had experienced bone-numbing fear.

Our entire group gathered at our common area in the center of the houses, staring at the sky. No one said a word until Jeremy came out with his TV.

"I've kept this thing fully charged because I was sure this would be happening soon." He set the TV down on a picnic table and we all spread out so we could see it.

When Jeremy tuned into a channel, it confirmed that the "friends from the Universe" had arrived.

They were the weirdest assortment of beings I had seen outside of a Marvel movie. Yet they were real—not some CGI-created virtual monsters.

These "friends" were met by the Pope and a number of world leaders in a large stadium. A huge platform had been set up in the middle of the field, and the "friends" were escorted to it.

Everyone in the entire stadium sat in hushed silence as the "friends" approached the platform. Our group waited with bated breath, glued to the TV screen.

The Pope began introducing them to the world leaders.

After he made it through a few, a tall, blue "friend" who carried a wicked spear-pitchfork thing stopped the proceedings.

The blue creature called several of the other "friends" forward to offer gifts for the planet to help provide food, but then made an unexpected statement. He said that they wouldn't deal with the fractured, squabbling governments of the world.

Instead, they had selected their own human liaison. They would only deal with him, and he could be their spokesperson to the rest of the world. He would be the one to distribute the gifts they brought.

The blue "friend" called forward a tall, dark-haired man who appeared Middle Eastern. None of us recognized him. He was introduced as Liame Emanuel.

Mr. Emanuel made the rounds on the platform, greeting all the world leaders, none of whom appeared happy with this development. Then, he walked by several of the "friends," stopping briefly to whisper something into the ear of a voluptuous pink woman with seaweed-like hair. The pink woman smiled seductively.

The tall blue "friend" saw this exchange and flew immediately into a volcanic rage. With no warning, he slashed out with his spear and split Mr. Emanuel's head in half.

Screams and cries erupted from the stadium. Pandemonium broke out among the world leaders.

Members of our community who were watching cried out in shock as well. One woman, who was standing close to me, fainted.

Emanuel's body dropped to the platform floor, blood pooling around the gaping wound in his head.

The TV lost power and went dark.

We were left with our own stunned silence as the crickets hummed around us in the unnatural dark.

CHAPTER 32

"He's dead?" I heard myself say. "For a 'friend of the Universe,' that wasn't very friendly. I thought this Emanuel guy was supposed to be the one-world leader or Anti-Christ or whatever...."

"We did, too." Dan sounded perplexed. "I have no frame of reference for this."

"The book of Revelation is basically our textbook right now." Mark spoke to everyone. "But I think we can all expect some twists and turns."

"This was a *big* twist." Jarl let out a sigh. "What now?"

"Yes, what now?" several people asked.

I heard my sister's voice before I saw her.

"We go to Petra." Tessa's familiar lilting voice brought joy to my heart.

Jarl flashed by me to grab Tessa in a hug and swing her around. I was annoyed that I didn't get the first hug until I saw the grin on Tessa's face. Grudgingly, I decided to wait my turn. She was his fiancée, after all.

Aneera caught my eye. I thought I saw her wink, but it was hard to tell in the darkness. The two of us went up for our hugs and greetings afterward.

I tried to be content with that.

—ɯ—

Our group was given a time frame to pack up to leave for Petra. We didn't have much time to decide whether we wanted to stay or go.

Katherine announced loudly that she was going to stay, and marched back into her house.

The rest of us packed up.

I saw Jarl giving Tessa a brief introduction to multi-presence. She practiced with childlike glee.

Within a few hours the group members were ready to go, except for Katherine. We met in the common area where we had recently watched the "friends from the Universe" fiasco on TV.

We jerked our heads up to the sky when we heard an odd screeching sound above us. It sounded like an incoming missile.

Something caused a fiery explosion a few miles away. The ramifications of what was happening stunned us.

Then, there were more of the awful screeching sounds.

"Meteors!" Mark yelled. "We need to get out of here!"

Jarl and Tessa went into multi-presence and began grabbing group members, encasing every person in a spacewalking bubble before disappearing.

Katherine came out of her home, seeing the meteors falling. Fear filled her face. "I'm coming with you." She raced inside to grab a few items.

Can't say I blame her for changing her mind.

Katherine ran out and was immediately grabbed by a Jarl. They disappeared.

Tessa appeared in front of me. "Hold on, Quinn." Her

arms encircled me. I saw fiery meteors mixed strangely with large hailstones destroying the streets and houses in our neighborhood as we quickly left.

—ᴍ—

I still wasn't used to these abrupt entrances and exits from the quantum realm. They weren't quite as disruptive as my first trip with Harnel, but still, my legs were rubbery and my head was woozy.

Sheesh. I'd better get my spacewalker bearings soon. This is ridiculous.

When I could walk without feeling like the ground was tilting, I moved forward and gazed at the red dust surrounding me. There were literally tons of sand interspersed with intricately carved rock surfaces. It reminded me of an *Indiana Jones* movie.

Tessa and Jarl were back in their original forms, standing close together and talking. Jarl had apparently gotten hurt. He sat on a rock and rolled up his pant leg. I watched Tessa hurry off, presumably to get something to help him.

Aneera walked up to me. "Isn't spacewalking fantastic? I feel completely energized, like the very first time when I went to my Universe Healing team meeting." She did a happy turn, then threw in a few dance moves.

"I'm glad you like it." I took my backpack off and moved to stand in the shade. Enjoying the cooler temperature, I leaned against a towering rock face. "I haven't had quite the same experience. Although I like that dance routine you did." I grinned at her. My equilibrium was back enough for me to grab her and give her a couple of spins with my own dance moves.

"Wow." Aneera's face was flushed and her eyes were

bright. "I didn't know you had it in you."

"I'm full of surprises." I had never wanted to kiss her as badly as I did now. As she smiled up at me, I drew her in close.

Unfortunately, Tessa walked up to us right then. She glanced quizzically between Aneera and me while we grew red.

"I was showing Aneera a few of my stellar dancing skills." My expression dared Tessa to make any comment.

Tessa's amusement was plain to both of us, but all she said was, "Aneera, Jarl's leg got hurt when he rescued Emily's cat from under a porch. Can you come check it out? I've cleaned it already."

Aneera disengaged herself from my arms, but her expression promised we would pick up where we left off at a later time.

I watched her go, anticipating our next encounter.

CHAPTER 33

There were other people besides our group in the ruined, ancient city of Petra. They had been brought by other spacewalkers, rescued as we had been when the planetary disasters became exponentially worse.

Everyone found places to stay within the carved tombs and caves scattered throughout Petra. Since our group was a smaller one, we found a cozy cave and settled in.

One evening Dan gave us a mini-lecture on Petra around the fire. "Petra was built by the Nabatean people, although other peoples lived here long before that time. This became the capital city of the Nabateans around the fourth century BC."

Dan poked the fire for a few moments and threw more sticks on it before continuing. "At its peak, around twenty thousand people lived here. Archaeologists have been interested in this area for at least two centuries, and the country of Jordan has had it open to tourism for many years—until the current world situation became what it is."

We were all lost in our thoughts for a while, contemplating the "world situation," which had changed radically again yesterday. After we had seen Mr. Emanuel wind up dead while being introduced to the world, our questions hadn't abated.

The planet blocking the sun had moved out of the way, and Jeremy was able to charge up his small TV a couple of days after we came to Petra. Miraculously, he found a satellite to connect with that wasn't destroyed by the meteor storm.

Once he got his TV running, we watched the news repeatedly playing on every channel. For some revolting reason, the cameras were trained on the lifeless body of Liame Emanuel. Flies crawled over the congealed blood on his head.

It made me sick to my stomach.

As we watched, morning sunlight hit Emanuel's head. It was the third day since he had been killed. Movement began subtly. His right index finger twitched. His eyelid flickered. Then, slowly, the two halves of Emanuel's head came together and re-sealed themselves seamlessly.

I wondered what diabolical evil this was.

The fallen man blinked, sat up, then moved blood-encrusted hair out of his eyes. He smiled in triumph as he stood up, faced the cameras, and declared,

"I am he who has risen from the dead. Peoples of the Earth, BEHOLD YOUR GOD!"

Personally, I was getting tired of earth-shaking events that left us all in stunned silence. Yet here we all were again, standing together, appalled and speechless.

Jeremy powered the TV down and walked back into the cave without saying a word.

Loraine broke the silence. "Well, I suppose that removes

all doubt as to who Emanuel is."

"I suppose it does." Mark rubbed his hands through his hair. "The Beast of Revelation 13 has arrived in living color."

"Yes, the color of blood." Dan was somber. "He's going to drench the Earth in it."

On that terrifying note, I decided to take a walk. I needed to think.

—⟋⟍—

My walk passed several other groups of people from different parts of the globe. I smiled and waved, but kept on moving until I reached an uninhabited place in the old city. I walked until a flat bench-like rock presented itself.

Plopping myself unceremoniously down on the rock, I craned my head back to see the clear blue sky between tall rock walls.

"These last few years have been crazy." I was half-muttering, half-praying. "How is any sane person supposed to handle this?"

"The way sane people have dealt with difficult times throughout the ages." The Shepherd walked out of the shadows toward me, off-white robes swirling around him. "They built their spiritual and emotional houses on the Rock.[17] Those houses remain standing when the storms come."

The Shepherd gave every indication of being completely at home in his flowing Bedouin-style robes.

"You could have stepped from the pages of the Bible in ancient Israelite times." I admired his desert chic. "Are those

---

[17] Matthew 7:24-27

robes *really* comfortable?"

"They keep you cooler than you might expect. And they camouflage bad body odor well." His teeth flashed white against his tan skin when he laughed.

"It's nice to see you." The Shepherd's presence provided a handhold to stop my figurative slide into the depths of despair. "But why are you here?"

"As one of my Golden Ones, it is time for you to learn how to hold increasing amounts of glory in your 'vessel'— inside yourself." He pointed his staff at my heart. "You need to hold it and then release it safely at the proper time."

"Isn't that part of what I'll be doing when I'm on the Universe Healing Team?" That assignment loomed a few years in the future.

The Shepherd nodded. "Yes. And no. If you attempt to hold what you'll need to when you are a Universe Healer without proper preparation, it will destroy you."

"I don't like the sound of that."

Fast-forward towards despair again.

"Neither do I." The Shepherd appeared pleased. "Which is why your secret missions will begin now."

Secret missions?

"Who are these missions a secret from?" The picture of a debonair James Bond flashed in my mind.

"Everyone." The Shepherd's grey eyes pierced mine, lightning rolling in their depths.

"Do I get awesome spy equipment?" I gave him hopeful puppy-dog eyes.

He shook his head, sighing. "And they say movies don't affect people." Then, he smiled at me. "You'll be equipped for every mission. As I recall, you were after Harnel to tell you what else you needed to do to prepare for your Universe Healing. Here's your answer. This will give you several kinds of practice, including spacewalking."

Sheepishly, I dropped my head. "I should probably apologize to Harnel for yelling at him."

"You'll get your chance. He understands how temperamental humans can be." There was no condemnation in the Shepherd's statement.

I squared my shoulders, and sat up straighter. "All right, when do these missions begin?"

"Right now, of course." The Shepherd's raised eyebrows made me think I should have grasped this immediately. "Follow me."

He turned and walked back into the shadows.

I stood up and, with tentative steps, trailed along behind him.

PART 2
ADVENTURE FINDING

CHAPTER 34

"Do you remember when I asked if you believed in time travel?" The Shepherd's voice bounced eerily off the walls of the narrow canyon we were walking through.

"Yes, I do." I increased my pace to catch up to him.

"What do you think now?" He glanced at me over his shoulder.

"You said you 'owned time,' as I remember. I think if you own something, you have the authority to decide how it's used." It seemed logical to me.

The Shepherd stopped and faced me. "That's a good answer, Quinn. You *have* given this some thought." He began walking again, but took an abrupt right around a tall, weather-rounded rock pillar a few yards in front of me.

When I followed him, all I saw was a blank wall.

What the dickens just happened?

I reached out and touched the wall. Solid, cool rock. After I rapped it gently with my knuckles, I took a step back.

Maybe my first mission begins right here?

"What's the password?" I heard coming from somewhere in or behind the rock wall.

"You've got to be kidding." I paced in front of the wall. "What password? You mean, like 'open sesame' or something? Let's see... 'Time lord'? or 'He who created time'? or 'The Elvish word for Friend'?" I wracked my brain. "Heck, I don't know."

Chuckling echoed around me. "How about 'Please'?"

"Sure thing. That should have been right at the top of my 'password through a rock wall' list. *Please* may I come in?" I couldn't help smiling.

A hand reached out, grabbed my forearm, and pulled me through the wall.

—᨝—

The interior of wherever we were was nothing like the dusty, red exterior rock outside.

Golden, liquid light surrounded me. It had substance to it, and a certain amount of weight.

The Shepherd appeared different. His robes were now dazzling white. He was shinier, and his face was indistinct—swallowed up in the golden light.

"Observe, Quinn." The Shepherd swept his hand forward, and a large, round, open area appeared.

We walked into the open space. The Shepherd pointed his staff outward as he turned in a full circle. Dark holes, equidistant from each other, appeared in the golden atmosphere. I could see a rounded rock roof high above me.

We're in some sort of cave.

"These." The Shepherd pointed at the holes. "These are your time-splicing gateways."

"Why does time need to be spliced?" This was beyond my understanding. "How can that even occur?"

"This entire Universe is finite. It had a beginning, and it

will have an end. Like an old garment, it will be rolled up and discarded[18] when the eternal arrives." His words began creating pictures.

A 3-D type of display grew in front of me. It started with the Earth, then zoomed out through space. Our galaxy became a dot, swallowed up by larger clusters of stars. We backed out of the light-studded darkness until the whole of the Universe lay stretched out before us, undulating like a blanket on a clothesline in a gentle breeze.

"Are we… are we looking at the entirety of the Universe right now? My Universe?" My mind spun with the enormity of what I was seeing.

How is this possible? Is it true?

"You've heard of the fabric of space and time—about how they bend and flow. You know that they will be rolled up as a scroll[19] or changed like a jacket when you come in from the cold." The Shepherd had disappeared in the light. I only heard his voice.

I nodded dumbly.

"Consider, now, a master weaver of tapestries." His voice surrounded me.

"Tapestries?" My mind flew to the intricate and enormous tapestries I had seen when I toured the Palace of Holyroodhouse in Scotland when I was in school.

"Yes. If you are able to grasp it, the Universe is a tapestry. All living things, from the most incomprehensibly large to the most infinitesimally small, are woven together to create beauty so wondrous you can only observe the fullness of it when you're with me in eternity."

---

[18] Hebrews 1:10-12
[19] Isaiah 34:4

With all this talk of fabrics, my mind felt like it was beginning to fray at the edges and unravel like the hems on my old jeans.

"Then, if everything is woven together like you're describing, why does any splicing need to occur?" I rubbed my temple, trying to get my brain to cool down.

"Think about that for a moment, Quinn. Is the Universe perfect now?" the Shepherd asked.

Easy answer to that. "Hardly. If it were, there would be no cataclysmic events right now or a need for Universe Healing Teams later on. Not to mention all the evil, mayhem, and death that has happened throughout the ages."

"Why is that?" The Shepherd's voice still came at me from all angles. I couldn't see him.

"Sin. Rebellion against God." This was a quick, Sunday School answer.

"You're right. But where did that rebellion originate?"

This question caused me to pause longer. "On Earth, I would say it began with Adam and Eve in the Garden of Eden."[20] The early chapters of Genesis sifted through my memory.

"Did it?" The Shepherd's question caused me to review what I knew about the beginning of sin. Unlike many of my neighborhood buddies, Tessa and I had actually paid attention in Sunday School.

"The Serpent talked to Eve in the Garden of Eden. Sadly, she believed him, disobeyed God, and talked Adam into doing the same thing. Death and destruction have been the norm ever since." I was walking back and forth in the golden light, feeling it flow caressingly over my skin. "Of

---

[20] Genesis 1-3

course, this begs the question of where the Serpent came from. He was already in rebellion against the perfect order God had created—or really, against God himself."

"Precisely." The Shepherd's voice boomed out, causing the light to quiver. "His rebellion, at its core, intends to place him in the position of Creator—of God. As a created being himself, one who was perfect when originally made, but who became proud and sinned, he is doomed to eternal failure[21] and eventual judgment."

The Shepherd sighed. "As a deceiver and the father of lies, he has deceived even himself about his appointed end. Because he believes he has a chance to become a god and lures those who follow him with that same message, he has attempted many times to ravage and thwart the time frames I have set in place. He also convinced many other angelic beings to join him."

Finally, I was getting ahold of a concept that made sense. "So, the Serpent is the one who has broken parts of time or cut threads in the tapestry of the Universe in order to change his fate?"

"That has been what he has attempted. He is limited in the scope of what he can comprehend. Therefore, his action against me is also curtailed, although he refuses to accept this fact. Regardless, he has affected parts of the tapestry that need to be repaired."

The light in the open area became brighter. "You, Quinn, will be receiving glory in ever-increasing amounts to go and splice together the time strands that have been severed."

"Oh, is that all?" My lighthearted response did a poor

---

[21] Ezekiel 28:11-19

job of covering up my internal quaking. I was petrified. "How does this time-splicing affect the future Universe Healing?"

The Shepherd responded, "You will go to places where my timeline has been severed and necessary events didn't occur. You will splice the proper threads together with the glory you receive. The power and glory you will have originates from the fact that Jesus paid for all sin when he came to Earth, died on the cross, and rose again. He is the restorer of all things and opened the way for this to be possible."

The Shepherd's form reappeared out of the light. "What you do, Quinn, will bring everything into order so that the Universe Healing will proceed as planned. You will already know how each mission is to be resolved because you know what the Bible says."

He pointed at a gateway with his staff. I watched as the interior lit up and began pulsing with a purplish-blue light.

He grinned at me. I could now see his grey eyes full of laughter and anticipation. "Are you ready for your first adventure?"

Absolutely not!

Still, I gave him an uncertain nod of agreement and began walking toward the pulsating gateway.

CHAPTER 35

I cast one backward glance at the Shepherd before I set foot in the purplish-blue light. He gave me an encouraging smile, along with a hand wave that indicated, "Go on."

Stepping inside the gateway was like nothing I had ever experienced. The light sucked me into it, but then I sucked the light into myself.

Is this the glory I need for this time-splicing job?

My fingernails glowed with the purplish-blue light. I had no way of knowing what the rest of me looked like.

My kneecaps were cold. Glancing down, I saw why.

Why am I wearing a skirt?

It wasn't a skirt exactly. I was wearing two layers that came down to my knees. The underlayer was an off-white, thin, soft cloth that reminded me of a sheet, while the outer layer was thick, woven, dark-colored wool. A leather belt with a hook-type closure that fit into holes drilled into the leather cinched the clothing together at my waist. The sleeves stopped above my elbows.

I really miss my jeans. This style is a little drafty.

A knife in a sheath, along with a leather pouch that clinked when I touched it, were attached to the belt. Tough rawhide sandals, tied with leather thongs, were on my feet.

My hair was longer than I ever wore it. It brushed the tops of my shoulders. I discovered a beard when I ran my hand over my face. There were also two bracelets on my wrists – one glowing dull green on my left wrist and the other glowing blue on my right wrist.

What time am I in?

The open plain I was standing in had no signposts or markers. I saw hills in the far distance to my left. A path, possibly a road, lay to my right. It went into a section of exceedingly tall trees. They reminded me of sequoias that I had seen in pictures.

I turned in a circle, searching for something—anything—to give me a clue as to *when* I was.

The only thing I noticed was brief movement inside the tree line. A glimpse of light-colored fabric moved between two shrubs, then disappeared.

This aroused my curiosity, so I headed for the tall trees. When I got closer, I saw that all the vegetation was enormous. I could have built a shelter out of two or three leaves. If I was able to reach them, that is.

Vibrations came from the ground through the soles of my sandals. Something was running. Something big.

A herd of elephants coming my way?

Crouching down behind a tree root for cover, I tried to discern which direction the vibrations were coming from.

Peering around from my hiding place, I was startled to see a woman watching me from behind a large plant several paces away. Only a portion of her face was visible. She had brown hair and blue eyes and was clutching a folded-up piece of cloth under her arm.

Her physical proportions were larger than any woman I knew. She would have most likely been around six and a half feet if she was standing. Her outer garments were the same type of woven wool as mine.

She raised a finger to her lips, indicating a need for silence.

Rustling through the bushy undergrowth grew louder. Whatever was running would be visible in the next few moments.

When the creatures came into view, I had to blink several times to be certain I wasn't dreaming.

Twenty-five-foot-long raptors with large men riding them burst into view. The raptors reminded me of those in the *Jurassic Park* movies, except that their skin was muddy green with streaks of brown running through it. The pattern brought zebras to mind.

Their claws and teeth were vicious. The beasts had thick metal harnesses that went through their mouths and were attached to metal bands around their bodies.

The five men I saw had the same larger proportions as the woman. They seemed like normal humans, only everything was bigger. I guessed the men were between seven or seven and a half feet tall.

I could understand why the woman was hiding. These men gave off cruel vibes. Several had necklaces of small human skulls. They all carried sticks around four feet long that had thongs with sharp rocks or thorns tied into the ends of them. I was sure these whips could lacerate flesh down to the bone in a few seconds.

One of the men yelled, "Come out, woman! We only want to see what you've woven into that blanket you're carrying. We won't harm you."

My dull green bracelet buzzed lightly and tingled against my skin. It stopped when the man stopped speaking.

I get it. A mini-translation orb. Nice!

The men snickered at what the first man had said. Somehow I wasn't convinced they meant this woman no harm.

The silence hummed with insect and bird life. The woman remained frozen, hiding in the bushes.

"Come out, you stupid she-dog!" another man yelled. "Do you think we don't know what your crazy father-in-law has been saying all these years? He's insane, and so are his sons. We need to rid the world of you all."

"When we find you, we'll rip that baby out of your belly and add its skull to one of our necklaces." A man with reddish-brown hair jangled his skull necklace loudly.

I glanced over to see the woman biting her knuckle hard. Blood trickled down the side where her teeth cut into her skin. Tears dripped into the dirt she crouched in, but she remained motionless.

"You made a mistake when you ventured outside that protective barrier you've all been living behind. Did you think we wouldn't notice that your large, strange-looking house is finished? Or all the animals that have shown up and gone inside? I've never seen some of those creatures before now." The tallest of the men moved his raptor through more bushes as he spoke in a conversational tone. "Don't worry about my companions. I'll keep you safe and take you back to your big... what have they called it... ark."

The other men fanned out and began moving through the vegetation.

Ark? Did he say ark?

Noah. I'm in the antediluvian time before the Flood. And this is one of Noah's son's wives.

These men were going to kill one of the wives of the

men who were going to repopulate the Earth after the Flood.[22] Noah had three sons, which meant they would wipe out a third of the future population of the world. Here. Now.

I'm supposed to stop this? "Welcome to your first time-splicing adventure," *my foot!*

I knew what had to happen. This woman had to live and make it onto the ark.

But how?

---

[22] Genesis 6-10

CHAPTER 36

Sweat ran into my eyes. I slowly, quietly, raised my hand to wipe it away.

The way I figured it, the woman had done something to sever the proper timeline. If it wasn't immediately restored—or "spliced" back together—history would be radically altered.

"Why me?" I internally pray-yelled. "No, really, *why me?*"

I didn't expect an answer. The big man on his raptor was getting closer. He began swinging his whip through the bushes, shredding them with the sharp objects tied into the thongs.

In a few more steps, he would be in our hiding spot.

Why didn't I work on my spacewalking more?

The thought occurred to me as I noticed the glow from the blue bracelet on my right wrist. The blue light winked up at me.

No, not spacewalking. Glory.

This was about holding the glory light I was given and releasing it at the proper time.

Some instruction on how to do that would have been helpful.

Getting the woman and myself into the glory was paramount. All I had on my belt was the small knife and pouch that clinked. I didn't even know what was in the pouch, although I suspected it might be fire-starting tools. It didn't matter. The noise would be a good distraction.

I quickly untied the pouch. It had weight to it—enough weight that it would make a good amount of noise when I threw it.

Palming the pouch, I hurled it as far as I could in the opposite direction. It made a satisfying racket as it crashed through the bushes.

"There." One of the men pointed in the direction I had thrown the leather pouch. All the men and raptors sped to where my pouch landed.

In the commotion, I ran to the woman and whispered, "I'm here to help." My green bracelet buzzed. The woman nodded like she understood.

Now, what to do?

How was I to safely release the glory I was given? My fingernails still glowed the same purplish-blue that my bracelet pulsed with.

I felt all around and under the bracelet on my arm. Nothing happened.

"It's a trick!" the large man yelled. "Keep searching. She's somewhere close." The men scattered again.

I saw the skull-necklace-shaking man coming toward us.

Help! How do I release the glory?

The woman saw me fiddling with the bracelet and the quickly approaching man on his raptor. She clamped her hand over the center of my bracelet with a grip that I thought would crush my arm.

Apparently, that released the glory. Light poured from my fingernails, then crawled up my arm until my skin glowed. The woman and I were encased in light. As soon as it covered us, the light acted like a giant, colorful vacuum. It sucked us into itself right as raptor claws slashed through our hiding place.

—m—

We emerged from the light—or, rather, were spit out of the light—onto the ground close to what could only be the ark. The enormous wooden structure rose to a great height beside us. I heard the sound of many animals. A ramp to the door on the side of the ark was a few feet away.

The woman fell to her knees, then kneeled forward with her face to the ground, weeping loudly. Her pregnant belly made an impression in the dirt where she knelt.

Men rushed to her, along with an older woman.

"Sherena," one of the men said, gathering her tenderly into his arms. "Where were you? We couldn't find you. I was so worried...."

The woman continued to sob incoherently into his chest. She made a flailing motion toward me with her hand.

The other two men walked over to me. One of them grabbed the front of my clothing, lifted me off my feet, and growled into my face, "Who are you? If you have hurt her, it will be the last thing you ever do."

Before I could speak, a grey-haired man walked up. "Put him down, Ham. What's going on here?"

Noah. I'm looking at Noah! Right... This... Second.

"Sherena vanished," the older woman said. "We scoured the building area and inside the boat while you were organizing the food for the animals, but we couldn't find her. She appeared a moment ago with this stranger."

Noah gazed down at me, then at Sherena, who was still

weeping.

Everyone is so tall here. Noah must be pushing eight feet. I guess people were larger before the Flood changed our atmosphere.

"Who are you, small man? What have you done to Shem's wife?" Noah's wife came to stand beside him as he questioned me. They glared at me, oozing hostility.

Great. Getting a biblical patriarch and his wife angry at me was just what I wanted to do today.

"You… don't understand." Sherena gasped out the words. "He saved my life." She stood up, still clutching the folded material under her arm. Shem stood as well, keeping a protective arm around her.

Sherena tried to wipe the tears away, but they continued to flow. "I am so sorry. I am ashamed. I knew we weren't supposed to go beyond the angel-fence, but I couldn't bear to leave our family crest behind. I meant to get it earlier. We were so busy getting the animals settled that time ran out. I worked so hard on it. I thought I could quickly run to get it and be back before anyone missed me."

"Did someone find you? Did they hurt you?" Shem asked.

"Feron's raptor riders saw me. They chased me into the Glimwoods." Sherena's tears still fell.

Shem blanched. "Dear Holy One in heaven." He took a minute to get himself together. "How were you not killed? Was it only them? Did they involve the giants, too?"

"Only them." Sherena shook her head. "I hid in the bushes. It was only a matter of time before they found me…." She started hyperventilating. Shem stroked her back until her breathing became more regular. "They said they would rip me open and put my baby's skull on one of their necklaces…."

Noah's wife went and put her arms around Sherena.

"Shhh... you're safe now. You're all right. Shhhh...." She gently caressed Sherena's pregnant belly.

Two other women walked up to Shem. They stared between Sherena and me in confusion.

These must be the other two wives.

Shem turned to me. "Stranger, thank you for rescuing my wife. We are to board the ark tonight, at the Holy One's command. Will you join us and be spared from the destruction coming upon the Earth?"

"I don't think I'll be staying that long, but thank you." I stared hard at Noah and his family, imprinting their faces in my mind, then shifted my attention to the ark. I wanted to remember as many details as I could.

"I do have a request, though." I pointed at the fabric Sherena still gripped. "May I see your family crest?"

With shaking hands, Sherena unfolded the woven piece of fabric. It was a small tapestry.

It showed a man's foot with the heel crushing a snake's head as the snake sank its fangs into the man's heel.[23]

Prophetic foreshadowing at its finest.

"Look!" One of the women pointed to a purplish-blue ball of light that was growing in size.

"That's my ride." I waved good-bye as I walked into the light.

---

[23] Genesis 3:14-15

CHAPTER 37

Shevril's monstrous bat-like wings unfurled and flapped while he roared with incoherent rage. He perched, talons gripping a balustrade, on the second floor of the Council chamber.

Gone were his perfect alabaster skin and flowing hair. His shining raiment had been swallowed up in a robe blacker than deepest night. His eyes glowed red in a heavily scarred face. The other twelve members of the Council of 13 watched him in concern, although Racil seemed to be holding back secret amusement.

"What is the *point*," Shevril spat, "of being able to track Quinn's movements through time and other dimensions if we can do nothing to hinder his actions?"

Draven rose from his chair. "Calm yourself. Racil has provided us information we've never had before. Our previous limited access to time only let us know that 'something' saved the woman, Sherena. We were never able to discover what it was, especially since she was securely in the trap we had planned for her demise." He inclined his head toward Racil. "Thanks to Racil's tracking device, we can discover much of the enemy's tactics."

"And why are you so concerned about the time flow we are currently unable to manipulate?" Gomert said, a sneer curling his upper lip. "Our efforts need to focus on that which is outside of time altogether. We need to find the despicable Book."

Jaburn agreed. "Quinn will travel outside the timeline at some point. Then, we will meet him in our own territory and take what we seek."

Shevril released his grip on the railing, gliding to the floor and landing heavily in front of the Council members. His talons flexed and unflexed, seemingly perturbed at having nothing to puncture. He resolved this by grasping Draven's empty chair in his right claw and methodically ripping the chair to bits with one of his left talons. Draven's eyes were black and angry, but he made no move to stop Shevril.

When the chair lay in unrecognizable pieces around Shevril's thick legs, he asked, "What about the time-worms? Are they able to bore through both time and space fast enough to meet Quinn in his travels?"

"We would have to know in advance where he was going." Quovern spoke up, cautiously moving away from Shevril's gruesome bat-creature persona. "I thought we didn't want to stop Quinn until he had the Book?"

Shevril abruptly resumed his former golden appearance. His golden robe with its arcane symbols once again covered his glowing form. "We are assuming the book is outside this Universe. We don't know that. I want the option of quickly reaching Quinn anywhere he goes."

"Prynk. Vander." Shevril motioned to two of the Council members. "Work with Korfal on increasing the time-worms' ability. They need to be faster—nearly instantaneous."

Prynk and Vander inclined their heads, then stood up and disappeared from the Council chamber.

—◊◊◊—

The purplish-blue light deposited me back in the room with the Shepherd.

"So," the Shepherd said. "What do you think?"

"No one will ever believe that I met Noah and his family." I still couldn't believe it myself.

"That's why this will literally be 'our little secret.'" The Shepherd's serious gaze met mine.

This pained me. "I can't tell anyone? Not Aneera or even Tessa?"

He shook his head.

"I'll explode! There has to be some outlet for these experiences." A thought occurred to me. "Can I draw them?"

"That would be a good way to relieve the pressure," the Shepherd agreed, "as long as you don't explain your drawings to any observers."

"I'll make sure I describe them as 'the ponderings of my artistic imagination,' which they will be." I grinned at the Shepherd, anticipating getting a hold of my sketch pad and charcoal pencils.

"However." My thoughts returned to the present. "I have several questions about this whole time-splicing thing."

"Go ahead." The Shepherd sat down on a rock, seeming like he had all the time in the world. Which, I suppose, he did.

"I've always thought of time as inflexible. Rigid, in that the past can't be changed or tampered with, and future events, or at least *certain* future events, as absolutely set in stone. These things *will* happen. That's because I believe the

Bible is true, and what it talks about will definitely happen, if it hasn't already happened. Right?" I turned to the Shepherd for affirmation.

"This is true," the Shepherd said, "but it's not complete."

"What would make it complete?" My curiosity continually got the best of me these days.

"A clearer understanding of a closed system operating inside an open system." The Shepherd tapped his staff on the sand for emphasis.

I'm sure I exuded perplexity.

"Come, let's reason together." He patted a rock close to him.

I walked over and sat down, wondering what this time spent with the Shepherd would reveal next.

CHAPTER 38

"What is a 'closed system'?" The Shepherd directed the question my way while running his hand over his staff.

"A system where nothing gets in or out?" I was guessing. "Like a closed vault with no ingress or egress points."

"In thermodynamics, mass can't escape a closed system, although energy can." The Shepherd checked my face for comprehension. "However, in closed-system time, certain events are predetermined and unchangeable. They are similar to mass. You could almost call them 'time mass.' In open-system time, time can flow like water around these rocks in eddies, waves, or rapids, yet never dislodge them."

The headache that was becoming, unfortunately, all too familiar began above my left eye. My synapses were almost smoking trying to follow this discussion.

"It sounds like you're describing time as two different things. Part of it is unchangeable and part of it is in changeable motion. Am I hearing you correctly?" I rubbed my throbbing temple absentmindedly.

"Yes. It's the perfect pairing of omniscience with the gift of free choice." The Shepherd said this as if this statement was the epitome of reason.

My glazed expression must have let the Shepherd know that my brain was on the verge of turning into mush.

"Let's go back to the tapestry idea," he said.

"Okay." I shook my head hard to get the blood flow ramped up.

"Humans are not the only beings in the Universe who can choose to follow God, although they are the *only* beings made in the image of God."[24] He continued to assess my level of understanding.

No problem. I can grasp this idea.

I inclined my head in agreement.

"Good. The created angelic beings who rebelled, the one known as Satan being the chief, have embarked upon a war bent on destroying created order and all things I hold dear. As spirit beings, they have limited access to the finite timeline embedded in eternity. This is open-system time. However, although they refuse to acknowledge this, they can neither fully recognize nor dislodge events within the closed-system time."

"That's an idea I can hold on to. It reminds me of the place where it said, '...the hidden wisdom which God predestined before the ages to our glory; the wisdom which none of the rulers of this age has understood; for if they had understood it, they would not have crucified the Lord of glory....'"[25] A glimmer of hope appeared that I could get a handle on this discussion.

"That fits nicely with what we're talking about." The Shepherd smiled proudly at me, like a father would give approval to a son who had provided a good answer.

---

[24] Genesis 2
[25] I Corinthians 2:7-8

"So…." Things were clicking in my mind. "Jesus' crucifixion was part of 'closed-system time'—it would have occurred one way or another?"

"It was decided before time began or the world was made,"[26] the Shepherd said.

"This 'closed-system time' reminds me of the outlines I had to do for term papers in high school. I knew the points that absolutely had to be included in the paper, but not all the ways I was going to reach those points—until I had written the paper." Mrs. Hinkle's face popped into my mind. She was a good high school English teacher, but was overly insistent on outlines. Or so I had thought at the time.

"Take that idea and apply it to the tapestry concept. All of time within this Universe is weaving together to create something of astounding beauty." The Shepherd got up from his rock and walked a few steps in front of me, gazing at something I couldn't see. "Oh Quinn, if you could only comprehend now how amazing it is."

I really wish I was able to see it.

The Shepherd recollected himself and began again. "'Outlines'—if you will—of events in time can be seen by the fallen angels who are bent on destruction. They attempt to sever the strands incorporated in the overall pattern in order to thwart the completion of the final picture."

These ideas coalesced in my mind. "And because the strands that I am to 'splice' in time are part of 'closed-system time,' they *will* be repaired in order to complete the eventual final picture."

"You've got it, my boy!" The Shepherd nodded enthusiastically.

---

[26] 2 Timothy 1:9, 1 Peter 1:17-21

After a pause, I asked, "But, can't you splice them yourself? Why involve a person?"

What I meant was, "Why involve me?"

"Because I mean what I say." Lightning crackled in his grey eyes. "Earth was given to mankind to have dominion over. The first people chose wrongly and opened the door for Satan and his forces to rule." Pain washed over his expression. "As you know, the destruction from that choice has been horrific throughout the ages and continues to this day."

I nodded soberly, eyes downcast.

"You also know that the story doesn't end there. This is the story you are a part of. Your choices matter, as do the choices of every person throughout time. These choices will have ripples that will flow through time and into eternity."

He walked over to me, tilted my face up, and looked into my eyes. "Remember who you are and choose wisely."

CHAPTER 39

I walked out of the rock face I had been pulled through by the Shepherd. Shadows had grown long on the canyon walls. Leaning my head back, I saw that the sky had a purpley-pink tinge to it and noticed the air was considerably cooler. Dusk was falling fast. I wasn't wearing a jacket and decided to walk briskly back to our cave to put on an extra layer.

The Shepherd said he would let me know when my next time-splicing mission would be. I was still in a state of mild shock after rescuing Sherena. My fingers twitched, wanting to get a hold of my sketch pad and draw every detail I could remember.

I picked up my pace, longing for a blank piece of paper and unhurried time to draw.

—⟋⟍—

The next morning, with a cup of manna-made tea and sandwich beside me, I perched on a rock a short way from the mouth of our group's cave and began my sketching. Charcoal pencils lay on the ground close to me.

My fingers flew as I sketched, although I caught myself rubbing my right wrist often. It was sore, and bruises shaped like Sherena's fingers were beginning to form. The pain quelled any lingering doubts I might have had that my time-traveling jaunt was real.

I drew a series of scenes, starting with the huge trees and vegetation when I walked into the forest's edge. Hiding and seeing Sherena, the fear I felt when I saw the raptors with their riders, and releasing the glory that zapped Sherena and me back to the area in front of the ark took shape on the pages of my sketch pad. I made sure that I was faceless or turned away in these sketches so as to appear as a generic part of the action.

I had begun outlining the altercation with Ham when a shadow fell across the page. I lifted my head to find Aneera standing over me.

"You're completely absorbed in your work. Didn't you hear us calling you the last few minutes?" She perused the scenes I had finished.

"Sorry, no. I do get lost in my own world when I'm drawing. What's happening?" I reluctantly set my pencil down.

"A meeting has been called at the amphitheater. Would you like to come? It sounded pretty serious." Her green eyes were dark with worry.

I set a mental bookmark in my mind at the spot I was sketching, then gathered up my supplies. "Let me put these in the cave and I'll join you."

Aneera, Gemma, Emily, and Gary were waiting for me. Loraine was already on her way with a friend. We all headed toward the large, red rock amphitheater to find out what the meeting was about.

Hundreds of voices rose and fell as we got closer. It was

loud, even in the open space. We scanned the people until we saw a few of our group members and joined them.

"What's this about?" I asked Stella, who was sitting on my left side.

"Not sure yet." She shrugged.

I was surprised to see Mark and Dan with a selection of other group leaders on the open stone pavement used to address the audience.

The leaders called for quiet before they took turns explaining in the different languages that the borders of Jordan were surrounded by Emanuel's forces. Even though Buddy had provided plenty of almonds to provide a protective cover over the whole country, these hostile forces had discovered where we were and intended to wipe us out.

Dan was the one who helped to move our collective fear away from the troops surrounding us and back toward worshiping God. We were reminded of the praise singers who went before the armies of Israel in Jehoshaphat's time and how the Lord completely destroyed the invading troops.[27]

The whole amphitheater full of people took Dan's words to heart. After a half-hour or so of worship, singing, prayer, and dancing, we heard a loud noise over our heads.

A missile had hit an invisible barrier high above us and exploded. Several volleys of missiles followed the first one, all with the same result.

Rumbling began under our feet. It grew louder and louder until I had to cover my ears. The vibration thrummed through my chest. I couldn't tell how long the rumbling went on, but it stopped abruptly. For a few moments, the

---

[27] 2 Chronicles 20

silence seemed as loud as the rumbling had been.

Our heads turned toward a shout from the top of the canyon walls. One of the runners who delivered information was there, waving his hat vigorously. He rappelled down the ropes set up for this purpose and ran to the leaders on the stone pavement, talking to them and gesturing excitedly.

Dan fell to his knees, weeping, then fell forward in a prostrate position. The other leaders burst into shouts of praise and thanking God.

When they had calmed down, Dan told us the runner had heard from the short-wave radio operators spread throughout Jordan that the ground had split open and swallowed up all of Emanuel's troops. All the tanks, guns, and missiles fell into the open crack, which then closed over them.

After all the leaders had relayed this information in the different languages, there was shocked silence. A man yelled, "Praise God!" Then the amphitheater exploded into sound. Weeping, shouting, and singing blended into a beautiful cacophony. I joined in with gusto.

We had been delivered from certain annihilation.

Praise was the only proper response.

No mention of the decisive defeat of the army surrounding Jordan's protected borders was mentioned by the news coming from Jeremy's TV later that afternoon.

"That's no surprise." Mark shoveled another bite of chili into his mouth. "Emanuel wouldn't let a whisper of anything negative about his plans out over the airwaves."

"I suppose not." I continued working on my sketches, enjoying the companionship of our group as we ate a late lunch. I had nearly finished the last scene of my time-splicing adventure. The ark loomed large in the background as Noah and his family faced toward where I had been standing. Sherena's tapestry waved gently in the wind, clearly visible.

"The detail in this sketch is amazing," Aneera said as she peered over my shoulder. "It's more like a photograph than a drawing. I could almost imagine you were there...."

"Let's see," Dan said, holding out his hand. He made his way through the sketches, oohing and ahhing, then passed them around.

Tessa was the final one to see all the sketches. Her eyes narrowed as she glanced over at me, pausing before she handed back the sketchbook and saying, "Yes, it's almost like you were there taking a picture."

I grinned innocently and took a big bite of my sandwich.

CHAPTER 40

Life in Petra was finding a happy rhythm. Jarl and Tessa, along with a number of other quantum spacewalkers, had been traveling around the world in order to rescue those who belonged to Jesus. These were people who hadn't made the initial trip to the protected area of Jordan. When they arrived, they were added to the groups scattered across the country. The influx caused our numbers in Petra to swell.

Greeting new people and hearing their stories as they got settled became one of Aneera's and my favorite activities. Not only were we performing a useful task, but we also got to spend time with each other. That was something I always enjoyed. The more time I spent with her, the deeper and broader my feelings grew.

Violent catastrophes continued unabated in the outside world. Meteors of various sizes decimated one-third of the oceans, wrecking the shipping trade and destroying marine life. Fresh water sources were poisoned over much of the globe, with people dying from the deadly waters in huge numbers.[28] Plagues spread through the populations, killing many.

The net Emanuel was creating to bring people under his control was a dystopian nightmare. The Pope was his right-hand man in enforcing every person receiving the infamous "mark"[29] in order to buy or sell. Anyone who resisted or who was caught without it was executed, many of them by beheading.

It got to the point where we couldn't let the children watch the news reports. They were too grisly.

Regular coverage showed piles of the heads from those who were executed, decaying and fly-covered. The reports were the stuff of nightmares, made all the more terrifying by their reality.

—⁂—

One morning, I was heading out to join Aneera and welcome a new family in Petra when I heard my name.

"Quinn, meet me at the wall."

I didn't see anyone, but the Shepherd's voice was unmistakable.

Jogging up to Aneera, who was waiting for me at our favorite rock, I told her something had come up. She was disappointed but went ahead to greet the new family.

Heading into the recesses of the old city, I hoped I could remember where to turn in order to find the right rock wall again. I needn't have worried. An invisible string kept tugging at me, making it clear where I had to go.

---

[28] Revelation 6
[29] Revelation 13:11-18

Once I arrived at the wall, I said, "Please may I come in?"

It worked last time, right?

A chuckle, then a "Sure, come on in," was the response I received. However, no hand reached out to pull me through the wall.

Okay. Here goes my first spacewalking solo attempt.

I envisioned the interior room where the Shepherd had created all the time-splicing gateways. Putting my hand on the rock wall, it began to liquefy under my palm. I pressed into the wall. It brought to mind what it must feel like to try and push my whole body through thick pudding.

Shouldn't this be easier? And faster?

Working my arms and torso through the wall, I saw the Shepherd's smiling face in front of me. The rest of my body followed, but I was so pleased to see the Shepherd that I forgot to take the final step through the wall. My concentration was broken and I found my left foot stuck inside the rock.

This isn't good.

I tugged on my foot. Nothing doing. It wouldn't budge. Somehow, it and the rock had gotten mixed up together.

"Um… a little help here, please." I gazed pleadingly at the Shepherd, expecting an immediate rescue.

He regarded me with interest. "Well, now you've done it." He came closer, bending down to examine where my calf stopped and disappeared inside the wall. He poked my calf with his finger. "Very interesting. How do you feel?"

"Stuck." I shifted the position of my other foot to change my center of gravity. The awkward angle of my trapped leg was getting uncomfortable. "I feel very stuck."

"I bet you do. So, get unstuck. I'll wait." He walked over to a rock in the approximate center of the circle of gateways and sat down.

"You're not going to 'un-stick' me?" I was incredulous.

"I don't need to. You already have everything you require to get unstuck. Hop to it." He smiled encouragingly.

"Ha. Very funny. I'm not even sure I *can* hop in place at the moment." I wasn't amused.

"Think, Quinn. What should you do?"

Moving in the quantum realm was the same as moving in any spiritual realm. It was by faith. Jesus was the one who upheld all things by the word of his power,[30] providing for this type of travel.

Fear and distraction worked actively against faith.

"Okay. Refocus." I took a deep breath.

Reorienting my thoughts to move through the rest of the wall brought instant results. The quantum particles of my foot and the rock wall separated, then slid into their proper places. I was free.

"That was a truly weird sensation." I shook my foot, wiggling my toes inside my boot. "I actually felt the particles separating."

"Remember what you just did. You'll need it for this next mission."

With that said, the Shepherd pointed his staff at a glowing orange gateway.

---

[30] Hebrews 1:1-3

CHAPTER 41

The orange light pulsed in the gateway, beckoning me.

"Where am I off to this time?" I grinned at the Shepherd, hoping for a clear, concise mission dossier.

"That's for me to know and you to find out." The Shepherd winked at me but then grew serious. "Expect opposition, Quinn. You're being hunted by those who want to use you for their own purposes."

"Do you mean the fake Golden Ones? What can they do? I thought they weren't allowed to travel through the timeline of history." Dread crept into my mind.

"They can travel through the timeline by using dimensional portals, but have limited access to it. They cannot undo what I have done, although that doesn't stop them from trying. You don't need to trouble yourself over their personal plans for you right now. It's their pets you need to be on the lookout for while you travel." The Shepherd blew out a disgusted sigh.

"Pets? What kind of pets?" My thoughts leapt to the hideous dog creature I had seen in my London neighborhood.

"These fallen ones have long attempted to tamper with

the created order. What was originally created for good, they have taken and warped into something monstrous." The Shepherd stood up, appearing grim. "Take the humble earthworm, for example. This marvelous creature works in quiet, unobtrusive ways to cultivate the soil and break down organic matter. Worms like this help the soil become more productive for many things, including growing food."

A suspicion grew. "Have these fake Golden Ones done something awful with earthworms? Or is this only an example?"

The Shepherd stared directly at me. "They have engineered a creature they call a 'time-worm.' It is also a type of hybrid. They can be all different sizes, from regular earthworm size to large enough to consume planets."

"There are worms out there gobbling up planets?" I shuddered involuntarily. "What do I do if I meet one of these things?"

"Destroy it."

Easy for you to say.

"Any tips on how to do that?" My knees grew weak. "This isn't a Jonah and the great fish kind of thing, is it?[31] I don't have to destroy them from *inside*, do I?"

"Not unless you want to." Amusement was written all over the Shepherd's face.

"The thought of hungry worms hunting me creeps me out." Now my skin was prickling. I wasn't handling the thought of evil, galactic worms very well.

"Curb your imagination. These time-worms don't want to eat you. They want to pinpoint your location for their masters, which is almost impossible for the fallen ones to do

---

[31] Jonah 1:15 – 2

when you are traveling inside the glory."

"Because…?" I cocked my head inquisitively.

Yup. Information assimilation headache beginning… now.

"Because they have set all their hopes on thwarting my purposes by intercepting you at the right moment. They are part of Satan's multi-pronged plan to bring my rule of the Universe to its knees. After that, they intend to conquer eternity." Power radiated from the Shepherd in waves, washing over me. "Therefore, if you ever see any of these worms, destroy them."

"Absolutely! How?" This, to my mind, was the crux of the matter.

"Jarl already gave you the weapon you need. The prophetic declaration is effective on these hybrid entities."

"Now why didn't I think of that? Since these time-worms are also hybrids, the declaration of 'In Jesus' name, I prophesy to your breath, that it be taken away,' is all I need?" I was nearly giddy with relief.

"Yes. The trouble is seeing them coming. They travel through black holes, and their specialty is ripping a hole in the fabric of space-time to create a temporary portal for their masters so that they can access this Universe." The Shepherd pounded his staff into the sand for emphasis, eyes flashing.

"Hold on a sec. Wouldn't a 'time-worm' travel through a wormhole, instead of a black hole? And, why can't the fake Golden Ones pop in and out of this Universe whenever or wherever they want to?" This was news to me. "How did they keep showing up in my life when they did?"

"Black holes are actually portals between the Second Dimension and this Universe. Wormholes only operate within this Universe." The Shepherd nodded encouragingly. "That is a good question, Quinn. As for the rebellious Golden Ones, they have used other established portals between dimensions. These aren't always where they want to access this Universe, so they are attempting an 'override.' However, the time-worms aren't always successful in creating a portal. Many times the portals are unstable and collapse, destroying the worm and blocking the fallen ones' entrance or exit. But they keep trying." The Shepherd shook his head sadly. "They are optimistically deluded."

I grinned wryly. "That describes most of the people in the world right now. 'Optimistically deluded' that things will improve while everything crumbles around them."

"They refused to love the Truth, with a capital 'T.'[32] Fortunately, you do love the 'Truth' and have every reason to be simply *optimistic*. You are free from living under any strong delusion." The Shepherd strode toward the glowing orange gateway.

"Time to go." He made a gesture similar to Vanna White on *Wheel of Fortune*, pointing to the time-splicing gateway with a flourish. "Your next adventure awaits."

---

[32] John 14:6, 2 Thessalonians 2:10-12

CHAPTER 42

The butterflies in my stomach grew to medium songbird size. They began flying in formation, causing my interior to rumble.

Am I going to get this nervous before every mission?

I paused a few seconds to quell the flutters. They didn't cooperate.

Yep. Probably.

Walking forward, I tried to appear confident while reminding myself that I would be equipped for each mission I faced.

The orange glow enveloped me as I entered the gateway. A slight burning sensation began when the glory wrapped around me, then was sucked into me in a similar manner as it had been in my first time-splicing trip.

Little tendrils of what felt like flame ran up and down my body, pulsing in rhythm with the blood coursing through my veins. I was alight with energy and purpose.

Even if I wasn't sure what that purpose was.

—ɯ—

Tauren said, "He's in Nimrod's[33] court, or possibly his dungeon. It's hard to tell." He motioned with his elegant hand for Racil to come examine the floating map where events intersected with time and space. "Which is it? The court or the dungeon?"

"Quinn is still moving," Racil observed. "He hasn't settled into a specific spot yet."

"Should we release a time-worm?" Prynk looked askance at Shevril, who glowered at him from his seat at the Council table.

"Haran and Abram are to die today, if we have our way." Shevril smiled wickedly at the seated members around the table. "What a delightful turn of events it will be when we intercept Quinn and keep our timeline as the predominant one. It will reshape thousands of years of history."

"Is that actually possible?" Chorne asked, considering the layered timelines on the floating map. The timeline the Golden Ones wanted to keep glowed red amongst the lines.

"Abram is a lynchpin in our Enemy's plan throughout the ages. If this 'pin' is pulled, his house of cards tumbles down, and history will be radically changed, as will the opportunities we have for finding the Book," Jaburn said, tapping his chin thoughtfully. "The Enemy would have to find another human to be part of his plan. Who knows how long that might take." He slapped his hand on the table. "I think we should attempt it."

Shevril gave a cold smile. "Draven, Nipher, and Vander, prepare for travel. Korfal, release a time-worm."

---

[33] Genesis 10:8-13

Dark stone walls faced me when the glory deposited me through the gateway. Lamps were placed in holders drilled into the rock. The air was dank and smelled of smoky oil, human excrement, and decay.

Lovely. Where am I now?

My translation bracelet was on my left wrist again, but I had no bracelet on my right wrist. Instead, I carried a type of scepter. It was made of intricately carved reddish wood and had a glowing orange stone embedded in its tip.

Taking stock of my clothing, I saw that I was covered in flowing, embroidered robes. I had a heavy gold chain around my neck from which several large keys dangled.

Footsteps approached me rapidly from behind. I turned to see a red-faced servant coming toward me at a run.

"Your handkerchief, my lord." He stopped in front of me, panting. "It has three drops of mint oil on it as you prescribed in order to cut the smell." He extended the fine cloth to me.

"Thank you." I took the handkerchief and brought it to my nose. "You are dismissed."

The servant bowed, then trotted away in the direction he had come.

Nice. The mint does help ward off the stench.

With the cloth firmly pressed to my nose, I continued down the long hallway, wondering where and when I was.

I was bearded again with a long beard-braid hanging below my chin, intertwined with golden thread. I wore a skull cap of thick material over my closely cropped hair.

Too bad I don't have a mirror to check out how I look in this get-up.

Enclosed leather shoes of a surprising softness covered my feet, stitched with an intricate starburst design on each shoe.

The fancy attire nudged me toward feeling regal.

As I rounded a turn in the hallway, I saw wooden doors with bars across the peepholes. This confirmed that I was in a dungeon, but it didn't tell me why.

I stopped in the hallway, checking at each door, waiting for some sort of inspiration. None came. There was also no one else around to ask.

Deciding to ask the prisoners their names, I rapped on the first cell door to my right with my scepter.

"Who are you in there?"

A string of violent curses met my inquiry.

Okay. Moving on.

I tried the next door. Only low groaning answered me.

Strike two.

The same question got a legitimate response on the third try. When I rapped on the third door, a deep voice answered me. "I am Haran, son of Terah, and I am unlawfully imprisoned in this stinking cell. I demand an audience with Nimrod."

Haran? Am I possibly speaking to Abraham's brother?

"Who are your relatives?" I attempted to sound official.

"Why do you want to know? So you can imprison them as well?" Hostility filled Haran's voice.

"No. To serve to confirm your identity. Please, tell me who your relatives are." I projected an air of authority.

Grudgingly, Haran said, "My brothers are Nahor and Abram. Terah is our father. Both Abram and I are imprisoned here because I dared to defy Nimrod's order to sacrifice to his 'moon god.' He's trying to eliminate my whole family."

Abram was a prisoner, too?

Cold sludge began to fill my stomach. Or it felt that way. This was awful. The little I knew about Nimrod didn't make me think he would be inclined to be merciful if someone defied him.

"How long have you and your brother been in here?" It was imperative that Abram be set free so that he could eventually go on to make a covenant with God and become *Abraham*.[34] The fate of the entire race of Jewish people was hanging in the balance.

"For two months." Haran pounded the door angrily. "I demand an audience with Nimrod!"

A voice came from the cell across the hall, startling me.

"Keep your voice down, brother." Turning, I saw two eyes and a shock of dark brown hair through the peephole. "Have faith. The God who spoke to me will get us out."

Haran snarled, but didn't reply. I walked over to the other cell door. "Are you Abram?"

"Yes, I am." He blinked at me and moved the hair away from his face. "Who are you?"

---

[34] Genesis 12-15

CHAPTER 43

Staring into the eyes of the patriarch of the Jewish race was surreal. Meeting someone who had such dramatic impact—or should have such an impact—on world history left me in silent awe.

"Who are you?" Abram asked again.

"A friend who intends to free you from this dungeon." I wondered if the keys hanging from my neck had any practical purpose here. I tried them in the cell door lock. The last key turned with a painful screech, and I heard the lock click open.

Removing the key, I swung the door wide. Abram walked out, wearing filthy clothes and looking generally unkempt. He was, however, grinning widely. He wasn't as tall as Noah and his family from my previous mission, but he was still several inches taller than me. I had to tilt my head back to make eye contact.

I guess people have shrunk as history has progressed. I used to think I was tall at 6' 3".

Clapping my shoulder, he gave it an almost painful squeeze. "Thank you more than words can express. I wondered if I would die in there." He nodded at his brother's cell door. "Would any of your keys open the door to my hotheaded brother's room?"

"I can certainly try." I walked to the door and started checking out my keys in the lock. The third one worked and, soon, Haran was free.

"We need to leave." I began to escort the men out of the dungeon, but Haran stopped me.

"Where are you taking us?" He glared at me, appearing every inch the hothead his brother had described. "You're dressed in the official robes of Nimrod's court, but I don't recognize you."

"I'm from a… distant province." I was at a loss as to how to describe who I was. I didn't even know who I was supposed to be in this time period. "I've been sent to release you and get you to safety."

"By whom?" Haran spat the question out. "How do we know if we can trust you?"

Okay. Enough with the questions.

"The Holy One, who has spoken to Abram, sent me. We need to leave. You're free to stay if you want to." I turned and headed down the corridor, happy that no other guards or people had yet shown up in the hallways. I was hoping to extricate all of us without showing off any spacewalking moves. I had no idea if the Shepherd intended me to travel that way with these men, so I opted to use more "normal" means of getting around right now.

Abram followed closely behind. We wasted no time moving through the dungeon corridors. Haran cautiously trailed behind us, letting out grunts every few minutes that I didn't try to interpret.

Haran and Abram looked strikingly similar. I pondered this as we moved up a set of stairs, getting ever closer to freedom.

"Are you and Haran twins, by any chance?" I said over my shoulder to Abram as we walked.

"No, we were born a year apart, but many people mistake us for twins. Haran is a little taller and broader than I am, though. It's easy to see the difference if we're standing next to each other." He spoke so quietly that I had to strain to hear the words.

The entrance to the dungeon was in sight. Relief hit me as I picked up my pace.

What is that odd gnawing sound?

The strange gnawing intensified. I stopped so abruptly that Abram bumped into me. "Do you hear that? Do you know what it is?" I faced Abram and Haran as I asked the question.

They shook their heads.

Suddenly, the rock wall to the right several feet in front of us shattered. Debris hit the far wall like machine gun fire. A sickly-white anaconda-sized creature slithered out of the hole. It had rows of jagged teeth.

I barely stopped myself from screaming like a girl.

The slithery creature wasn't interested in us. It turned back to the hole and tore large hunks of rock out to enlarge it. Flickering golden light emitted from the hole.

This can't be good.

This hideous thing must be a time-worm. I wasn't going to wait until I saw what walked out of that hole.

Completely forgetting to kill the time-worm, I decided immediately that it was time to spacewalk. I grabbed the wrists of Abram and Haran after tucking my scepter into my belt. I set my mind on the space outside the dungeon doors, and I began to envelop all of us in what Tessa described as a "spacewalking bubble."

An elegant golden hand came out of the hole and

wrested Haran away from me. He was pulled out of my bubble as Abram and I left the dungeon and instantaneously appeared beyond the prison walls in a quiet, unoccupied alley.

Frantic, Abram struggled to free his wrist from my tight grip and head back into the dungeon for his brother. I released his wrist but quickly captured his shoulders, forcing him to meet my eyes. "You have to go get your family and belongings and leave this city immediately. Do not delay. I will go back to see if I can find your brother."

After several long moments of indecision, Abram hurried away and was lost in the crowd.

Dread filled me, but I forced my thoughts back to the dungeon passage. I arrived close to the open portal that the time-worm had created. Merry laughter with a sinister edge emanated from the hole in the dungeon wall.

"I can't believe we actually got him. Shevril will elevate our rank at the Council table. As soon as Nipher returns and confirms that Abram is dead, we can go. Delivering him straight to Nimrod was a stroke of genius. Nimrod will execute him immediately when he learns he was trying to escape."

"Shouldn't we go after the other one, Vander?" The laughter slowed to a chilling giggle. "Are you sure we got the right one?"

"He is exactly the same as I remember him. I'm sure it's Abram." There was a pause before Vander said, "But… you're probably right. It's best to be sure. Let's find the other one."

Oh, no you don't.

I pulled my scepter from my belt, walking purposefully toward the portal. The orange stone embedded in the stick glowed with encapsulated glory.

I reached the portal opening at the same time as the two fake Golden Ones were walking out. Swinging my scepter, I struck the top of the portal. Glory with a distinct orange hue was released. The time-worm, sensing the imminent collapse of its portal, slithered behind me, knocking me off my feet as it escaped through the shrinking portal doorway.

"In Jesus' name, I prophesy to your breath…," I yelled. I never got the rest of it out. The time-worm was gone, although I saw a high-velocity rock shard rip through its belly. The Golden Ones were sucked backward, clawing the air and shrieking like the unholy things they were. I watched this in seeming slow-motion as I fell onto my back.

I was being pulled into the portal as well. Doing my best to backstroke in the gravel of the hallway, my hands and feet scrambled furiously. I was almost out when the portal closed, trapping me from the knees down inside the stone.

Panting and clutching my scepter, I lay on the ground and stared at the ceiling, realizing my predicament.

Focus. I need to focus.

Footsteps echoed in the dungeon corridor before I could.

"What do we have here?" Mocking black eyes in a golden face glared down at me. "Ah, Quinn. You've completely failed. Abram is dead. I watched as he was eviscerated before his father.[35] Nimrod laughed, then sent Terah home with a warning to never defy him again."

It was only after the Golden One finished gloating that he saw the portal was gone. His mocking became a guttural growl.

"You fool." His elegant fingers began transforming into

---

[35] Genesis 11:28

unnervingly sharp knife blades. "You incalculable fool. You'll pay for trapping me here with your life."

The excitement of the past few minutes left me in a quandary. I was having a hard time processing this new development.

I guess I should be concerned about this Golden One's plans for me. This doesn't seem to be what the Shepherd intended.

The Golden One lifted a knife-bladed hand to plunge into my torso. Anticipating him, I swung my scepter up as he pounced. The glory entered him, causing him to disintegrate from within as he writhed and screamed.

After mere moments, which felt like several years to me, there was nothing left and I was alone in the dank, echoing corridor.

CHAPTER 44

It was an uncomfortable, but not painful, sensation having my lower legs quantumly interspersed with the dungeon wall. This was obviously why I needed to refocus on my freedom as I had inside the "gateway room" back in Petra. I was thankful for that lesson now.

If I can only have a few uninterrupted moments....

I turned my concentration to the alley where I had recently been with Abram. Immediately, I arrived there. My relief was tempered by the sight before me.

A group of people, weeping, were bearing a type of litter with a body on it through the street. The body was covered with a sheet, but blood soaked through it. Members of the group stooped down to grab handfuls of dust and fling it into the sky as they wailed. An older man with a strong resemblance to Haran and Abram was leading the mourners. Dust covered his face and hair. He walked bent over, leaning on his staff, with his face twisted in agony.

This must be Terah.

I watched the sad procession pass by from my place in the shadows and wondered what the fake Golden Ones would report to the other Council members.

If all went as I hoped, Abram would be preparing to leave the city of Ur at this very moment. His father and nephew would join him, and then Abram and Sarai would once again be on track for their meeting with the Holy One.[36]

The stone in my scepter pulsed with a familiar orange glow, growing brighter as it encased me.

Time to go home.

—⋙—

Shevril paced in the Council room. "Where is Nipher? How is it that you two are here without him? And in this sorry state?"

Draven and Vander stood in the doorway of the Council Chamber, their once perfect skin sliced where they had inadvertently clawed each other when they were sucked back into their dimension. Black blood seeped from their wounds, dripping on the dying time-worm at their feet.

Korful ran over and carefully picked up the head of the time-worm, speaking to it softly. "I'm so sorry, my boy. I wouldn't have sent you if I knew this would happen." He caressed the worm as it gave a convulsive shudder and died.

Standing to his feet, Korful was nearly spitting with rage. "How could you? How did this happen?" He glared first at Draven and then at Vander.

Vander ran his hand over his arm, absentmindedly wiping it on his shining garment and smearing blood over the golden fabric in a long, black streak. "Everything was going perfectly—even better than we planned. The time-worm

---

[36] Genesis 11:31-32

was able to create a portal quickly when we discerned the precise moment to intercept Quinn, Abram and Haran."

Draven picked up the conversation. "Nipher grabbed Abram as Quinn was attempting to escape. He delivered him to Nimrod, who we knew would execute him immediately. Everything was perfect...."

"Not perfect at all." Tauren laughed mirthlessly. "We apparently lost Nipher, along with one of Korfal's time-worms. What happened to him?"

"Quinn showed up again as we went to search for the brother who got away. He collapsed the portal with some kind of scepter. Nipher wasn't back by then." Vander stared blankly as he recited this information.

Shevril came to stand in front of the two battered Golden Ones. They straightened up hopefully before the Council leader.

Instead of the expected praise, Shevril's eyes smoked with a rage that burst into flames, illuminating the dark depths with terrible fury. "Nipher grabbed the wrong brother. The timeline is essentially unaltered. All we accomplished to change the timeline was that Haran died several minutes sooner than he would have otherwise." His voice was low and deadly until he turned back to the other Council members. Then, he roared, "We accomplished nothing. *Nothing!*"

"So, Nipher is trapped in the timeline until he finds an exit portal?" Racil asked with an undercurrent of glee.

"Or worse," Fraynt said. "Find him with your tracker implant." He swiped his hand in the air to produce the multi-layered timeline map they had used previously.

Racil walked up to the map and searched it thoroughly. "I can't find him anywhere. He didn't access any of the other exit portals and I can't see his signal at any level of any time frame." There was concern in Racil's smooth face. The glee was gone. "He may have been obliterated."

A hush fell over the Council. "Obliteration" meant that the one in question was removed and kept in an eternally dark prison until the day of final judgment.

"Twelve is an abominable number," Shevril said after a long silence. "We need a replacement immediately."

"Seat yourselves," Chorne said, then motioned to Prynk. "Produce the list."

The Council of 13 minus one sat at the table and began the process of finding a new member.

I walked through the gateway into the open area. The Shepherd was singing a strange, beautiful song. The song seemed to be creating, or recording, the events at the ark with Noah and the recent escapade with Haran and Abram on the rock walls. I was mesmerized.

Walking over to the first gateway I had gone through, I ran my hand over the rock pictures chiselled in the walls, marveling at their cleanly-cut lines. Unlike my sketches, I saw myself clearly represented in each picture, taking part in the action.

The Shepherd finished his song, pointing to his work.

"You're part of the history of the ages now, Quinn."

His smile filled me with a deeper satisfaction than any I had ever known.

CHAPTER 45

Aneera and I held hands as we strolled through the red dust pathways of Petra, dodging the occasional thorn bush.

"You know, the only thing I miss from Texas is the sculpture you made of me and Emily. I couldn't find a way to fit it into my pack." Aneera's eyes were sad. "I know it's too heavy to be lugging with me all over the Universe when we start Universe Healing, but it brought me joy every time I saw it."

"What if I make a sketch of it for you?" My heart lifted, knowing she prized the gift I had given her. "That's certainly lighter than ten pounds of solid clay." I gave her hand a squeeze.

"Ooooo… yes, I'd like that." She stopped, then reached up to give me a kiss on the cheek.

I grabbed her around the waist. "None of that, now. I need a proper kiss if I'm going to go to *all* the work to do this sketch for you…."

She giggled, then pulled my head down, giving me the proper kiss I wanted.

My breathing intensified. Soon, Aneera and I would also be having a "proper" talk about us and where we were headed.

Soon.

—◊—

The horrors the outside world was experiencing under Emanuel's reign of terror rarely touched our day-to-day lives, but the changes in the natural order of things did.

We were protected from the one-third of trees being burned up for the first Trumpet Judgment, and we weren't affected by the oceans and fresh water sources turning to blood and being poisoned from the second and third Trumpet Judgments[37] because we were provided with our eternally full water jugs that Tessa had brought from the planet Maqualan.

However, the fourth Trumpet Judgment drastically affected us by reducing both the day and night by one-third. Time was literally speeding by.

Jarl, Tessa and other spacewalkers still made occasional rescue blitzes to get people who would otherwise be caught by Emanuel's forces, but most people who had refused to take Emanuel's mark[38] had either been rescued or killed by this point.

The plague of demonic hybrid locusts from the fifth Trumpet Judgment were the hardest to watch on Jeremy's TV. The suffering they inflicted was terrible to behold. One broadcast sickened me sufficiently that I avoided TV news reports after that.

The groups in Petra regularly converged in the amphi-

---

[37] Revelation 8:6-12
[38] Revelation 13:16-18

theater for singing, worship, news updates and teaching. These were joyous times. I had never experienced large-scale get-togethers like this before and I found I liked them.

Choirs were formed, as well as drama teams. I discovered a natural acting flair when I joined a team that did skits. Aneera often helped me practice my lines. More often than not, we would find ourselves howling with laughter over my messing up a word or phrase although her attempts to mimic my Welsh accent were even funnier.

The juxtaposition of a world experiencing ever-increasing levels of evil and our world that experienced peace—for the most part—was a continual source of fascination for me.

We all knew that battles raged in the physical and spiritual realms, and those battles were leading to an ultimate showdown.

What no one else knew about were the dramas unfolding throughout the timeline where I was repairing and re-weaving broken tapestry strands into the proper eternal picture.

Even though a few suspected.

—〰—

I walked into our cool cave to escape the late afternoon heat. Flopping down next to Tessa, I saw that she was thumbing through my sketchbook.

"I've never known you to sketch things entirely out of thin air." She gave me a pointed look. I could feel her intuitive twin-superpower trying to crack my mind open and read what was there.

I hated avoiding her unasked question so, instead, attempted a light-hearted response to keep the mood upbeat.

"Perhaps your stodgy brother is plumbing heretofore unknown depths of talent. My brain is expanding even as we speak...."

"Mmm-hmmm...." She rolled her eyes and carefully closed the sketchbook. "Perhaps."

Giving me a wink that said she knew there was more to the story, she gave my shoulder an affectionate pat before using it to lever herself to her feet.

"C'mon." She grabbed my hand to pull me up. "It's almost time for your evening performance."

Indeed, it was. I gathered my props for the skit, then joined her outside the cave for the walk to the amphitheater.

CHAPTER 46

Mission #3 found me.

We were in Petra for our third year. Anticipation was rising because we knew that only six months remained of the three and one-half years that Emanuel was to have unhindered rule over the Earth.

I could see why Jesus said these days had to be shortened or no life would be left.[39] The planet, and all life on it, were being completely devastated.

It had been over a year since my last time-splicing mission involving Abram and Haran. I had only seen the Shepherd once in that time. He had reassured me that things were on the proper trajectory for my life. He had said, "Use your time wisely, Quinn, before your next mission. Aneera isn't a woman you can expect to know well in a short while. Spend the time to delve deeply."

I had taken him at his word. Aneera and I were learning about each other on progressively deeper mental, emotional and spiritual levels. When emotions ran too high and we

---

[39] Matthew 24:22

wanted to make the same progress physically, we made a pact to run to the safety of our ever-present group of "chaperones." Lately, we were spending a lot of time with these "chaperones" as our emotions grew more entangled. I had never imagined how fiercely these feelings could pull me.

Jarl was gone fairly often on different assignments, and I once caught him looking at me suspiciously when he returned. He apparently hadn't gotten the memo about Aneera's and my growing relationship, although nearly everyone else knew. I guessed this was because he was so utterly enthralled with his own relationship with Tessa. I hoped I wasn't as bad as the two of them, always making googly-eyes at each other.

Aneera laughed when I mentioned this to her. "Oh, yeah. We're just as bad." She patted my arm reassuringly. "I wouldn't have it any other way."

When my next mission came up, I reluctantly extricated myself from my obligations, providing vague excuses. It was harder to go into the unknown now that all of these relational ties held me.

Is this how soldiers feel when they go into battle?

Nevertheless, when I heard the Shepherd's call, I answered.

I made it through the rock wall into the time-splicing gateway room with no trouble this time.

The Shepherd was nowhere to be seen, but the gateway next to the one I had gone through to rescue Abram pulsed red across the open circle. When I moved into the center of the cavern's room, I saw a note scratched in the sand.

"Walk through."

A cryptic note, to be sure. It could only refer to the pulsing red gateway.

I walked forward… into a maelstrom.

—⟫⟫—

Violent forces tore at me. I was being shredded at a quantum level. Explosions of light and pain engulfed me.

WHAT IS HAPPENING HERE?

That was the last conscious thought I had until I was flung onto the ground, waking up as red shining glory was being sucked into me. My hands were glowing red and burning.

Sinister laughter echoed around me. Was it in the wind? Was it in the spirit realm? I couldn't tell.

I gasped while I fought to sit up and take in my surroundings, noticing there was no green translation bracelet on my wrist. I wore a knee-length, rough woven tunic and I had a lasso in my right hand.

A young man lay to the left of me in a growing pool of his own blood. His clothing was slashed across the midsection and slowly turning red as blood seeped into it from his wounds.

Sheep were scattered in the distance. I heard a lion's roar nearby.

Fighting disorientation and the waning pain from my trip through the gateway, I struggled to make sense of the scene before me as I stood up.

A hand-harp, sling and staff lay scattered around the bleeding, semi-conscious man. A knife lay gripped in his hand.

Is this… could this possibly be David? The future killer of

Goliath, the giant? The future king of Israel?

The implications slammed into me. David—if this was who this was—was dying on the ground while I was trying to get myself together.

*Stop the bleeding. Stop the bleeding **now**!*

I dropped my lasso next to me as I fell to my knees and ripped open David's tunic. The gashes from the lion were deep. I tore pieces from the tunic and applied pressure to the wounds. The man groaned.

Help! What am I supposed to do?

My internal prayer received a prompt answer. I saw a picture of glory leaving my hands and healing David's wounds.

Ah. The glory.

I removed the blood-soaked tunic pieces and placed my glowing hands directly on the gashes in David's abdomen. Glory poured out of me at an astonishing rate, bringing burning so intense I cried out. The red hue of the glory mixed with the red of David's blood, somehow turning into blinding light that was absorbed into him as it sealed his wounds.

When it finished, I rocked back on my heels, pulling in deep breaths like a man who had just been rescued from drowning.

David blinked several times, then sat up and ran a hand across his abdomen, which was now completely restored.

He tilted his head up and gave me a half-smile, but then paled as his eyes went past my shoulder. He cried out, pointing with one hand while he scrambled to his feet and grasped his knife with white-knuckled fingers in the other.

The lion.

I grabbed my lasso and was up in a flash, pivoting as I rose. The lion, his mouth covered in blood from the sheep he had killed, was charging us.

Lassoing a lion. This will be a first.

My arm moved instinctively from years of practice with Granny's hog. The lasso sailed and snared one of the lion's feet, exactly like when I caught our six-hundred-pound porker. I threw all my weight against the rope.

Tripping, the lion's face plowed into the ground and stopped inches away from David's feet.

The lion was up again before I could re-tighten my grip on the rope.

But David was ready.

He grabbed the lion by the furry beard under its chin. When the lion rose up to try to throw him off, David plunged the knife up to the hilt into the lion's heart.[40]

With a final roar that trailed away in the wind, the lion collapsed and died.

The wind continued to whistle around us. David and I stared at each other with wide eyes, adrenaline causing us to suck in great gulps of air.

Abruptly, with no prior warning, I was tugged backward into pulsing red light.

I was ejected from the time-splicing gateway into the open room with force. I lay on my back, stunned, and contemplated the rock formations in the ceiling.

I hope my next mission doesn't involve me laying on my back, staring at the ceiling. This is two in a row.

"Perfectly executed," I heard the Shepherd say.

When I thought I could move again, I carefully rolled over onto my hands and knees. Wobbling a little, I stood up.

"That was intense." My voice was shaky. "Why was that

---

[40] I Samuel 17:34-36

so intense?"

"Timing... was of the essence." The Shepherd's eyes glowed with affectionate irony. "Those who made sure David was wounded thought they had accomplished the task of killing him. They needed to leave before you arrived."

I remembered the fading, evil laughter.

Drawing one more deep breath, I nodded. My equilibrium was back, although my heart rate was still high.

"Come and have a seat, Quinn." The Shepherd pointed to a rock close to where he sat down. "Refresh yourself."

It was then I saw a small rock table filled with goodies and a large cup of something frothy and fruity-smelling.

My stomach rumbled. Adventures always made me hungry.

"Don't mind if I do." I took my seat and started in on the refreshments.

CHAPTER 47

When I had devoured the food in front of me and polished off the fruity beverage, I stretched, sighing with happiness.

"What have you noticed about the glory on the missions that you've undertaken?" The Shepherd's grey eyes met mine.

"It's getting stronger." My hands were tingling even now from the glory they had released into David's wounds. "Releasing the glory was painful this time."

"Do you feel any lasting effects from that?" His eyes were now unreadable. I sensed that my answer mattered a great deal, although I wasn't sure why.

I did a mental check over my body. My pulse was normal now, my mind was clear, and my emotions were settled. "I feel quite good, except for a bit of tingling in my hands still."

A slow smile spread over the Shepherd's face. He gave a quick nod and said, "I'm glad to hear it. Have you checked yourself in a mirror after these missions?"

"Not right away." What an interesting question. "Why?"

"Look at your skin." He pointed at my forearm.

I held my arm up to the light. There was a slight sheen

to it. I rubbed my finger over it. Tiny gold bits came off on my fingertip.

"Whoa! That's different. This reminds me a little of how Granny appeared covered in gold after that prayer time when she swept up gold flakes off the table." I moved my finger, watching it glitter in the light.

"Perhaps a rinse-off is a good idea before joining the others from here on out—at least for the next few missions." The Shepherd pointed with his staff to a new addition to our time-splicing gateway room. "I've prepared a pool for you."

Steam rose from a subtly-lit pool at the back of the open cavern. Bio-luminescent rocks were strategically placed for ambiance. A towel waited for me on a nearby rock.

"That is incredibly inviting." With no further urging, I walked over, stripped off my clothes and lowered myself into the warm water. "Ahhh... I've always wanted my own hot tub."

"Perks of the job." The Shepherd grinned at me and rose to leave. "You did well today, Quinn." With that, he walked through the wall and left me to luxuriate in the water.

Refreshed, I made my way back to our cave under a starlit sky.

Sliding into an opening next to Aneera around our evening fire, I went over the events of the day in my mind. I was surprised that I wasn't exhausted. Instead, I was humming with energy.

Aneera leaned over and gave me a sniff. "Someone got cleaned up today." She winked at me. "You smell nice."

Putting on my best Elvis impersonation, I said, "Thank

you. Thank you very much."

"Charming." She grinned at the others, announcing, "He's my favorite Welsh Elvis."

"I feel a new skit coming on…." Loraine laughed as she moved her hands dramatically. "Welsh Elvis runs onto the stage, a bevy of suntanned beauties crooning behind him. A pause, then he bursts into *Hound Dog*…."

"Except *this* Elvis," I said, pointing at myself, "can't carry a tune in a bucket."

"Too bad." Loraine looked disappointed, then brightened. "I have a better idea. What about 'rope trick' Welsh Elvis?"

My mind flashed to lassoing the lion. "No thanks! I'm more interested in getting the girl." I jumped to my feet, then pulled Aneera up after me. "What do you say, suntanned beauty? Do you want to croon to me under the starlight?"

Linking her arm with mine, she grinned at the others around the fire. "See y'all later. I have some crooning to do."

We walked out of the cave, leaving the laughter and catcalls behind us.

CHAPTER 48

Jarl and Tessa were gone now. Jarl had been tasked with retrieving the Revelation 19 sword that Jesus would use in his return to Earth.[41] The sheer enormity of how important this mission was made me shake my head in wonder.

Tessa had gone to wait for Jarl in the 5th dimension at the base of the Blue Mountains. That's where he was to meet Jesus and give him the sword after he had retrieved it. Our cave felt a little empty to me without them there.

Excitement was high in Petra, and throughout Jordan, from the reports we heard. Nearly everyone was anticipating Jesus' return. They knew they would be bodily transformed to be with him when he came to get them before his eventual physical return to Earth.[42]

Aneera and I, as well as the few other Universe Healers in our immediate vicinity, were gearing up for something different, however.

Any day now, we would be called to our training.

---

[41] Revelation 19:11-21
[42] 1 Corinthians 15:50-58; 1 Thessalonians 4:13-18

—w—

"Are you packed?" Aneera's question shook me out of my reverie.

"Yes, I only have a couple of things left to fit in my pack whenever we get called to go." I was sweating, but not for any atmospheric reason. The early evening air was cool.

Granny's wedding ring felt like it weighed a thousand pounds in my front jeans pocket. Granny had given it to me shortly before she died, for when I found "that special girl."

"That girl" was walking next to me, holding my hand.

Blast all these other people out strolling tonight.

I was seeking the perfect place for privacy. The one or two places I thought would work had too many people milling around.

Hence my sweating.

We kept walking until the only thing surrounding us was silence. Just in case any stray people showed up, I pulled Aneera behind a large boulder.

Don't stammer. Please don't stammer.

Taking Aneera in my arms was the easy part. Getting the words out of my mouth was considerably harder.

"I love you, Aneera." Starlight reflected in her eyes. "I'm not sure how or when, but I want to marry you. Will you marry me?"

She stared at me with wide eyes. She didn't answer immediately and the silence lengthened.

Have I made a mistake? Misread things?

My worry disappeared when she flung her arms around my neck, saying, "Yes, I'll marry you! I love you, too." Tears were sparkling in her eyes.

I slipped Granny's ring on her finger, hoping it would fit

properly. It seemed snug enough, so my concerns about it sliding off were eased. Aneera held it up to the little light we had, watching it shine.

Drawing her close, I wrapped my arms around her. The silence lengthened again after that for another reason entirely.

———ᴕᴕ———

Excited voices were coming out of our cave when we got back. I heard Jarl's and Tessa's voices inside.

Mark, Dan, and all our group members surrounded them, peppering them with questions.

Tessa saw us come in and ran over to hug me. Then, she hugged Aneera. Tessa seemed to be glowing with joy.

Mark's animated voice reached us. "You'll never believe it, you two!" His voice was high and he spoke rapidly. "Jarl got the Revelation 19 sword, but got waylaid by Satan...."

"It was awful," Gemma chimed in. "Satan tried to trick him by showing him pictures of us getting slaughtered...."

"Evil deceiver," Dan said.

"Except that Tessa really did get killed by a demon in the 5th dimension," Loraine said.

Shock drained the blood from my face. I didn't realize I was crushing Aneera's hand in a death grip until she gently extricated her hand from mine.

"It's okay, Quinn." Aneera reached up to touch my cheek comfortingly. "You can see she's all right now."

"Jesus resurrected me." Tessa smiled up at me. "It was an interesting experience, being dead for a little while. I'll tell you about it someday."

I grabbed her in another hug and didn't release her for a while. "I am so glad you're here. Alive." My mind was reeling.

"We got the go-ahead to get married after I gave Jesus the sword." Jarl walked up to us and put an arm around Tessa. "Soon, because Jesus will be coming for everyone in a few days. He gave us the option of going with him or living on Haven, where we've both spent time. We could help out the Universe Healers on Haven with the lodge keepers, Ted and Geneva." He smiled at Tessa. "We decided on that."

Jarl noticed how closely Aneera and I were standing together. "And there's something I've been meaning to ask you, Quinn." He stared at me with a glint of brotherly protectiveness. "What are your intentions toward my sister?"

Aneera blushed and smiled.

I confidently stared Jarl straight in the eye and said, "I love your sister and want to marry her."

There. It was out for the world to know.

"We're engaged!" Aneera added, blushing again and smiling widely as she held her hand up for everyone to see the engagement ring on her finger.

Congratulations exploded around us. From the looks of things, talking and planning would go on late into the night.

We settled around the fire and got immersed in organizing the events that would happen in a mere couple of days.

CHAPTER 49

Jarl and Tessa's wedding was two days later. It was impressive, considering the limited resources we had. Aneera helped scrounge up appropriate wedding attire for Tessa, me, Jarl, and herself. Gemma and Loraine organized an enormous cake and manna-made meal. Dan led the ceremony. One of the more interesting additions was the elaborate flower arrangements and bouquets that Jarl's large hummingbird friends delivered from the Gardens of Laranda in the 8th dimension. They transformed the amphitheater into a colorful desert jewel.

All the groups in Petra and a large number of space-walking friends from around Jordan filled the amphitheater for the wedding. These were joined by many of the angelic trainers who had taught the spacewalkers how to travel through the quantum pathways. It was a time of honor to the God who brought Jarl and Tessa together, as well as a boisterous celebration.

Jarl and Tessa were whisked away to their honeymoon in the Gardens of Laranda by hummingbird taxi after a few hours at their reception. We waved good-bye then feasted and sang late into the night.

—m—

A day later, flush with the happiness of being newly engaged, I decided to show off a little.

Since no one knew about my time-splicing missions, I thought it would be safe to demonstrate my increasing skill in spacewalking by suggesting a practice run.

Aneera seemed a bit skeptical.

"Are you sure we shouldn't wait until we have a more experienced spacewalker with us?" She lifted her eyebrows questioningly.

"I'm sure we can handle it. Don't you think this will let our trainers know we're eager to learn?" My confidence knew no limits.

"Maybe...." She smiled wryly. "Go ahead."

I pointed to an enormous boulder in the distance. "I'll go up there."

Aneera nodded. She was trying to be supportive, which I appreciated.

"Tessa said to focus on the place you want to go." I closed my eyes and said in a commanding voice, "In Jesus' name, move to the boulder."

I realized my mistake as soon as I said it, but it was too late. I made it to the boulder, all right. Unfortunately, half of me was out of it and half of me was mixed up in the rock. From the waist down, I was entangled with the boulder.

Good grief. You'd think I'd be past this by now. That's what I get for showing off.

Aneera ran over to the boulder and called up to me, "Are you all right?"

My arms flailed around, trying to signal her somehow. "I'm okay, but I'm stuck."

"I'll go for help."

I heard her footsteps leaving. Drumming my fingers on the red dust, I debated what to do.

It would be easy to extract myself from this situation after having practiced it a couple of times already. However, that might show that I was more advanced than I should be at this spacewalking thing.

Swallowing my pride, I waited to be "rescued."

I heard Derrik's voice call up to me. He was a spacewalker who had gone on many missions with Jarl and other teams.

Aneera echoed Derrik, asking, "How are you doing?"

"I'm fine up here, just stuck." I stifled a groan at my stupidity.

Ah, the humiliation of it all.

Derrik appeared next to me. His snickering became guffaws of laughter when he saw my predicament.

I stared at him glumly. "It's not funny. A little sympathy would be helpful."

This made him laugh harder. He wiped tears from his cheeks, then said, "Okay, Quinn. Sorry." He tried to suppress his chortling. "You know how this works. Refocus on being on *top* of the boulder."

As a good student would, I took a few seconds to refocus, and quickly stood beside Derrik. We spacewalked together to where Aneera was waiting.

Aneera was relieved to see me. She hugged me, even though my top half was coated in red boulder dust.

"All right. I'll wait to do that again until we have more instruction." Conceding defeat seemed like the best option facing me. "Think I'll go get into different clothes."

Aneera linked arms with me as we headed back to the cave.

Harnel and Darion, our angelic trainers, showed up the next day to collect us for Universe Healing school.

The next leg of our adventure was upon us.

CHAPTER 50

We stood in front of our backpacks, facing our group and a few other assorted friends. Harnel and Darion waited for us a few paces away.

Aneera was holding back tears. I was feeling a swirling mixture of emotions myself. Grief at being separated from these people I had grown to love and appreciate. Nervous excitement at the beginning of our training as Universe Healers. Secret curiosity about how my time-splicing missions would work in a Universe Healing context. So many questions were yet unanswered.

We hugged our group members before we left. A tear did slip down Aneera's cheek when she hugged Emily and gave a fully-grown Strawberry a quick chin scratch, making the cat purr. She turned away quickly, giving me a look that told me we needed to hurry up and leave or she would completely lose her composure.

With a final wave, we walked over to our packs, shouldered them, and joined the angels. They extended their hands to us.

The moment we took them, Petra disappeared.

—⟋⟍—

An orange sun was shining cheerfully in the sky. The light glimmered off short shrubs and plants before us, but seemed to be absorbed into the bright orange dirt at our feet. I had thought the dust of Petra was red. This dirt, however, put it to shame. The bright orange color was like a fluorescent orange soda pop.

I watched as Aneera bent down and pinched some dirt between her fingers and tasted it. She quickly spat it out.

Laughing, I walked up to her and flicked a few orange specks off her lip.

"Scientific curiosity. Tastes like dirt." She grinned sheepishly. "I was sure it would taste like orange drink mix."

"It certainly looks like it should." Glancing at Harnel and Darion, I asked, "Where are we?"

"We are on the planet Shargram, the abode of the Wisdom Keepers for the Holy One." Harnel motioned to the beautiful—if unusual—terrain stretched out in front of us. "It resides in Quadrant 3 of this Universe."

A huge, magnificent hall was in the distance to our right. Massive columns held up the roof of the porch. Even at this distance, I could see pictures moving across the columns, like holograms or movies.

To our left, another well-apportioned white building lay. Stories were moving on the exterior walls of this building as well. Tall beings teaching eager, human students took up one part of the front wall, the etched stone moving as the lesson progressed. Martial arts training was shown on another section of the wall. We heard shouts and saw the exercises as the students ran through their drills, the stone shifting with their movement.

A glass roof topped the lovely white building, and there were many windows set in the stone walls. The entire structure radiated light and welcome.

Low, flowering vegetation created wide pathways for large, round objects to whiz past. No bushes were higher than three feet, presumably so the round things wouldn't bump into each other. Delicious fragrances from the flowers wafted over to us.

A rolling object exited the pathway nearest to us and came to a stop in front of the angels.

"Greetings, Universe Healers and brethren." The odd creature bobbed a greeting. "I am Partak, and will be the one to settle you in the Education Center."

I could never have imagined the creature in front of us. Multiple limbs extended from a round, central mass that was full of eyes. Willowy fingers extended from the end of each limb. There was no mouth I could see, yet I heard the creature's voice clearly in my head.

"Are you speaking in my mind?" I was dumbfounded.

A wave of surprise from the creature hit me, followed by, "Of course. Doesn't everyone?"

"Not everyone." I grinned as I wondered how to greet this creature properly. His limbs had undulating colors of reds, yellows, oranges, and pinks. He could have been a stationary sunset.

Should I shake a tentacle? Bow? Or what?

Amusement touched my mind.

Of course, he would hear me.

"Verbal greetings are fine," Partak thought to us.

"May I ask *what* you are?" I hoped I wasn't being rude.

"We are Ophenim, an angelic order in charge of stewarding all the knowledge and wisdom in this Universe for the Holy One." Partak stretched a limb in the direction of the distant hall. "That is our Wisdom Hall, where our archives are kept." He then pointed at the white building gleaming in the sun. "And that is our Education Center, where your training will take place."

Aneera smiled at me, wonder in her eyes. I inclined my head in silent agreement.

"Come." Partak motioned to us all. "Allow me to show you to your quarters." He slowly rolled toward the building as we followed behind.

CHAPTER 51

An Ophen rolled up to our group before we reached the steps leading into the Education Center. He had green tips on the end of each limb.

"Welcome, Universe Healers. My name is Rhondak, the main Wisdom Keeper on Shargram. The archives at the Wisdom Hall are under my management." He bobbed to us in greeting.

Aneera exclaimed, "Rhondak! My brother, Jarl, mentioned you."

Rhondak turned his attention to Aneera. "Was Jarl able to deliver the Revelation 19 sword?"

"He did, but it was extremely difficult." A troubled expression passed over Aneera's face, then cleared. "Jesus now has the sword."

Rhondak sent out a booming thought-message across Shargram. "Our Master has his sword."

The volume of his voice in my head made me wince. However, when he roared "Rejoice!" and all the Ophenim began yelling and singing, I was flattened. I was sure my head was exploding.

Vaguely, I sensed Harnel pick me up like a sack of potatoes and throw me over his shoulder, pack and all. Once we were through the doors of the Education Center, he set me gently on my feet. My legs were rubbery. I melted down to the polished floor, leaning on my pack with my legs splayed out in front of me. Thankfully, the level of noise in my mind was muted in the vast foyer.

It hurt to move my head. Groaning, I released my pack belt and slipped out of my shoulder straps. I sat forward, fighting nausea.

I saw Darion ease Aneera to the floor, where she sat shakily on the pack he had put down for her to rest on. If I was as white as she was, we must have looked ghastly.

Rhondak and Partak rolled into the building's entrance. I wasn't overjoyed to see them.

"My apologies." Rhondak's limbs undulated with a pinkish hue that brought to mind embarrassment. "I forgot that you don't yet know how to control your thought access."

"Whut's dat?" My mouth felt full of mush. It was difficult to form words.

"It is the ability to shutter and protect your mind from unwanted intrusion," Partak said. "You will learn how to do this in your training here."

"Oh good." My ability to speak was returning. I stood up slowly on wobbly legs. "That will be useful."

"I will see you tomorrow at our Dining Hall. Partak will get you settled." Rhondak gave another brief bob and rolled away.

A few other Universe Healers were carried in by their angelic trainers, followed by their Ophenim guides. They Healers were in pretty rough shape from the "thought assault" we had been through.

"Derrik!" I was surprised to see my recent rescuer. "I didn't know you were a Universe Healer."

Derrik grinned weakly from his seat on the floor and waved at Aneera and me. "We're quite the cozy bunch, aren't we? I'm one of the lucky ones who gets to do double duty—Quantum Spacewalking *and* Universe Healing."

"Well, what do you know about that?" Aneera returned his grin from her seat on her pack. She put her best Texas drawl into action. "Circle the wagons, boys. Trouble just arrived."

Derrik rolled his eyes, giving a short laugh. "Smart aleck."

Aneera chuckled. Partak, taking in this exchange, said, "I can see I have a lot to learn about humans." Waving a willowy limb at us, he motioned for us to follow him. "Come with me. I'll show you to your quarters."

I helped Aneera up, and we followed Partak while Harnel and Darion brought our packs.

Aneera and I were put in two different wings of the building. Partak and Harnel left me alone to get unpacked. After arranging things on the shelves and small desk, I examined all the flat surfaces in my room more closely.

Every surface was telling a story. The wall above my shelves showed a woodland dryad singing to a gathering of small animals. I heard her song softly emanating from the wall when I stepped closer.

My shelves were depicting battles—one on the sea, complete with muted booms of cannon fire—and another on a rolling plain involving horses, chariots and archers.

The desk showed a maiden being wooed by a man in old English-style dress. I supposed it was a story from Shakespeare's era.

Under my feet, ocean creatures swam across the floor. A sea turtle glided by, followed by a mermaid holding onto a dolphin fin.

At least a story I was familiar with was playing out on the ceiling. Cyrano de Bergerac, his prominent nose on full display, was attempting to woo Roxanne on her balcony from a place in the shadows.

I closed my eyes and stood in the center of the room. The soft sounds from all the stories intermingled.

"You enchanting baby fawn…," the dryad sang.

"Boom! Boom!" the cannons roared. "You scurvy dogs," said a sailor.

"Archers! Release arrows!" said a chariot commander.

"My love, the zephyr caresses your fair hair, the tendrils like strands of silk…," said the Englishman to the maiden.

Cyrano was plying Roxanne with gentle phrases.

And on it went. None of the stories was overly loud, but they all combined to produce a considerable undercurrent of noise.

What to do?

A bold approach might be best.

"Attention, all stories!" Instantaneous silence resulted from my statement. "While I have always loved a good story and am grateful that you are included in the wisdom compiled on Shargram, the noise may make it hard for me to sleep or study. Would you be willing to mute yourselves whenever I'm in the room?" I made eye contact with each of the story characters.

They nodded cheerfully. The action resumed, but on silent mode.

Wonderful. Glad that worked. Now, I really need a nap.

My head still throbbed as I lay down on the comfortable bed and drifted to sleep.

CHAPTER 52

Sunshine hit me directly in the face, coming through the unshuttered window.

What time is it?

A knock on my door brought me further out of the deep sleep I had been in.

"Come in." My voice was filled with sleepy scratchiness.

An Ophen rolled in and set a packet down on my desk. "Good morning," he said. "This is your welcome and training packet. Breakfast will be at the Dining Hall in forty-five minutes."

Morning? Breakfast? Did I sleep all night long?

I sat up slowly. "Where is the Dining Hall?"

The Ophen rolled to the window and pointed with a colorful limb. I walked over to the window to see what he indicated.

A structure with what seemed like glass levels suspended in mid-air, with foliage of all types cascading down and through each level, was behind the Education Center. I wasn't sure how I could have missed it yesterday.

"It is less than a five-minute walk from your quarters." The Ophen gave a cheerful bob and rolled out of the room.

A slight headache throbbed behind my eyes from the thought assault yesterday. I was feeling grungy from sleeping in my clothes and my teeth had that fuzzy feeling from not being brushed last night.

Tea first, then a shower.

Dropping a few grains of manna in my mug, I said, "Hot tea with milk and sugar, in Jesus' name." My mug was instantly filled with the delightful liquid. The hot mug in my hand filled me with gratitude for the manna Jarl had distributed to everyone in our group when we were back in Texas.

Manna. The gift that keeps on giving.

I sat on my bed, sipping tea and watching the dryad leading an exuberant dance of other dryads in an open meadow on my wall.

"Ms. Dryad," I said. "Would you mind if I heard your dance music?"

Instantly, a sweet, wild melody filtered into the room. It filled my spirit with joy. "Thank you. That's what I needed this morning." Finishing my tea and waving good-bye to the stories, I gathered my towel and toothbrush, then headed to the bathroom for a long-overdue shower.

—⟋⟋⟋—

Cleaned up and feeling fine, I went in search of Aneera. I was hoping to walk with her to breakfast. The foyer in the Education Center was crowded with Universe Healers and angelic trainers, all greeting each other and chatting.

Aneera emerged from the hallway where her quarters were located a minute after I arrived. When she saw me, she threaded her way through the crowd to where I was.

"The walls and tables are alive!" She was alight with

excitement. "Even my ceiling has humming flowers on it."

"I know." I gave her a hug. "I drank tea this morning to the accompaniment of a dryad's woodland dance music."

"I wonder what other unusual things await us today?" Her anticipation was palpable.

"I'm as curious as you are." I saw Darion and Harnel approaching. "Maybe they'll give us some clues."

"Clues?" Harnel said. "Clues to what?"

"Clues about what to expect today." I glanced between Harnel and Darion.

"We wouldn't dream of spoiling the surprise." Darion comically closed his lips and mimed locking them with a key.

Aneera rolled her eyes good-naturedly at the tall angel. "Do you see what I have to put up with?"

I laughed, then saw that everyone was filing outside. "C'mon. Breakfast is waiting. That will probably be an adventure in and of itself, considering that the Ophens don't seem to have mouths."

Harnel corrected me. "They are Ophen*im*, not Ophens."

"Oops." I shrugged my shoulders at the mistake. How was I to know?

Aneera grinned at me, slipped her hand in mine and we followed our angels out the door.

Ophenim, apparently, didn't use chairs at their long, ornate dining tables. Later, I discovered they had mouths to eat with, but they didn't bother to use them to speak. Thought-communication was easier.

We dined standing up, filling our plates repeatedly from a stunning array of delicious foods I had never seen before.

We shared comments and observations as we ate, enjoying ourselves. A sense of excitement surrounded us from the Ophenim and our trainers. It was building in intensity, but I wasn't sure why.

Glad I'm not a picky eater. Some of this food looks questionable, but tastes great.

I exchanged nodded greetings with several of my Quadrant 4 Team members. Aneera came over to me after visiting with some of her Quadrant 3 Team members. I leaned over to give her a quick, unobtrusive kiss.

I was examining the structure of the Dining Hall's numerous glass levels, which were suspended by nearly invisible wires that must have been enormously strong. The lush, plant-filled alcoves were arranged for smaller groups while there were larger rooms for big meetings. Everywhere I turned, inviting spaces drew the eye.

A change in the atmosphere grabbed my attention. I followed everyone's gaze. They were looking at the entrance where seven majestic beings, each twelve feet tall and dressed head-to-toe in one of the colors of the rainbow, had appeared.

"Welcome, Your Excellencies." Reynel, the brilliantly blue-eyed head angelic trainer, glowed as he bowed before the beings. "We are honored by your presence."

"The seven Spirits of God,"[43] Harnel whispered in my ear.

I was immobilized by awe until I heard a crash behind me. A Chinese woman had dropped her plate, fallen to her knees, and bowed in reverence. The rest of us quickly followed her example, setting our plates on the floor and

---

[43] Isaiah 11:2

bowing with our faces to the ground.

"Dear children, we are pleased to be with you," the Spirit dressed in brilliant red said. "We are happy to beginning your training sessions in the art of Universe Healing after breakfast." When his brief greeting concluded, the seven Spirits disappeared.

Darion glanced at Aneera and me once we stood up again. He winked exaggeratedly, then waggled his eyebrows.

Didn't want to spoil the surprise, indeed.

CHAPTER 53

Walking back to the Education Center after breakfast, my head swarmed with questions.

How will this training progress? What role will I play? How will Aneera and I ever have any time together?

"You'll need your introductory packet," Harnel told me.

Jogging back to my room, I dashed in to pick up my packet. The stories immediately muted themselves when they saw me.

Leaving just as quickly, packet in hand, I waved to them all and said, "Carry on." The low hum of song and voices resumed.

I saw my Quadrant 4 Team assembling in the foyer. Before I could join them, Reynel stepped in front of me.

"Quinn, you are needed to join three others—one from each Quadrant's Team—for a special assignment on Earth." His brilliant blue eyes burned into me like lasers.

"What assignment? Are we going right now?" It was inconceivable to me that I would be pulled out of training before it even began.

Reynel observed my reaction gravely. "You'll stay on Shargram until day nine of the training, then will be gone for two weeks. Derrik, Tyrus and Claudia will also be on Earth during this time."

I raised my eyebrows, not sure what to say.

"You will receive special sessions to get you caught up when you return so that you will have all the information needed for Universe Healing." After delivering his news, Reynel left to join Aneera's team as they followed the yellow-clad Spirit of Understanding down a hallway.

Questions flooded me once again as I watched him go.

*Special secret missions. Now, a special assignment? Some days being **special** isn't all it seems cracked up to be.*

Aneera caught my eye and blew me a kiss before following her team. That lifted my spirits. I pretended to catch it and hold it to my heart. Smiling, she disappeared down the hallway and I went to join my own team.

The imposing, indigo-clad Spirit of Knowledge led our Quadrant 4 Healing Team into a round chamber. It was a room with a lofty feel, the smooth walls shooting up to a skylight. The sun's rays came through the ceiling window, then were cleverly directed down the cylindrical walls by a series of mirrors. The light was then focused into a series of differently shaped prisms suspended in the center of the room by clear threads. The color dispensed through each prism changed as the sun progressed across the sky. Currently, we were enveloped in orange light with a hint of red showing at the edges. This light-refracting masterpiece excited my imagination and admiration.

I would love to create something like this if I'm ever so fortunate as to have a house of my own with Aneera.

I perused my teammates' faces. I hadn't spent time with

these people since our introductory meeting seven years ago. A wave of loneliness hit me. Suddenly, I missed the familiar faces of my group in Petra. And I missed Aneera, even though she was in the same building.

"Quinn." Harnel bumped my shoulder. "He asked you a question." He indicated our indigo-clad instructor.

Startled, I looked at Harnel, then at the Spirit of Knowledge. "I'm sorry, Your Excellency." I bowed briefly. "What was your question?" I flushed as everyone's eyes turned to me.

"What do you consider your main skills to be, Quinn?" The Spirit smiled gently, amused.

"Well…." My *main* skills? "I throw a mean lasso." Visions of Granny's hog and the charging lion flashed to mind. "And I can do nearly anything with metal and almost as much with wood, if I put my mind to it."

"How did you acquire those skills?" our instructor probed.

"Practice. Lots of practice, and a willingness to try new procedures or ways of creating something." Fond memories of doing these things brought a smile to my face.

"I'm surprised you didn't mention your artistic endeavors," the Spirit of Knowledge said.

"Yes, me too." I laughed, and the other team members joined me. A little of the uncomfortable strangeness in the atmosphere broke and everyone relaxed.

"But, is that your *main* skill?" The Spirit gazed at me expectantly.

This puzzled me. "I'm not sure what other skills I have that you could be referring to."

"Perhaps you don't think of it as a skill yet," the Spirit said, "but you will."

"What do you mean, Your Excellency? What is my main

skill?"

The Spirit of Knowledge glowered at me, abruptly fierce. The change in his countenance startled me and made my heart beat faster.

"Your main skill, Quinn, is *remembering*."

—ɯ—

Trying to pay attention to each of my team members' responses to the Spirit of Knowledge's questions took intense effort. The memories of the many times the Shepherd had told me to "Remember who I was" kept intruding into my thoughts.

Tulok's "Walrus Hunting Dance" finally helped keep my attention in the present. The short, compact Inuit man gracefully danced through the motions of a traditional walrus hunt. Apologizing at the end, he explained, "There are usually five dancers for this performance, to show where each hunter's position should be. I'm afraid one dancer can't give you the full experience."

We all applauded enthusiastically. I was impressed with the thoroughness of the dance, and planned to tell Tulok that later.

"All of you," the Spirit of Knowledge said, "are gifted with many useful or beautiful acquired skills. However, in the Universe Healing you will do, none of these skills will take pre-eminence."

We glanced at each other, wondering where this was going.

"You have heard that the Earth will be filled with the knowledge of the glory of the Lord as the waters cover the sea?"[44] The Spirit of Knowledge walked in front of each of us, seeking our acknowledgment.

We all nodded or said, "Yes, we have."

"This knowledge will also fill each of you and will go out to the ends of the Universe." The Spirit then looked at me. "And beyond."

Beyond?

Indigo flames erupted from the Spirit's hands. "Are you ready to receive?"

I swallowed hard. Glancing at my teammates, I noted that they all had concerned expressions.

Unexpectedly, quiet Dottie, the Wyoming librarian, stepped forward and extended her hands, palms facing up. Her hands shook slightly, but she said, "I'm ready."

Indigo fire leapt from the Spirit's hands onto Dottie's outstretched palms. Flames wreathed her hands, then were absorbed into her. We saw the indigo fire traveling under the skin up her forearms, then farther up her arms until they were no longer visible under the fabric of her short-sleeved shirt. The flames were visible again when they went up her neck into her face. A short time later, we saw them burning in her eyes.

"And we will know fully, as we have been fully known…,"[45] she murmured. "Amazing."

The rest of us extended our hands, palms up. Indigo fire flew into them, filling each of us with the burning knowledge of the Lord as it danced its way through our veins.

Knowing—deep and wide—filled me. My own lack of

---

[44] Habakkuk 2:14
[45] I Corinthians 13:12

knowledge was submerged in the fiery tidal wave rushing through me.

This is only the first lesson? Can it get better than this?

Hunger for more from all of these Spirits, I now knew, would propel me forward until I was filled to the point of bursting.

CHAPTER 54

"Welcome to the Council of 13, Gruxen." Shevril, dressed in his ornate robe, pointed with his golden hand to the open chair waiting for the new member at the table.

Thick golden hair, with streaks of black that matched his eyes, fell to the new Golden One's waist. He was taller than most of the others at the table, and he exuded a power that might rival Shevril's.

Moving forward to take his seat, Gruxen said, "I gather my election to the Council did not come about through happy circumstances." He looked around the table at each member, judging their reactions.

Tauren shook his head and blew out a resigned breath. "It did not. One of our members was unexpectedly obliterated, which created this opportunity."

Gruxen's eyes narrowed. "And you opened the Council seat to me? Why?"

"We heard of your interest in timeline disruption events. You could be a valuable asset in our pursuit of the ability to break into the timeline at a precise point." Jaburn's half-smile wasn't entirely welcoming. He then indicated Korfal. "Korfal has developed a breed of time-worm that can travel to designated parts of the timeline and create a portal, which has worked well a few times. It's not an exact science."

Korfal nodded, eyeing Gruxen cautiously.

"Why do you need to access the timeline at a certain point?" Gruxen drummed his black-tipped fingernails on the table.

"We seek a certain object of the Enemy's," Chorne said, shuttering his expression.

"Don't we already have plenty of the Enemy's trinkets? Crowns, mantels of the blessed, scrolls of destiny—we've collected these things for millennia—keeping them from being used by the Enemy's pawns." Gruxen scoffed at the Council members. "While their absence may have temporarily hindered the Enemy's advances, it seems a way was always found around them."

Gruxen stopped drumming his nails on the table, giving Shevril a challenging glare. "What could you possibly hope to intercept that would make any difference in the Enemy's plans?"

"The only Book that holds the eternal destiny of each human." The weight of Shevril's tone made each word a heavy stone that crashed down in the midst of the Council. "The Book of Life."

Shock filled Gruxen's face, but then a gleam grew in his dark eyes.

"Excellent." A sly smile spread across his face. "I'm in."

We were to have three weeks studying with each of the Spirits, for a total of twenty-one weeks, according to our introductory packets. Starting out with the Spirit of Knowledge was advantageous, because his fire—which now coursed through my Healing Team's veins—would make it easier to assimilate the lessons from the six other Spirits.

It was with regret that I was pulled from my classes on day nine. I had told Aneera that I was to go back to Earth with Derrik, Tyrus, and Claudia, but we were all in the dark as to why.

Our angelic trainers walked with the four of us who were bound for Earth as we made our way to the departure pavilion. It was set a short way out of the Education Center's back doors. Our feet crunched through the orange dust until we stepped up onto the stone platform where we would have our send-off. I turned back to the Education Center and saw Aneera standing at a second story window with her hand raised in farewell. I waved to her before directing my attention to Harnel.

Each angel handed his trainee a small paper. "These are the coordinates for your spacewalk to Earth," Harnel said to me.

Every person had a different destination. Derrik, from the Quadrant 2 Team, would be in Jerusalem actually witnessing the return of Jesus to Earth and the Battle of Armageddon. Then, he would work in Jerusalem for two weeks.

Lucky fellow.

Claudia, from the Quadrant 1 Team, was to go to Iceland to escort an aged woman of enormous influence over a tribe of people to meet Jesus in person after his return. This old woman had resisted all of Emanuel's coercion and evil attempts to force her people into his system. She had, against all odds, kept herself and her people unmarked and free. And, amazingly, alive. However, she said she would never accept any supposed Savior of the world unless she met with him eye-to-eye and knew he could be trusted.

Claudia dipped her head, acknowledging her assignment, after receiving her slip of paper. Her Nordic features, hollowed-out cheeks and imposing stature made her seem like she would fit right in with Icelandic people.

Tyrus, from Aneera's team, grinned hugely when he received his paper. Onthel, his angelic trainer, said, "I thought you would be pleased."

"I can't believe it." A tear slipped down Tyrus' cheek. The tall, Maasai warrior gave every appearance of being fierce in his traditional dress with a spear in his right hand. This vulnerability surprised me.

"How did they survive?" Tyrus asked Onthel.

"Your extended family utilized a spell for invisibility that your grandfather taught them and they went into underground caverns few were aware of." Onthel spoke reassuringly, but there was a note of warning in his voice. "They evaded Emanuel's forces, but that doesn't mean they are friendly toward Jesus. They are involved with the same evil spirits your grandfather knows. Satan's kingdom is not always unified and there are internal factions that war with each other. You will need to use caution in retrieving them and spacewalking them to Jerusalem to meet Jesus. Prepare yourself in case they don't all choose to accompany you."

Tyrus nodded, his wide grin still spread across his face.

Finally, it came to me. I held my slip of paper and glanced at Harnel with surprise. He regarded me with an encouraging smile.

I was going back to Petra.

CHAPTER 55

My coordinates landed me back in the time-splicing gateway room. Our angelic trainers had remained on Shargram.

The gateway cavern was empty when I arrived. Taking my pack off, I laid it on the ground and went to see the walls. The Shepherd had updated the etchings in the wall to include my escapade with David and the lion. The same adrenaline rush hit me as I saw the carving of me lassoing the charging beast.

What a crazy day that was.

The lights were dim in the cavern and none of the gateways were lit up. The Shepherd's presence always made the rock walls shine. Now everything had an empty feel to it, like no one had been here for a while.

What to do?

I was unused to waiting. My last few weeks had been filled with activity of one sort or the other. I had been itching to resume sketching my adventures, but had no opportunity until now. With the stone etchings on the wall to inspire me, sketching was exactly what I wanted to do.

Pulling my sketchpad out and getting my favorite charcoal pencil, I decided to first continue working on a sketch of Aneera. She had been enticingly beautiful in her borrowed bridesmaid's dress at Jarl and Tessa's wedding. Flowers with colors I had trouble describing from the Gardens of Laranda were entwined in her hair. Her expression had been a mixture of joy and longing. This expression was what I was struggling to get just right.

She told me after the wedding that she had such an unusual jumble of feelings going on during the ceremony. She was so happy for Jarl and Tessa, but also felt twinges of envy and longing.

I had watched the emotions flow over her features, wanting to capture each one. My pencil worked slowly. I didn't desire to rush the process.

My skin began crackling while I worked. Indigo sparks burst inside my skin, causing a slight "ping" of electricity each time they exploded. My pencil moved faster. Knowing rushed up from my abdominal region, guiding me as my pencil started to race across the paper.

Ten minutes after I began, I finished. The portrait was so lifelike I almost expected to see Aneera smile as her eyes found mine. I had never done something that looked so *real* in such a short amount of time.

Whoa. Spirit of Knowledge fire on display right now.

I jumped, dropping my pencil, when the Shepherd said over my shoulder, "That's a spectacular drawing, Quinn."

Heart pounding from the surprise, I leaned over to pick up my pencil before saying, "Thank you."

"Your artistic heart will be useful in your next mission." The Shepherd watched me fondly, light flashing in his eyes. "You don't need to worry about falling behind in your lessons on Shargram. The Spirits' fire that you receive will infuse you and enable you to keep pace when you return."

"That's good news." I recognized that a small part of me

had been concerned about this.

Standing up, I put the sketch pad and pencil back into my pack, then faced the Shepherd. "I'm glad to be here, but why now? Why am I one of the privileged four to be pulled out of training?"

"It would be hard to explain your absence adequately to everyone on Shargram if you disappeared. This scenario makes it simpler." The Shepherd pointed to a gateway that began pulsing with deep, living green light. "And, this mission will be more extensive than your other ones up to this point."

"It will? Can I ask why?" My curiosity was aroused.

"You can ask." The Shepherd smiled. "It will be more of a case of *show* over *tell*."

"Oh, one of those." I smiled wryly. You would think by now I would know better than to ask.

The Shepherd pointed with his chin toward the glowing green gateway. I got the hint.

Squaring my shoulders, I marched over to the gateway and was absorbed into the light as soon as my foot entered it.

Emerging from a darkened hallway where the gateway had deposited me, green glory light finished getting sucked into me as soon as I stepped out into the afternoon sunlight. I stood still for a moment and took in my surroundings.

A fountain to my left rhythmically showered droplets from the open mouth of a leaping porpoise. The water landed in a catchment pool at the statue's base.

An intricate, intertwined pattern of spirals was laid out in the mosaic pavement in front of me. I leaned closer to appraise the sparkling mosaic pieces. These were no cheap pieces of cracked tile. There were opals, cut glass and other semi-precious stones intermixed with precisely cut tile pieces. The wealth represented in the floor I was to walk on gave me the idea that I was around some type of royalty.

Taking notice of my clothing gave me something new to contemplate.

What frippery is this?

The toes of my shoes curled up and had small stones sewn into them. My mind ran to "Aladdin's Cave," but this didn't seem like Arabia. A solid white linen sheath went down to my ankles and was covered with a deep green, thickly embroidered outer robe. My beard reached to the middle of my chest and smelled of perfumed oil. When I reached a hand up to feel my head, I discovered a tall hat complete with tassels on the top. I took it off to examine it and saw that it was the same green as my robe and embellished with tiny, sparkling beads.

Movement across the courtyard made me quickly replace my hat and turn, but not before I noticed the translation bracelet with its small green orb on my left wrist.

Whew. Glad to see that.

I also held rolled documents in my right hand, but had no opportunity to examine them before I was hailed by a man exiting from a hallway on the other side of the pavement.

"Good! You've arrived, and I see you've brought the drawings. Please hurry. King Ahasuerus awaits."

CHAPTER 56

The man who hailed me, dressed in official-looking red robes, hurried across the pavement. "The king is seated in his receiving chambers. Let us make haste. He is not the most patient of men."

I fell in step beside the man, easily keeping pace with him because he was nearly a foot shorter than me. My mind was bouncing through the biblical stories of what I knew about King Ahasuerus.

Am I in the time period before Queen Esther[46] is crowned or after?

Deciding to venture a question to garner more information, I asked, "What is the king hoping to see from me today?"

Without breaking stride, the man said, "Surely you updated your drawings, Master Martus, and included the place setting for the large jewel in the top section of the scepter?"

"Naturally. I wondered if he had decided on which jewel to use?" I was floundering, but at least I now knew this

---

[46] Book of Esther

involved a scepter, and I knew my name here.

"I am unaware of his decision. That is not within my province." We approached two gigantic, dark-skinned men guarding a tall doorway. "This way." The short man nodded to the two large men, one of whom moved to open the door for us.

Walking into the lavish receiving area of King Ahasuerus, I strove to keep my expression neutral and not appear as impressed as I actually was. "Master Martus," my present persona, would have already seen this room, so I better not be gawking over it.

We approached the king, who sat on an ornate, cushioned chair. I followed the short man's example, bowing deeply before surreptitiously giving the king a quick once over.

King Ahasuerus was older than I expected, possibly in his early fifties. I had always visualized the king who married Queen Esther as a younger man. Clearly, I needed to brush up on my history.

"Ah, Master Martus. Good to see you again." The king rose from his chair, indicating I was to follow him as he walked over to a broad table.

"And you, Your Majesty." I followed him, then laid my drawings on the table within his reach. I noticed several huge jewels of different cuts and sizes laying on a rich, purple cloth spread out before us. My eyes were drawn to the ruby glinting in the light.

"The men who had the temerity to steal my scepter have been caught and publicly hung." The king wore a disgusted expression. "However, the scepter was not recovered. And what is a monarch to use to hand judgments down within the noble city of Susa if he is deprived of this symbol of his grandeur and authority?"

Thinking quickly, I rejoined, "With a new scepter, sire, of even grander, more impressive design."

The king laughed. "A good answer, Martus. Let us see what you have brought."

Unrolling the documents, I made a quick note that there were three sheets showing the dimensions of an intricately designed, two-foot-long scepter from the front, side, and back views. The top section had a generous space for a large jewel.

"Yes, these are excellent. The area for the jewel is just as I described." He swept his hand forward to indicate the jewels on the table. "Which jewel do you think will be most appropriate?"

"A proverb springs to mind, sire." I hoped I wasn't overstepping my place. "An excellent wife, who can find? For her worth is far above rubies. The heart of her husband trusts in her, and he will have no lack of gain."[47] I picked up the ruby, placing it on top of the drawing where the jewel would go. "This jewel catches the light with a unique brilliance."

"So it does." The king inclined his head approvingly. "A proverb I learned from the Hebrew people also comes to my mind. 'Do you see a man skilled in his work? He will stand before kings; he will not stand before obscure men.'[48] What do you think, Martus? How long will it take to make this?"

I quickly did a few mental calculations. "To complete it, sire, will take about one and a half weeks."

"Very good." He nodded to the short man. "Barzel, see that Martus has all the equipment and supplies needed. You may requisition the jewel when it is to be placed in the

---

[47] Proverbs 31:10-11
[48] Proverbs 22:29

scepter."

Barzel bowed and said, "Yes, Your Majesty."

King Ahasuerus nodded in dismissal and went back to take his seat while I gathered my drawings and followed Barzel out the door.

CHAPTER 57

This was why my absence from Universe Healing school had to be so long. I was to make a new scepter for a temperamental king because someone or other had stolen his previous scepter.

I can guess who goaded the thieves on.

My thoughts pondered the machinations of the fake Golden Ones. How could the king extend a golden scepter to Queen Esther in her hour of need if he didn't have one?

If my guess on timing was correct, Queen Esther had been in her station as queen for quite some time. Haman had advanced his murderous plot against the Jewish people—Esther's people. Someday soon, Queen Esther would risk her life, at her Uncle Mordecai's urging, to go into the King's Court and plead for the lives of her people.

The king required a golden scepter to extend to the queen, granting her life according to the laws of the land along with the freedom to make her request of him.

This is time-splicing at its finest.

Barzel's voice brought me back to my present, which was also the distant past. "We've arranged temporary quarters for you to stay in so that you can be close to your workroom.

Hushan will see to your needs." Barzel called a waiting servant who stood nearby. "Bring food and drink to Master Martus, and anything else he requires."

The servant bowed and left quickly.

Barzel was relieved by the progress we had made. "The king was in a good mood today. He seems pleased with your design. I'm sure I don't have to tell you how important this is to him."

"I know it's important. I will need to get several tools from the workshop at my home. This will take me a few hours tonight. I should be able to start work tomorrow. I will need the bronze core according to these dimensions." I opened the first document to show Barzel.

Barzel was smug. "The core you requested, the wooden staves and your tools have already been put into your workshop in the palace."

"You went through my home workshop?" Angry heat began to rise in my face.

The smug expression fled. "No, no Master Martus. Your assistant procured what we requested."

I relaxed. "All right. Please direct me to the workshop so that I can get things in order."

Barzel turned to our left, motioning for me to join him. "Follow me."

I didn't grasp how all the knowledge of "Master Martus" was being melded into me, but little blocks of information kept clicking into place. My backstory in this era unfolded over the next two or three hours as I familiarized myself with the palace workshop. I was a well-respected craftsman in the city of Susa in the ancient Medo-Persian Empire. I worked well in my two favorite mediums—metal and wood.

This is going to be fun.

Catching a glimpse of myself in a polished bronze mirror gave me a start. I was older, with grey hairs sprinkled amongst my black, shoulder-length hair. My beard was edged in grey. I hoped it made me appear wise and distinguished.

The tools at hand for my use were simple, but adequate. I checked the foot-powered lathe with slight consternation. A practice wooden stave or two would probably be needed before I got the hang of it in order to shape the scepter's wooden shaft.

All in all, I was pleased as I headed to dinner in my quarters.

Work began in the morning.

—◊—

My quarters were luxurious. The king didn't skimp on his working guests.

A traveling leather bag on my bed held several changes of clothing and toiletry items. I laid everything out for inspection. Work clothes and a well-used leather apron would be what I spent most of my time in, but I had two changes of official meet-with-the-king type of outfits. I was confused by a short, fine-toothed comb in addition to a regular wide-toothed comb. I fiddled with the smaller comb while I ate dinner, trying to discern its purpose. It was only after I brushed food out of my beard for the third time that I had an "ah-ha" moment.

This goofy little comb is for my beard.

Long beards were definitely the fashion for men in the palace. I decided that I would only have a short beard if I ever decided to grow one in my regular life. Running that little comb through my beard-tangles to get the food out was no small chore.

Before bed, I took a stroll out to the beautiful mosaic pavement I had crossed earlier. I sat on a bench in the twilight, listening to the plashing of the porpoise fountain while I mentally reviewed the scepter's details.

Noise to my right made me turn my head. An almost preternaturally beautiful woman, dressed as royalty, exited one of the numerous hallways. Her beauty was accentuated by the warm glow of the lamps lighting her way. She was flanked by two large bodyguards.

I couldn't help staring.

She must have felt my gaze, because she turned and locked eyes with me. Her brow was furrowed and she appeared troubled as she glanced away and continued on.

That had to be Queen Esther. Her beauty wasn't exaggerated in the Bible's account.

I wondered if she had been informed of Haman's evil plan right before I saw her. *Something* had disturbed her composure.

Leaving for my quarters soon afterward, I headed to sleep with the expression in the queen's eyes haunting me.

CHAPTER 58

"He disappeared." Racil was incredulous. "I was tracking him normally, but then he vanished." Racil shook his interdimensional tracking device, frustration marking his smooth features.

"Have you calculated for the time-slips?" Gruxen came over to examine Racil's device.

"Of course!" Racil was agitated. "As well as the day the Enemy stopped the Earth's rotation,[49] along with the time he reversed the rotation."[50] Racil waved his hand and produced a map of the Earth with its layered timelines. "The implant has been working perfectly up until now. Quinn was in Petra."

"Are you sure he is still on the Earth?" Jaburn joined the conversation. "Perhaps there are some dimensions inaccessible to your tracking device. Or the implant's function has been disrupted."

Troubled, Racil paced in front of the Earth map. "This

---

[49] Joshua 10:12-14
[50] Isaiah 38:8

was a concern when he began training as a Universe Healer. There was a brief disruption I noted during his first week on Shargram."

Shevril growled, the disturbing sound causing the Council table to vibrate. "Blast those Wisdom Keepers." He slammed a fist down. "We need to find a way to 'disrupt' them. Quovern, Fraynt." He waved a hand toward the two Golden Ones. "Go see the shield-penetrating division. See if we can get through to the ground on Shargram."

Quovern and Fraynt rose to leave.

"They need to know that nowhere is safe for their treacherous trainings." Shevril fixed his gaze next on Racil and Gruxen after the two other Golden Ones left. "And you two—find Quinn."

—⁓⁓—

Working on King Ahasuerus' scepter was a delight. I had roughed out the wooden stave and drilled through the length of it. The wood was sound after this procedure with no cracks or splinters. I filled the hollow with melted resin, after which I inserted the three-eighths inch, lightly-heated bronze core. The bronze ran the length of the stave, providing stability and the right amount of "heft" to the scepter.

While I waited for the resin to solidify, which would glue the bronze core in place, I worked to hammer out two sheets of gold.

When I had the gold at the proper thickness, I began etching in a lion with wings from a sketch I had made. It would go around the lower part of the scepter, where the king's hand would cover it, representing his power and authority. Geometric designs would be etched into the rest of the gold that would wrap around the scepter.

The carving of the top part of the scepter, which would house the large ruby, would be the most time-intensive portion of this task. The intricate design for the very top of the scepter would wrap around the large ruby in such a way as to give the impression that the stone had grown there organically. The indigo fire of the Spirit of Knowledge "pinged" under my skin until I executed the design perfectly. The final result was regal.

Before subjecting the scepter to the foot-powered lathe for shaping, I practiced on two spare wooden staves in order to get the speed and pressure correct when I shaped the actual scepter before wrapping it in its new golden clothing. It was a good thing I practiced because the first stave splintered on me and went to pieces. The second worked well, but not perfectly. I decided to work on a third practice stave. I was pleased with my third attempt and decided to begin shaping the real scepter the next day, after which I would requisition the ruby so that I could make the final adjustments for placing it in the top of the scepter.

Hushan came in with a tray brimming with food and drink, as he had daily while I worked away in solitude.

"Great timing. I was getting hungry." I grinned at Hushan.

The servant bowed quickly and left. I set my tools down, rinsed my hands off, and fell to eating.

I paced unhurriedly around the porpoise fountain that evening. Tilting my head back, I soaked in the starlight and thought of Aneera. The lamp light flickering along the hallways didn't impede my view of the constellations. The air was pleasantly cool as it ruffled my hair and beard.

I began to have an odd sensation, like someone was calling me. I didn't see any other people. Prickles crawled over my upper back and up my neck. The air grew heavy. The atmosphere on the other side of the fountain began to waver, as if someone was trying to press their fingers through an opaque veil. I was alarmed.

I don't think whoever that might be is a friendly visitor.

This wasn't the time for interruptions. I would finish the scepter in the next two or three days. The king, who had been on a trip to inspect one of his army units, would return to his throne room and resume overseeing matters of state. And Queen Esther would need his royal pardon with this new scepter.

The distortion in the atmosphere became more intense. I saw the air begin to ripple and split. Golden light began to leak through.

Release the glory.

After receiving this internal command from the Shepherd, I extended my hands without hesitation. Blazing, green-tinged light flew from my fingers and bashed into the burgeoning rift, penetrating it and disappearing inside. It sealed the opening when it went through, leaving only clear, calm night in its wake.

Gruxen looked down at the smoldering, blackened remains of Racil and a medium-sized time-worm on the Council chamber's floor. Then he turned to Shevril and the other seated Council members.

"It appears that hanging out with this Council is a dangerous business." Gruxen maneuvered around Korfal, who was aghast at the loss of another, younger time-worm. The time-worm had only just succeeded in opening the portal into Quinn's presence.

Bending over to pluck up the charred tracking device from what was left of Racil, Gruxen saw that the device offered a faint red blip on the screen before going dark.

"Quinn is definitely in ancient Susa." Gruxen tossed the device to Shevril. It skidded across the table until Shevril reached out to intercept it. Gruxen then gave a mocking smile. "You almost had access to him. Too bad. You'll have to devise a different tracking method from here on out."

CHAPTER 59

Barzel nodded to the two men standing on guard outside of the throne room. They reached over and pulled the large, thickly carved doors open.

My appointment with the king came early in the day at the end of the one and a half weeks. Sunlight filtered through high windows in the walls as I walked forward with measured steps.

Dressed in my best clothing, beard properly combed and oiled, I carried the finished scepter on an ornate pillow to present to the king. The eyes of nobles, councilmen and princes followed me as I moved slowly down the long open floor, flanked by tall pillars, to the throne.

Having never been particularly keen on "pomp and circumstance," I appreciated the coaching Barzel provided on making this presentation. I hoped I remembered everything he had said.

When I reached the foot of the steps going up to the throne, a shaft of sunlight struck the ruby set in the gold filigree close to the top of the scepter. The light created a burst of vibrant red splashes of color all around the throne. An audible gasp rose from all those present.

Magnificent! Couldn't have planned it better.

I knelt before the king, the pillow in my outstretched arms, sunlight still bringing the ruby to life.

King Ahasuerus quickly came down the steps from his throne. Picking up the scepter, he examined it closely, taking in the fine etchings, the lion with wings, the engraved golden caps on the top and bottom, and the intricate setting for the ruby.

"You've outdone yourself, Master Martus. Rise, so that I may bestow my praise properly."

I rose before him, holding the pillow in both hands, head bowed in reverence.

The king returned to his throne, scepter in hand. I raised my head and saw him lift the scepter to decree, "Master Martus is hereby one of the chief craftsmen of the realm. He will have a yearly royal stipend from the treasury and will create objects of beauty and usefulness for the king's household."

Murmurs of approval rose from those in attendance.

"Thank you, Your Majesty. I am honored." I bowed before him.

A stir arose behind me. I heard the doors open, and there were again gasps from those present.

I looked to see what had happened, even though it was against protocol to turn away from the king.

Queen Esther, stunningly beautiful in her royal robes, walked across the throne room floor. Her head was held high and the flush in her cheeks only accentuated her loveliness.

Whispers began. "She wasn't summoned." "It is against the law." "She is forfeiting her life."

I moved away from the steps to the throne and joined the officials at the side.

King Ahasuerus' eyes were locked onto the queen. His bodyguards moved to intercept her, but stood down when the king gave them a subtle shake of his head. He heard the whispers of the nobles and princes, but made no rejoinder.

The queen arrived at the foot of the steps leading to the throne. She bowed and waited there, never saying a word.

The king glanced briefly at the ruby in the scepter he held in his hand. I heard him mutter quietly, "Her worth is far above rubies...."

A hush blanketed everyone.

Slowly, the king arose and walked down the steps.

And extended the golden scepter.

—ш—

Exiting the throne room later, I exhaled the breath it seemed that I had held for hours.

I actually saw it. I saw Queen Esther rise and touch the scepter, then issue the invitation for the king and Haman to come to her banquet.

Dazed, I made my way back to my quarters. Time had been spliced in a momentous way today. A broken tapestry strand had been rewoven. I couldn't imagine a more wonderful mission.

When I walked through the door to my quarters, I found myself back in the time-splicing gateway room in Petra. The Shepherd sat on a rock, waiting for me.

Restored to beardlessness and my jeans and T-shirt, I walked over to sit close by the Shepherd.

"Wow... just wow." I shook my head.

What else could I possibly say?

"I agree with King Ahasuerus. You really outdid yourself on that scepter." The Shepherd's grey eyes twinkled at me.

"I'm sure the fire from the Spirit of Knowledge had a lot to do with it." Smiling, I remembered the process. "Especially with figuring out the setting for the ruby."

"You still had to bring it into existence." The Shepherd reached over and ran a finger over my arm. He showed it to me. Larger flakes of gold glinted on his fingertip.

I checked out my hands and forearms. Sure enough, gold flakes covered them.

"You're improving in holding and releasing greater amounts of glory, Quinn." The Shepherd's thoughtful nod encouraged me. "You're on schedule."

Schedule? What schedule?

"I'd like you to do me a favor before you resume your training, if you would." The Shepherd smiled at me with lifted eyebrows. "A fellow needs to be rescued and taken to Jesus."

"Has Jesus returned yet?" A great end to a mission *and* a chance to meet Jesus face-to-face. I loved my life.

"Imminently." Lightning crackled in the Shepherd's eyes. "But you won't see that. I need you to go find a fellow named Herbert after you rinse off in the pool." He gestured toward the hot pool that I so enjoyed. "I spent a lot of time with him in a cave recently...."

"Okay. Where is he?" I stood, gold flakes fluttering to the floor around me."

"Scotland, in the town of Whithorn."

How hard could this be?

CHAPTER 60

Leaving the gateway room in Petra, I spacewalked to the village of Whithorn in Scotland, close to the war memorial on a downtown street. On a rare school field trip as a boy, we had driven the eight or so hours from Dinas Island to come explore St. Ninian's Cave and other historical landmarks. My classmates and teachers had stayed in Whithorn and used it as a home base from which we had our daily outings. I was allowed to stay with my Aunt Jenny, Mum's sister, who had moved from Dinas Island to this area of Scotland not long after my parents' deaths.

My pleasant memories of Whithorn were nothing like the present reality. The village had been wrecked by war and natural disasters. The war memorial that had so fascinated me as a boy was now merely rubble with twisted sections of fence still trying to maintain their curacy around it. I was saddened to see it, as I was also sad to remember Aunt Jenny's passing not long after Granny's.

I studied the streets, but didn't notice any people.

How am I supposed to find this Herbert person?

I walked through the village in the direction of St. Ninian's Cave, which was a few miles out of town. That was the only cave I could think of in the area where the Shepherd might have spent time, as it was the largest. Other caves were shallow and too close to the sea.

Approaching the edge of the village, I heard voices. There were three or four people speaking. They didn't sound friendly.

I was hoping for a good place to duck into in order to avoid notice. I had my pack on but no weapons of any sort handy. Before I could quietly slip into an alley, I was spotted by a group of men coming around a building.

"Hey Bruce, look! A stranger!" A scrawny, unkempt fellow pointed toward me.

I started searching for a weapon in earnest. There was nothing close by.

Should I wait? Should I spacewalk? What I wouldn't give to have some glory available right now.

"Grab him! Maybe he has some food," the fellow I guessed was Bruce yelled.

Definitely time to spacewalk.

Backing into the closest alley, I was focusing on St. Ninian's Cave when I was hit from behind.

Falling to my knees, I put my arm up to block another blow. A foot caught me in the side and I felt my ribs crack. The other group of men reached me and jumped into the fray.

Focus. Get out of here. Quick!

Screaming like a banshee, a skinny, disheveled man appeared from a doorway in the alley. He was nearly bald and wielding a pick-axe.

I'm going to die. There's no way I can concentrate to spacewalk.

Instead of killing me, the skinny man went after my attackers. Bruce got a pick-axe to the chest. When he fell, another attacker got hit in the neck. He fell near me onto the ground, his lifeless eyes staring into mine.

My other attackers scattered. I heard footsteps disappearing down the street.

I tried to move carefully, but sat up faster than I should have. My head immediately started swimming. I groaned.

"They're gone for now." The skinny man dropped to one knee beside me. "Can you move?"

"I think so. I'm pretty sure I have some broken ribs." Gasping in pain, I tried to get my feet under me. My rescuer offered a hand to help.

"If we get through this doorway, I can bar the door. It's sturdy. I don't think anyone can get in." He let me hold onto his arm as we made our way inside.

"Thank you for helping me. What's your name?" It hurt to talk.

The man's haggard face broke into a smile before he said, "I'm Herbert. Who are you?"

Herbert helped me take my pack off, then offered me some of his water. I gratefully accepted, rinsing the blood out of my mouth where my teeth had cut into my cheek and lip, then taking a long swallow. Moving my jaw around, I could tell it was bruised but not broken.

"There are a couple of small gangs in town. I've learned to avoid them, mostly. They think I'm crazy, especially since I've had to defend myself a couple of times with ole' Betsy here." He patted the pick-axe.

"Were you in St. Ninian's Cave?" I spoke slowly. It was difficult to breathe deeply.

"How did you know that?" He glared at me suspiciously,

hand gripping the axe.

"The Shepherd sent me to find you. I was supposed to 'rescue' you and take you to Jesus. I never suspected you would be rescuing me. Thank you!" Needing to let the pain subside, I stopped talking and took a few deliberate, shallow breaths.

"I'm not a trained medic. I used to be an accountant. However, I've had to learn a thing or two during these past years." Herbert motioned for me to lie down. "I can hopefully ascertain if you've damaged any internal organs, if you'll let me."

When I nodded, he began to work his hands over my torso. "This will probably hurt."

"Uh huh." I gritted my teeth as he probed my ribs and abdomen.

"You do have a couple of cracked ribs, from what I could tell, but I don't think they've punctured anything." He sat back on his heels. "So, you say the Shepherd sent you?"

I sat up stiffly. "He did. You get to go meet Jesus in person." To my surprise, tears began rolling down his cheeks.

Herbert dropped his face into his hands, shoulders shaking. When he could speak, he said, "I saw him, you know. I saw him return. It was unbelievable…." He cried quietly for a few more moments before wiping his face with a filthy sleeve. "He filled up the whole sky. There were huge numbers of people with him. I watched until he descended too low for me to see any more." He was silent for a few moments before asking, "By the way, do you happen to have any food on you? I haven't eaten for the better part of a week."

Smiling carefully with my sore face and split lip, I nodded. "I have just the thing. You'll be happy to know you'll never have to be hungry again." Digging my container of manna and plate out of my pack, I set the plate on the ground and put three grains of manna on it.

Herbert's eyes bugged out as the manna multiplied to form a tidy mound spreading over the plate. I pulled out a baggie and put several grains of manna from my container into it, then handed it to him.

"What is this stuff?" He shook the bag curiously.

"Manna. It's how God fed the Israelites in the wilderness for forty years[51], and it's how he feeds his people today." I pointed to the pile on the plate. "What would you like to eat?"

"Seriously? You're not joking?" Hope and caution warred in his expression.

I shook my head. "Nope."

"Fish and chips with loads of malt vinegar." He licked his lips in anticipation.

I spoke to the manna. "In Jesus' name, become a pile of fish and chips soaked in malt vinegar."

Instantaneously, the food presented itself. Herbert picked up a piece of savory, steaming fish and started crying again. Between tears and bites of food, he kept saying, "Thank you. Thank you."

When the food was gone, he held his plate out longingly. "You don't suppose... I could have some more?"

I leaned back against my pack, trying to find a more comfortable position. "You can have whatever you want. Take a couple of grains of your manna and put it on the plate. After it multiplies, put some of it back in your baggie for future use. Then, tell the manna, in Jesus' name, what to

---

[51] Exodus 16

become."

Herbert did this, giving a happy cry when the manna once more became a pile of fish and chips.

"Could you tell me about what happened to you and how you saw Jesus' return?" I fidgeted against my pack until I finally found a less painful way to sit.

Herbert told me his story while he polished off his second plate of food.

CHAPTER 61

Herbert, an old shepherd, and a fellow named Jack stayed in St. Ninian's Cave during the last few months of the hellish tribulation period on Earth.[52] They experienced many of the Bowl judgments,[53] and only knew about other judgments because the shepherd had brought a Bible with him and read about them out loud.

I don't think Herbert knows that the shepherd who was in the cave with him is THE Shepherd.

Jack was killed during the last Bowl judgment by what Herbert guessed was a one-hundred-pound hailstone. After that, the shepherd left to go "check on his old homestead" and Herbert came into Whithorn to try to find food. He had been in the town for a few days.

He described what he could see of Jesus' return[54] in the sky. It sounded magnificent. The Revelation 19 sword Jarl retrieved for Jesus was on full display. Truth be told, I was a little jealous of Herbert's experience.

---

[52] Matthew 24:4-31
[53] Revelation 16
[54] Revelation 19

"How are we supposed to get to Jesus? Transportation isn't easy to find these days." Herbert was cleaning in-between his teeth with a well-used toothpick, smiling contentedly. His belly bulged, obviously full.

"We'll spacewalk. We should probably go soon, now that I've rested up a bit." Moving wasn't easy. "Do you happen to know where I can find an old shirt or something I could use to bandage my ribs?"

"What is a spacewalk? You mean, like on the space station in orbit?" Herbert began rummaging in his pack, taking out his clothes and inspecting them. "Here. This can be used to make bandages."

The holey, ragged shirt Herbert offered was perfect. Using my knife, I cut strips out of it and tied them together while I answered him. "Quantum Spacewalking is moving instantaneously through the quantum realm from Point A to Point B."

Herbert nodded as he helped me get my shirt off and wrapped the strips around my lower torso. "Hmmm…. I'm not even going to ask how you do that, but it sounds a lot better than trying to figure out ground transportation right now."

"A little tighter." I winced slightly as Herbert complied, pulling the strips firmly. "That's good. The pressure helps me breathe a bit better." Putting my shirt back on was hard, but manageable.

At that moment, Derrik appeared in our room.

Herbert jumped up and grabbed his pick-axe, yelling "Who are you? How did you get here?"

"Whoa, Whoa." I motioned for Herbert to calm down. "This is Derrik. We… uh… work together."

"What happened to you?" Derrik took in my bruised face and ponderous movements. "Are you okay?"

"Not exactly, but I will be. I was jumped by a gang of guys." I pointed to Herbert. "This is Herbert. He rescued me. We were getting ready to spacewalk to Jerusalem and meet Jesus."

"So, this is why my trainer showed up and told me to come meet you." Derrik looked back and forth between the two of us. "I'm to take Herbert with me. You're to take yourself to Haven and get healed up."

"Aneera and I practiced praying for people a lot and saw many of them get healed. Why don't you pray for me now? Why do I need to go to Haven?" This didn't sit well with me. I wanted to get back to Aneera and my training on Shargram.

"Orders, my good man. Things don't always go as planned." Derrik grinned and handed me a piece of taffy. "This will give you the coordinates to Haven."

I sniffed the taffy, slightly baffled. "Taffy? This will give me coordinates?"

Herbert grinned. "At least you get something sweet. I love taffy."

"It's easy enough to use your manna to make some." I moved the colorful taffy around on my palm, poking at it.

"Right. I'm sure it won't take me long to get used to having delicious food at my fingertips." Herbert patted his stomach gleefully.

Derrik directed his attention to Herbert. "If you'll gather your things, we can go."

Herbert eyed Derrik a trifle suspiciously, but began putting things back into his rucksack. While he did that, I stood up. Derrik helped me get my pack on, concern on his face at the pain in my expression.

"You definitely need to get to Haven." He gave me a light, friendly punch on the arm.

"Ouch! Cut it out, tough guy." I feigned injury, but then twisted the wrong way, which really did hurt. "Since you were in Jerusalem and saw Jesus touch down on the Mount of Olives, why don't you describe that to us while Herbert gets ready."

Derrik obliged and described the battle of Armageddon and how the Revelation 19 sword had come out of Jesus' mouth to deal with everyone who came out for battle against him. When he was done recounting everything, he said, "Let's go, Herbert. We'll leave the drama king to make his own way out of here."

Popping the taffy in my mouth, I stuck my hand out to Herbert. "Thanks for your help. I wish I could go with you right now to meet Jesus. I'll see you around sometime."

"My pleasure. Thanks for the manna." Herbert gave me a genuinely happy, crooked grin as he shook my hand. "See you later."

With the coordinates for Haven firmly in mind, Whithorn and the two men immediately disappeared from my view.

This was the first time I had ever been to Haven. It was easy to see the appeal. Multiple waterfalls in sparkling colors within easy walking distance, lush foliage, and cool breezes. It was every vacation I dreamed of combined into one place.

Aneera has got to see this.

I stood on a gravel pathway leading to a building I could see peeking out of the trees ahead. Walking toward the building took effort, but I plowed ahead. My left eye was partially swollen shut, but I could still see well enough.

A beautiful lodge came into view. It was made out of

some kind of golden wood. The front door was open and I heard Tessa's and Jarl's voices engaged in discussion.

Without knocking, I walked inside. I slowly slid my pack off and followed their voices.

"I know we need furniture for the new house," I heard Jarl say, "but I don't think I'm the one to build it." Then, Tessa crooned softly and persuasively, although I didn't hear what she said.

Finally, I found the right room. "What's this I hear about you needing some furniture?"

"Quinn!" Tessa's eyes lit up until she saw my bruises. Then, in concern, she ran over to me and grasped my arm. "What happened to you?"

Jarl walked over to me. I stumbled a bit and he caught me, which jarred my ribs painfully. He called out for Ted and Geneva—the lodge's caretakers—to come check me over. Buster, the resident mop-like dog, joined us.

Within minutes of my arrival, I was whisked into an examining room by Ted, then plied with terrible-tasting healing tea by Geneva. When Ted and Geneva had finished with me, I was quizzed by Tessa and Jarl.

I sank into the loving care, glad that I had come here.

CHAPTER 62

I ended up staying over three weeks on Haven, which was far longer than I expected. I had regretted not being able to take Herbert to meet Jesus on Earth, but I was sure my stay here worked into the larger plan for my life.

Aneera was able to visit for a few days. Everyone, including her, prayed for my ribs and injuries. That, combined with Ted and Geneva's joint efforts in using the healing plants on Haven, eventually got me back into tip-top shape.

Herbert's tale of the Bowl judgments and seeing Jesus return, along with Derrik's description of the battle of Armageddon, kept everyone glued to the edge of their seats as I related the story after dinner one night. Jarl was particularly interested in how the sword came out of Jesus' mouth and decimated the armies that came against him on the plains of Megiddo in Israel.[55]

"Someday...." Jarl's eyes reflected the firelight in the Great Room of the large main lodge. "Someday, I want to see an instant replay of that entire event in heaven."

---

[55] Revelation 19:15-16

Ted chuckled. "I don't want to see only that. I want a holographic, interactive experience of everything from creation onward. I want to see it all." Geneva nodded in agreement.

He makes a good point. Me, too.

While my ribs healed, I helped Jarl and Tessa fill their new home with furniture. I had plenty of practice building wooden things on the farm, although metal was my preferred medium. Tessa was pleased with my efforts, which made me happy.

When Aneera visited, I left off furniture making for Jarl and Tessa and spent my time with her. We explored Haven and got caught up on the training on Shargram, interspersed with kisses and flirting.

I told her what I could about my visit to Earth, leaving out any time-splicing information. I hated doing that and hoped I would someday have the freedom to tell her all about those adventures.

She updated me on how each of the seven Spirits imparted their fire to the students and explained its uses as it related to Universe Healing. I marveled at the colors of fire moving under her skin, as the indigo fire from the Spirit of Knowledge also moved under mine.

Aneera's team had gone through the yellow fire from the Spirit of Understanding, the red fire of the Spirit of the Lord, the green fire from the Spirit of Counsel, and were now in the blue fire of the Spirit of Might. The orange fire of the Spirit of Wisdom, the indigo fire from the Spirit of Knowledge, and the deep purple fire of the Spirit of the Fear of the Lord yet remained for them.

"I never knew Isaiah 11:2 had such practical implications when it mentioned these Spirits of God." Aneera tapped her chin with a finger, musing out loud. "It's astonishing. On the first day, after the yellow fire of the Spirit of Understanding aided the complete cellular regeneration of our two oldest team members—Juan Carlos and Jemeem—I knew we were in for a wild ride. It hasn't disappointed me yet."

I almost slipped and told her about how the Spirit of Knowledge's indigo fire had helped me make King Ahasuerus' scepter, but I caught myself and said instead, "I'm going to have a lot to catch up on. It sounds a little overwhelming."

"I don't think it will be too hard. Once the Spirit imparts his or her fire, it seems to grow inside you and continues to teach." She gave me a reassuring smile and squeezed my hand. "You're a 'smaht coooikie.'" Her attempt at a Welsh accent was endearingly hilarious.

"What in the world is a 'smut cAHkie'?" I was pleased that my ribs had now healed to the point that laughing like this no longer hurt.

She rolled her eyes, giving a disgusted grunt. "Well, if you can't figure it out, you're not as 'smaht' as I thought you were."

Pulling her into a hug, I then tipped her chin up to gaze into her eyes. "I may not be smart, but you love me anyway."

Grinning, she pulled me closer. "Yup, I do."

The waterfall added background music as we kissed.

Jarl, for all his intelligence, was not a hands-on guy when it came to building things. Since I was, I helped design and construct couches, chairs, and other items for the wooden lodge that was being "grown" for them out of Haven's amazing soil. It was close to the main lodge where Ted and Geneva lived, but still far enough away that the newlyweds would have their privacy.

Shortly before I was to head back to Shargram, I discovered that I would be an uncle. That threw me for a loop, but I was thrilled. My last building project for Jarl and Tessa was a cradle to hold the little one when he or she arrived.

Tessa caressed the smooth, honey-colored wood and rocked the finished cradle gently. It glided perfectly. She gave a happy sigh, patting the slight roundness beginning to show in her belly, then looked at me with glistening eyes. "You'll make a great uncle. I'm only sad that you'll be Universe Healing during the first few years of this baby's life. What I wouldn't give for those handy video calls like we used to do."

My heart twisted. "Me, too. I have the sense that I won't be visiting until this is finished."

I would love to be able to come back here and live with Aneera.

"Are you ever going to explain those *very interesting* detailed sketches you did in Petra?" Her eyes were laser-like, trying to peer into my soul.

"Your curiosity will have to wait, sis." I grinned at her. "You'll have plenty to keep you occupied without worrying about my blossoming artistic abilities."

"Not quite what I meant." She gave me a knowing, Mona Lisa smile. "Keep your secrets, then. Just know that you'll have to come clean eventually."

I stooped down to give her a kiss on the cheek. "You'll be one of the first to know all about it, although Aneera may be a little ahead of you in line."

"As long as I get to hear *all* the details." She gave me a hug. "Eventually." She gave me an extra squeeze to emphasize the word.

I hugged her tightly. "All right. Eventually."

CHAPTER 63

Aneera was right. Even though I hadn't been present for nearly a third of the training on Shargram, when I dove back into it—aided by extra tutoring sessions from the Spirits whose training I had missed—I caught up easily.

Getting to know my teammates was more difficult. They had bonded during the time I was gone. Hanging around on the fringes, I definitely felt like an outsider in our class sessions as they played off of memories from each training module or shared inside jokes.

Not very fun, but what did I expect?

I gained some credibility, however, when the Spirit of Wisdom put me on the spot one day during class.

"Quinn, you have now received fire from five of my brethren." At her words, the different colors of Spirit fire played riotously under my skin, causing a most unusual sensation. "What do you think will happen when you receive the last two colors of fire?"

Spirit fire was having a heyday inside me, causing little starbursts of different colors to fan out from each pore on my skin. I could have been a human fireworks show.

My mind flashed to the collection of prisms hanging

from the ceiling in our first classroom with the Spirit of Knowledge. "God is light. In him is no darkness.[56] We will be filled with the brilliant white light of God himself, but be able to call forth the different colors of fire as needed. We will become living prisms."

The Spirit of Wisdom nodded in affirmation. "Correct." All my teammates' eyes were on me again but, this time, I saw respect growing there.

The Spirit continued. "Each of you will be able to diffuse this white light to bring forth what is needed in each Universe Healing situation." Orange fire arose from her hands. "My fire will assist you in knowing what is called for each time." She gazed at me serenly. "Use what you've been given, Quinn, to create something to bless your teammates."

The Spirit of Wisdom waited calmly, fire still rising from her hands.

I extended my hands. A different colored fire blazed from each finger. Indigo, green, red, blue, and orange—each color left my fingers in a distinct arc, wrapping around each other to create an intertwined, multi-colored, multi-limbed tree in the form of how I envisioned the Tree of Life. It hovered in the air at the front of the classroom.

I was forming the branches that would bear fruit when the Spirit of Wisdom sent forth the orange fire from her hands.

Luscious, orange fruit developed on each branch, glowing with fiery light. The fruit was like a cross between a peach and a pear.

The tree, with its laden branches, hung in the air with colors undulating through the branches in a similar way to

---

[56] James 1:17

how they undulated through the many limbs of the Ophenim. The different colors moved up and down each branch in kaleidoscopic wonder while an enticing aroma from the fruit blew around us.

Now that it was completed, the tree gently settled on the ground. "Pick and eat." The Spirit addressed my teammates. Seeing hesitation in their faces, she said, "Don't delay. This will be a blessing to you."

Misha was the first to grab a piece of fruit and bite into it. Orange juice ran down his chin. He closed his eyes in rapture. "I've never tasted anything so delicious." He devoured his fruit in three bites, core and all, and reached for another piece.

Ji Woo, our plump Korean chef, arose rapidly after Misha to get her piece of fruit. Soon, the rest of the team members followed, each exclaiming over the delightful taste and grabbing piece after piece of the fiery fruit.

There were only two or three pieces left on the tree. I had been observing this feeding frenzy, caught up in the team's enjoyment and completely forgetting about having a piece of fruit myself. I noticed Baktygul elbow her husband, Nurbek, and glance at me. Nurbek nodded, picked the last pieces of fruit, and brought them over to me. Placing them in my hands, he smiled and said, "We truly are blessed by your demonstration. Thank you."

I grinned at him, then sniffed a piece of the fruit in my hands. I couldn't think what to compare it to.

Mango-y papaya? Coconutty apricot?

Everyone else was trying to clean up their juice-covered faces, but they stopped when I took my first tentative nibble. Sweet juice burst onto my tongue and slid down my throat. I had never experienced a food item this intensely flavorful.

Good heavens. This is amazing.

Unashamedly, I nearly inhaled the fruit in my hands. We all looked at each other with our juice-stained faces and laughed.

Best team-bonding experience ever.

CHAPTER 64

I lay on my stomach, arms hanging off the edge of the bed while I observed the water creatures swimming across the floor. A sea-turtle, with mottled green markings on its legs, swam languidly by. Two colorful male seahorses sparred with each other close to my doorway, trying to catch the eye of the drab, but cute, female seahorse feeding nearby. Anemones waved in the current with small, brilliant fish darting around them.

This is much better than those computer aquarium screensavers.

Relaxing as I viewed this water-based "floor show," I reviewed the training from the seven Spirits of God. It was hard to believe that we had finished our lessons and would be graduating.

Igniting a fingertip with each color of the fire the Spirits gave us, I speculated on how it would be used in Universe Healing.

Yellow—for the Spirit of Understanding. I understood more than I had but realized how much more I needed to grasp. I sent the yellow fire from my thumb to meld with the orange fire next to it on my index finger.

Orange—for the Spirit of Wisdom. Rightly did she say that her color of fire would infuse every other Spirit's fire to make it properly useful.

Orange and yellow fire combined, then leapt to join with the red on my middle finger.

Red—for the Spirit of the Lord, burning with the fury of his love. For the first time, his fire made me aware of how passionately God loves his people and all of his creation. Why else would he have sent Jesus to purchase its redemption?[57]

The color I could best describe as "rorange" moved from my middle finger to the green fire on my ring finger, combining to create a reddish-brownish color.

Green—for the Spirit of Counsel. How interesting that this combination of colors was so muddy and confused. Good counsel usually helps clear things up instead of making them murkier.

I wasn't sure what I thought of this brownish fire when it leapt onto my pinky finger to meld with the blue fire of the Spirit of Might.

Blue—for the Spirit of Might. The blue, true to its characteristic might, took the lead and created an enthralling deep teal color.

Wow. I like that.

Looking at my other hand, only two colors remained.

Indigo—for the Spirit of Knowledge. I held a deep affection for this fire burning so brightly on the thumb of my right hand, remembering how it had assisted me with King Ahasuerus' scepter and Jarl and Tessa's furniture.

The fire from the pinky of my left hand jumped to the

---

[57] John 3:16

thumb of my right hand, combining to create a dark, bluish-purplish fire flickering there. A sense of anticipation grew behind my breastbone, close to my rapidly beating heart.

Purple—for the Spirit of the Fear of the Lord. Every time I experienced this fire in force, awe at the holiness of God and reverent respect took over everything else.

The colors on my right-hand thumb and index finger combined. We had never done this in our classes, so I wasn't sure what would happen.

Brilliant, blinding white fire filled my room as it leaked out of every pore in my body. I heard all the stories on my walls, ceiling and floor gasp loudly, even though they had been previously muted.

A sensation unlike anything I had ever experienced ripped through me. My whole body was vibrating. My teeth clenched, and my eyes felt five times larger than normal.

All the items in my room took on a golden iridescence and then they started to become transparent. I watched my desk more closely until I could see the empty spaces and the atoms holding all that space together. I saw electrons moving at phenomenal speed, then was astounded to discover I could single out one electron at a time and track its progress. I knew that shouldn't be possible, but I was doing it.

A tearing sound brought my focus to the middle of the room. The air was being divided like a piece of thin fabric being cut by a dull knife.

I peered into a throne room with an immense being seated on a blazing throne. Creatures with several wings were flying overhead. Myriads of beings were stretched out into the distance all around the throne. Music of a kind I had never heard saturated the atmosphere, perfect harmonies blending together.

Getting into a sitting position, I planned to step into that throne room. I *had* to be there. This was where I had wanted to be my entire life, even though I hadn't known that until just this moment.

"You're always welcome here, Quinn," the being on the throne said, "but your visit will need to wait. You're being summoned."

A disappointment so deep I didn't think I would ever recover from it was cruelly dumped over my joy, submerging it. "No, please let me come over there...." I moved forward.

My sentence was cut short by a banging on my door. Harnel burst into the room, quickly taking in the scene in front of him. He bowed before the throne. "Holy One," he said. After his greeting, he stepped between me and the throne room and began to close the torn dimensional veil.

"Wait! Stop!" I ran toward the shrinking opening, trying to get around Harnel. I pulled up short when I saw that he had completed sealing the last inch of the veil.

In my white fire infused state, Harnel was entirely different. He became a creature of vibrating light with distinctly changed, flaming features. And wings. He had wings.

"Quinn." Harnel touched my shoulder gently. "You'll see the Holy One in all his glory soon enough. Now isn't the time. You have your graduation to plan with the rest of your team. Come, we need to go join them."

With a snap, Harnel's touch broke the white fire into its respective seven colors. The room returned to its normal state. The stories on every surface, who had all covered their eyes or heads in order to hide from the blazing brightness of the light, resumed.

How can I possibly plan for anything after experiencing that?

I stood, numb and desolate, in the center of the room. I couldn't imagine moving ever again. Harnel took my arm and led me, dazed, toward the door. "This Universe will become normal to you again and your emotions and thoughts will return to an even keel shortly."

I heard his words, but I didn't believe them.

CHAPTER 65

"What happened to you?" Roger exclaimed. "Your skin is glittering!" My teammates all stared at me when Harnel led me into the meeting room.

"You look like you've had a shock." Gabriella reached out a hand to touch my arm, but then pulled it back like she had been burned. "Or maybe you're giving out shocks. Your skin is full of electricity." Her Spanish accent intensified as she rubbed her palm vigorously.

"Gold is a good conductor of electricity." Dottie peered at my arms and hands. "You're covered in it."

"Quinn got a glimpse of the Holy One's throne room. It was a surprise to him." Harnel nodded at the other angelic trainers. "And it brings up an important topic of discussion."

Burmel, Misha's angelic trainer, came to stand beside Harnel. "Quinn inadvertently discovered today what you will all need to know. When you activate all the colors of fire given to you by the seven Spirits *by yourself*, the white fire of the Holy One will infuse your body."

Elgarn, Tulok's trainer, spoke up. "You all need to be aware that the dimensional veil between this Universe and the Holy One's domain is extraordinarily thin for you at those times."

Fernie asked, "Is it dangerous for us to activate the white fire as we go about Universe Healing?"

Pyrel, Fernie's trainer, addressed all of us. "The only real danger to you if you activate the white fire alone will be the overwhelming desire to be in the Holy One's presence." He smiled at her. "If you follow through on that desire, you are free to be in his presence, but you will die in this Universe and not fulfill the Universe Healing mission assigned to you."

"We will *die*?" Tulok's expression was incredulous. "Just like that?"

Harnel saved my life?

"In this Universe," Pyrel affirmed, "but you will still be eternally alive with the Holy One."

"You would see the Holy One's face, in all his glory," Zimiel, Roger's trainer, said. "No mortal can see his untamed, undimmed glory and live."[58]

Well, this news would have been useful a few minutes ago.

The entire Universe Healing Team grew somber. I was still aching with the desire to be with the Holy One. Every quantum particle in me screamed to be in his presence, saturated in the love and life I had experienced for such a brief time.

Gold flakes fell off my arms and hair, floating to coat the floor around me. A soft groan pushed itself past my lips. Baktygul kept her eye on me with the concern of a kind aunt.

Harnel gave my shoulder a sympathetic squeeze. "Up to this point, you all have seen different facets of the Holy

---

[58] Exodus 33:20

One's loveliness. His magnificence is truly indescribable. We, who have lived in his presence for eons, know only a fraction of what can be known about him. You, as his adopted children through our Master,[59] will need an eternity to know him."

Kre'el, Ji Woo's trainer, said, "As a team, you will be able to access the white fire at any given time. This diffusion amongst your team members is a protective measure for each of you."

The other angelic trainers nodded.

Lemuel, Baktygul and Nurbek's trainer, said, "You, as a team, will practice this briefly now before planning for the graduation ceremony." He gave me a side-glance. "Quinn, you can sit this one out."

I poured myself into a nearby chair, gold dust still drifting around me. I closed my eyes. All I could see in my mind was the being on the throne, clothed in light. True, I didn't see his face. It was hidden in the light. I knew I would have seen it if I'd stepped through the veil.

And, I'd be dead.

At this moment, being with him seemed worth it.

Aneera ran up to me at our table in a cozy, private alcove in the Dining Hall. Her eyes glowed. "We're all set for graduation. Out of our team, I have a feeling that Evan will be winning one of the seven Spirits' awards...."

She looked at me, growing quiet. True to Harnel's word, this Universe was coming back into focus, and my emotions

---

[59] Colossians 1:13-14

were equalizing. Yet, I wasn't quite there at the moment.

"Something happened to you, Quinn." Aneera put a hand over mine. "What was it?" She was distracted by the gold on my skin, rubbing a finger curiously over my arm. "And what is this on your skin?"

"I saw the Holy One." The internal ache had dulled, but wasn't gone. "I almost left to go be with him. These gold flakes were on my skin after I saw him."

"Left? You mean, like, left this life?" Her face paled.

I gave her a barely discernible nod.

"Our team practiced the white fire today." Her hand gripped mine tightly. "Darion warned me about activating it by myself."

I laughed mirthlessly. "I was reviewing each of the Spirits' fires and joining them together in my room. I had no idea what would happen." I drew in a prolonged breath, then slowly exhaled. "Seeing him on his throne was like nothing I could have anticipated."

Shaking my head violently, I freed my hand from her grip and rubbed both hands over my face, trying to force myself back into the present. "I'm sad I can't be with him now. I'm also sad that you and I are on different teams. Seven years of Universe Healing without you seems far too long right now." Blowing out another deep breath, I took her hand once more. "I don't even have a picture of you."

Aneera's quiet sympathy for me gave way to a mischievous smile. "We can fix that. Here, give me your arm."

"What for?" I was nervous. "Does this involve any needles?"

She gave a short, unladylike snort.

That snort may not fly at elegant dinner parties, but I find it charming.

"Don't be a sissy! The Spirit of Knowledge's fire will

help me out." Brushing away the gold flakes, she covered my forearm with her hands while indigo fire played over them. After a couple of minutes, she pulled her hands away.

I discovered that she had burned a perfect, lifelike picture of herself on my arm. It was as beautiful as she was.

Wild love rocketed through me.

The only outward sign of this internal storm was the tear sliding down my cheek.

CHAPTER 66

I watched Aneera track the tear that slowly made its way down my face.

Brushing it away, I gave her a tight smile. "I'm not much of a weeper, but I think this is the best present I've ever received." Another tear followed the first one. I ran my finger over my new tattoo, picking up a few lingering sparkles of gold dust.

"You're more easily satisfied than I am." Aneera's chin sank toward her chest, her eyes sad. "I want the sound of your voice, the feel of your arms around me...."

Instantly, I knew what to do. "Give me your ring." I held my hand out.

With a question in her eyes, Aneera slid the gold band off her ring finger and gave it to me.

The Spirit of Counsel's green fire rose from my hands. I formed the fire into a ball, then continued to compress it down into a square, multi-faceted green jewel. More green fire created the space in the golden band to place the jewel and then secure it.

I handed the revamped ring back to Aneera. "It's my 'counsel' for you. Press the stone."

She put the ring on, then pressed the stone.

I sure hope this works.

A hologram of me appeared in front of Aneera. My likeness stood there and said, "Never forget that I love you, Aneera."

She burst into tears. I wasn't sure if that was good or bad, but I pulled her into a hug. We both needed something to look forward to, so I talked to the top of her head. "This Universe Healing won't last forever, you know." I gave her a squeeze and stroked her hair. "It only feels like it. We'll go explore this healed Universe together when we're done."

"Promise?" she sniffled out in a tear-soaked voice.

"Promise."

I meant it with all my heart.

—⚉—

"Come in, Warven." Shevril pointed to the empty seat at the table where the other members of the Council of 13 sat.

Warven's sharp ears, sticking out of his golden hair, twitched. He sniffed loudly, wrinkling his equally sharp nose at the lingering odor of charred time-worm.

"I haven't made up my mind, you know." Warven's thin, reedy voice held a plaintive note. "The Council of 13 is beginning to get a reputation. I'm not sure I want to be associated with all of you."

Shevril growled, pointing to the empty chair again with a long, black-tipped finger.

Warven sat.

"Now, we come to the business of a replacement tracking device." Shevril addressed the Council, but focused his eyes on Warven. He jutted his chin toward the new Golden One. "This is why our newest *member* has joined us."

Warven curled his upper lip back to reveal sharp, pointed teeth at the word "member." A mutinous expression settled on his face.

"You are a technological expert, aren't you?" Tauren asked Warven. "Didn't Racil consult with you when he made the first tracking device to keep tabs on Quinn?"

Glumly, Warven nodded, his reluctance obvious. "Yes, I helped him draw up the blueprints. It was a brilliant idea, but we were by no means sure it would work, especially across dimensions."

"Which, I'm sure, is why he tested it on us before giving it to Quinn." Jaburn's acidic tone caused Warven to cringe back in his seat. "Was that your idea?"

"At least that helped us determine that it worked properly." Warven's mutinous expression returned. "You should thank me."

"We need you to make another one and set it to specific human DNA." Shevril silenced the table with his demand. "How soon can you get it done?"

"It's a very intricate process…." Warven began.

"How *SOON*?" Shevril thundered.

"Possibly a few days, but I'll need fresh DNA." Warven shifted in his seat, drooping miserably. "I'm still not sure I want to do this."

Chorne stared at Warven, eyes dark and hungry. "I've been wanting to… visit … your lab for some time now. I may do that if you *don't* decide to help us." Chorne's hands began a menacing transformation into sharp claws.

Warven tried to control his distress. He appeared calm, although his reedy voice came out an octave higher. "I didn't say I wouldn't help. How quickly can you get me the DNA?"

"We'll have it soon." Shevril nodded to the other Council members. "It's time to go see some old friends on Shargram."

—ɱ—

Our graduation ceremony was a joyful blur. The Ophenim did a spectacular job of decorating the site in the Banquet Hall. The seven Spirits of God gave out awards to those who they felt excelled in their understanding and application of what was taught.

I was honored, as well as surprised, to receive a ring with a large green stone in it from the Spirit of Counsel. She had encouraged me to continue to listen to her counsel found in the green fire she imparted.

Aneera's and my rings almost match. How cool is that?

Aneera received a bracelet full of magnificent orange jewels from the Spirit of Wisdom. She let me examine it after the ceremony. The golden metalwork was amazingly complex. I enjoyed the sparkle as it radiantly adorned her wrist.

A beautiful addition to an already beautiful woman.

All our Universe Healing Teams gathered outside the Education Center after graduation. Reynel called us to attention. "Now that you've officially graduated, each of you will go with your trainer tomorrow to a practice planet selected especially for you." Reynel's brilliant blue eyes made contact with each of us. "Heal this planet with the tools you have learned during your stay on Shargram. Meet back here tomorrow evening."

I put my arm around Aneera, whispering into her ear, "It's about to get real."

"What do you mean 'about to'?" She stretched up to give me a kiss. "Bet I heal my planet faster than you." She arched an eyebrow, grinning at me.

"You think so?" I gave her hair a gentle tug. "We'll see about that."

Game on!

CHAPTER 67

Harnel and I spacewalked to my specific planet the next morning after breakfast. Aneera had sent me a challenging wink before we left.

When Harnel and I arrived, I was sure he'd made a mistake. The planet was in near total darkness, the surface resting under an atmosphere so thick I wasn't sure light could penetrate it.

Even the lightning in the tumultuous sky was dark. I only recognized a brief shift in the darkness each time it struck, followed by a crackle of electricity on my skin.

I bet everyone else got nicer planets than this one.

"Go ahead, Quinn." I sensed more than saw Harnel's hand gesturing encouragingly at the wrecked planet in front of us.

"Where are we?" I wasn't sure it mattered, but I was curious.

"Rahngara." Harnel's outline nodded. When lightning flashed, I could barely make out a distant look glinting in his eyes, like he was remembering. "It used to be clean and beautiful. A gang of my fallen brethren did their best to kill it."

We need light.

The Spirit of Understanding's yellow fire was what I would use to get started. The fire blazed from my hands and cast light out from us in the size of a football field. It illuminated boggy, impenetrable marshland. I happened to be standing on a small hillock of slightly squishy plant detritus that kept me out of the muck.

Harnel let out a chuckle at my disgusted expression. "The whole planet is in a similar state. The fallen ones destroyed large portions of the double suns that kept the foliage lush, turning the suns into dwarf stars on the smaller side. The only reason this planet isn't frozen is the geothermal activity at the proper distance below the surface to keep things barely alive. The foliage has decayed into what you see, but hasn't entirely disappeared. Very few plant species can function in the limited light."

"Are you telling me I have to heal the suns *and* the planet?" I shook my head despairingly. "Did anyone else get such a tough first assignment?"

"Aren't you glad you're such a good student, even with all the classes you missed? You probably had it better than everyone else because of the special tutoring you received." Harnel grinned at me. "I have confidence in you."

I saw a brief flash of white teeth when he grinned. "Great. I'm glad one of us does." Peering into the sky, I saw the dim glow of the damaged suns. "Well, Jesus is the light of our world,[60] so I'm guessing he can be the light of this one as well."

"This is true." Harnel was thoughtful. "Our Master worked in the power of the Spirit when he walked on Earth

---

[60] John 8:12

as a human before his death and resurrection. You will do the same."

"I need to repair those stars. Do I have to go to them or can I do that from here?" I looked to Harnel for guidance.

"Where is the Spirit of God?" Harnel's stance told me this should be glaringly obvious.

Which it was.

"He's Omnipresent. Everywhere."

Basic "God's Character 101."

"Exactly." Harnel waved his hand again. "Get going."

I joined the red fire of the Spirit of the Lord with the yellow fire burning in my hands, then added the orange fire from the Spirit of Wisdom. The fire dancing on my fingers grew to a crescendo.

My arms started vibrating. Soon, my whole body was shaking. Gathering the lively orange flames together, I compressed them to the size of a tennis ball—not unlike how I had made the stone for Aneera's ring. However, this time I shot the orange fireball at tremendous speed toward the two barely functional stars.

Harnel and I watched the orange fireball divide as it streaked toward its destination. We saw the flash when each fireball impacted its target. At first, nothing seemed to happen.

Did this work or do I have to go back to the drawing board?

Seconds stretched into minutes. After waiting for about fifteen minutes, we saw pinpricks of bright light in the center of each star.

Over the next half-hour, like a flower blossoming on a time-lapse camera, we watched the stars come back to life and expand in size. After an hour, they grew too bright to gaze at directly. Their brilliance and warmth grew to a level that seemed to satisfy Harnel.

"Excellent work. Now, what will you do for this poor planet?" His gaze was encouraging.

"Are there any animals still living here?" This would determine my next steps.

Harnel shook his head sadly. "No, not mammals. They weren't able to adapt and died off centuries ago. I think that it will be possible to transplant some suitable species from similar planets once Rahngara is healed."

With that hopeful idea in mind, I got to work. First, the blue fire from the Spirit of Might and the indigo fire from the Spirit of Knowledge enabled me to atomize multiple centuries of rotten plant carcasses before I terraformed the planet's surface.

Green fire from the Spirit of Counsel tenderly rescued the plant species that still clung tenaciously to life. They were held suspended in the atmosphere all over the planet until I finished preparing the ground.

Once the ground was ready, the plants rushed to their new homes. They quickly covered the rolling surfaces. The planet consisted of large plains with a few scattered forested areas but no mountains. Imbued with new, vibrant life, the plants grew and flowered with astonishing speed.

The purple fire of the Spirit of the Fear of the Lord restructured the atmosphere. I watched as the planet rotated into night. Standing between light and dark, I saw a watery mist rise up and shower the newly productive greenery, providing the perfect amount of moisture.

A picture of insect life grew in my mind. Insects resided in stasis under the planet's surface. They were hibernating until they could be roused to do their jobs again.

Thank you, Spirit of Knowledge, for that tidbit of information.

Tendrils of six of the Spirits' fire were sent to wake them

up. Harnel and I watched as fascinating and bizarre colorful creatures began coming to the surface. A few flew while others scurried around us. Humming, buzzing, and whirring filled the air.

As the tendrils of fire were finishing their work, I stared at them on my fingertips. I was seized with an overpowering desire to join all seven colors of fire once again and be back in the Holy One's throne room. Only one more color was needed.

Harnel saw my struggle. "Quinn, it's not time for that yet. There are things only you can do in the time allotted to the Universe Healers."

Mesmerized by the fire, I wasn't able to look at him. "Are you sure? Are you *absolutely* sure?" Aneera's face flashed in my mind, followed by Tessa's.

Could I leave them now? Could I?

"Yes, I'm sure. Leaving at this time would be premature." Harnel's confident voice helped to break my absorption.

Beating down the churning desire, I retracted the fire on my hands, then purposely shoved them into my jeans pockets. I had read stories of people who had near-death experiences. They had come back from meeting the Holy One with a renewed impetus to fulfill their purpose in life. I wanted to do what I was made for as well, but still, the pull to be immersed in the overwhelming love I had felt was strong.

"There are reasons to stay. You're right." I glanced at Harnel and couldn't help asking, "How do you stand being away from the Holy One after having lived in his presence?"

"I'm not away from him for long periods of time." Harnel smiled down gently at me from his seven-foot height. "I'm often in the throne room, but my purpose is different from yours. Your experiences with dimensional travel will be of another kind than mine."

"Dimensional travel? Really?" I laughed. "That certainly adds a new *dimension* to this job, doesn't it?"

Harnel rolled his eyes and groaned. "Come on, 'punny' boy. Let's go take a final overview of Rahngara's healing before we head back to Shargram. Catch me if you can!" Immediately, he disappeared.

I flung myself into spacewalking mode and followed Harnel's quantum signature as we zipped around the planet.

CHAPTER 68

I was satisfied with the state we were leaving Rahngara in. It might have been my imagination, but I thought I heard musical humming from some of the flowers. I leaned over tall, pink flowers that resembled ears of corn, listening more closely.

"Do you hear anything unusual, Harnel? Like music?" I bent down further to listen to a cluster of yellow tulip-like flowers.

"Certainly." Harnel cocked his head sideways, listening. "Several of the plant species are remembering the songs of their birthplace from the Gardens of Laranda. I believe Jarl told you of his visit to the Gardens in the eighth dimension. The majestic music these plants produce was one of the reasons the fallen ones hated this planet so much. Continuous praise rose to the Holy One. That's why they did all they could to shut it down. You'll find many similar kinds of destruction while out Universe Healing."

Harnel ran a hand over several of the tall, pink blossoms, causing the humming in the air to grow louder. Then, he "played" several of the flowers to create a happy melody.

Hearing this lit a small joy-fire in my heart. While the

warmth spread over me, I realized I needed to let Harnel know something. "I have a confession to make, Harnel."

The tall angel waited for me to go on.

"I've been a reluctant Universe Healer." I shook my head. "I never truly understood why we humans had to be a part of this healing process. I thought God should just 'do it.'"

"Are you still reluctant?" He paused, before playing another tune on the flowers.

"Not as much, even though I still wonder about my ultimate purpose within our team. Everyone else seems to have a specialty they will use during our Quadrant's healing." I shrugged my shoulders. "At least today I get a sense of the joy that comes from this kind of restoration."

"True." Harnel was thoughtful. "The trajectory is reversing."

"What are you talking about?" Sometimes this angel made no sense.

"When the Serpent—also known as Satan—deceived the first man and woman in the first Garden, the trajectory for the Universe was set on a ruinous course." Angry light flashed in Harnel's eyes. "The Holy One had created all things 'good.' The Earth was no exception—an agonizing, slow death spiral began with that first rebellion."

"So, you're saying the trajectory of evil that led to such devastation on the Earth and in the Universe is now reversing?" This was a new thought.

Harnel inclined his head. "Our Master is now ruling on Earth as he should. There is yet a brief period of time at the end of the next thousand years where evil will be allowed free rein, but it will be short-lived."[61] A brilliant smile blazed out from Harnel's suddenly glowing features. "Then... *then* all the healing restoration that has been done will be incorporated and transformed in the new heavens and Earth." He looked me in the eyes. "At that time, Quinn, you will understand fully how important the work that you are doing now has been in the larger picture of things."

My mind jumped to the Shepherd's description of the tapestry and the time-splicing missions I had already completed. The things in the past that had been mended would be a part of the end product as well as the future healing our teams would do.

Fascinating. I'm can't wait to see the final picture.

"We're done here." Harnel ran his hand over the musical flowers once more, releasing a cascade of riotous notes. "Let's head back to Shargram."

I took one final look at the two suns and the warm, humming landscape in front of me before turning my thoughts back to the Wisdom Keeper's planet.

Harnel and I returned to organized chaos.

"What happened here?" I met Harnel's troubled gaze.

"I don't know. I see Reynel over there. I'll be back after I speak to him." Harnel took off to meet with the other angel.

Shargram had been attacked. Holes were blasted in the ground and gardens. Columns from the Information Hall's porch had been pushed out of place and had crashed to the ground. The Education Center was the worse for wear with

---

[61] Revelation 20

blank spots on blackened walls where stories had fled in terror.

Several members from my Universe Healing Team and the other three teams were using Spirit fire to help the Ophenim restore the damage.

I saw Aneera working on re-setting the huge columns on the Information Hall's porch. We had recently viewed the columns before graduation. They had lively stories from before creation until the end of time. We had hoped to get useful glimpses of our future, but what we saw of our future was confusing and inconclusive. Now, however, the columns were blank.

When I reached Aneera, I saw that the stories had re-turned after she reset the columns, but they weren't moving. She sent a blast of fire toward the columns, which shud-dered when it hit them. The stories began moving again like a merry-go-round at a carnival slowly getting up to speed.

"What's going on?" I asked her after a quick hug and kiss.

"Partak said the shields on Shargram were unexpectedly breached by the fallen ones." Aneera's eyes grew dark. "They seemed to want to do the maximum damage possible. I'm sorry to say that your section of the Education Center was hit pretty hard. Darion and I were the first ones back from planet healing, so we've been helping since then. Everyone else pitched in when they returned."

"You *did* make it back before me." I gave her a weak grin. She lightly punched my arm, but there was only a glimmer of a smile on her face.

We walked to the Education Center. The exterior had been repaired, but once we walked in I saw that there was a lot left to do inside.

I was shocked when we got to my room. It looked like a

bomb had gone off, although it wasn't the kind of damage I had expected.

"Someone frisked your room." Aneera walked into the disastrous bedroom. "Unless you're just very, very messy."

"Ha ha." All of my drawers were emptied onto the floor and the contents of my pack were strewn across the overturned bed. "I've never been this messy. It would drive me bonkers."

Aneera and I jumped when a mermaid from the sea-story that had been playing out on my floor, spoke. "They took several of your personal items," she said to me. "They put them in the pillowcase."

"Who? What things? Why?" I was suspicious of any information from a mermaid, even if it was from a story that the Wisdom Keepers archived. Mermaids were hybrids and not to be trusted.

As if reading my mind, the mermaid said, "We're not all bad, you know." She pouted prettily. "We never asked to be made this way."

I nodded noncommittally. "Would you tell me what the people looked like who ransacked my room and what they took?"

The mermaid did a lazy flip in the water-floor. "They were tall and shiny. They seemed especially interested in your comb and a stinky pair of socks." She swam slowly after a sea turtle. "Ta ta. Have to go."

I had a bad feeling about this.

"What were you telling me about the strange visitors you used to have before you met Harnel?" Aneera appeared as uneasy as I felt.

"They called themselves 'Golden Ones.' They said I should get to know them because I was a 'Golden One' too." I remembered the bone-chilling cold and heavy paralysis from their visits. "I'm quite sure they are a type of fallen angel."

"Do you think this was them? Why would they want your comb and socks?" Aneera knelt on the floor and began organizing my scattered things into piles. "Is anything else missing?"

"I have no idea. It doesn't make any sense." I sifted through my things as I knelt beside her. "Oh man! They took my 'Lambs R Us' T-shirt. That was my favorite shirt from the high school agriculture program."

Aneera gave me a sympathetic smirk. "Umm... I know you loved the shirt, but it *was* mostly holes. You know that, right?"

"Beside the point." I huffed. "I don't see anything else missing. Where the heck am I going to get another comb on Shargram? It's not like the Ophenim need them."

"You're in luck. I always carry a couple of extra combs with me. I'm weirdly afraid of being without one." She blushed. "Must be my quirky, feminine vanity."

"Your quirks only make you more adorable." I pulled her in for an extended kiss. She sighed and snuggled closer.

"I'm really going to miss you." Her tremulous smile made me hold her even tighter as I rested my chin on her hair.

"Me, too." A heavy sigh escaped. "You would have thought someone would have figured out intergalactic communications by now."

"No kidding." Aneera slowly extricated herself from my embrace, giving me another lingering kiss. "I'll go get the comb for you. I also think you should talk to Harnel and the Ophenim about this situation."

"We'll go together after I clean things up." I rapidly began reorganizing my pack as she left the room.

CHAPTER 69

Partak fetched Rhondak to join our little huddle. The six of us made a unique group. Reynel and Harnel had listened to me and Aneera describe my room, the missing items, and what the mermaid had said.

Reynel called for Partak, who then got Rhondak, after which I explained the whole situation again to everyone, adding a few extra details.

"It's possible," Rhondak said, tapping a green-tipped limb thoughtfully on the ground. "It's possible that members of the Council of 13 accompanied the attack squad. They may have even been behind the attack."

"Members of the who?" Aneera rubbed an arm absentmindedly, her expression one of concentration.

"You said they presented as shining beings and mentioned being 'Golden Ones' when you ran into them previously." Reynel addressed me. "Is that right?"

I nodded.

Rhondak and Partak held a mentally-veiled conversation for a few moments.

"We think it is the Council of 13." Rhondak flexed several of his limbs with disgust. "They are near the top of

Satan's hierarchy and have, historically, been tasked with extremely strategic jobs. Everything they have done or attempted to do in the past has a deep eternal impact. They are immensely cunning and extremely dangerous."

"I have heard wisps of information about them." Reynel paced, as agitated as I had ever seen him. "Why would they steal things belonging to a human? Why take such insignificant items?" Reynel stopped, his blue eyes piercing me like lasers. "What do they want with you, Quinn?"

"I have no idea. They started to show up at random times after the Shepherd mentioned to me that I was one of his 'Golden Ones.'" My head was spinning. I was remembering the way they had almost derailed two of my time-splicing missions.

Which, of course, I couldn't talk about.

Rhondak sent a startled thought-message into my mind. "The Holy One has come to you as the Shepherd? How often has this happened? This is highly unusual! And extremely rare, although it makes more sense if you indeed are one of his 'Golden Ones.'"

Any lingering doubts are gone. The Shepherd and the Holy One are the same!

All eyes were on me now. "I first met the Shepherd when I was eighteen before I moved from our farm to London. We've seen each other a number of times since then."

"Wait a minute." Aneera gave me a perplexed stare. "I thought Jesus was portrayed as the shepherd[62] in the Bible. Are you saying God the Father has been talking with you in the form of a shepherd? Why?"

---

[62] John 10:11-15

Rhondak made eye contact with all of us simultaneously through his central mass of eyes before he said, "Like Father, like Son."

The staggering implications of this had to sink in. Aneera and I looked at each other in shock before staring at the ground, neither saying a word for a full five minutes. Then, another thought struck me.

Hang on. How did they find me?

The Shepherd had told me about the time-worms, and he had intimated that these Golden Ones were hunting me in order to stop me from carrying out my time-splicing missions. He had never said *how* they were attempting to find me. Things started clicking together in my mind.

"Theoretically, would it be possible to track a human interdimensionally or while spacewalking?" My question hit our group like a missile strike.

All the angels looked at each other while Aneera narrowed her eyes appraisingly. Harnel nodded to himself before pinning me with a stare. "I knew it. You've already been traveling in other ways, haven't you? Beyond regular spacewalking?"

"I'm only asking a question." I lifted my hands in protest.

Aneera gave me a knowing glance. "What he means is that he can 'neither confirm nor deny' interdimensional travel. I think his question is a valid one. Is it possible?" She leaned toward me and whispered, "I've suspected you've been taking some side trips you haven't told me about. Don't worry. You don't have to answer."

Trying to keep the "deer-in-the-headlights" expression out of my eyes, I gave my best neutral smile.

"It is possible." Rhondak moved many of his limbs expressively. "Your essence as a person is retained in your quantum particles, then re-assembled however or wherever you travel."

"Is there a way to know if he's been compromised by some sort of tracking device?" Reynel's gaze was intense. "If he is, this could potentially endanger his entire Universe Healing Team."

What a terrible thought.

The scene that overwhelmed my mind right now was the bug crawling into Neo in the first *Matrix* movie. It turned him into an unwilling spy. Is that what I was?

Desperately, I gripped my hands together. "There has to be a way to find out." I tried to remain calm. "A scan or something like that?"

Rhondak and Partak appeared extremely uncomfortable now. The colors in their limbs undulated faster. Partak finally answered. "There is a scan to check for genetic anomalies, but we've never used it on a human. It has only been used on creatures we've rescued from places the fallen ones have destroyed."

"That's why they wanted the items they took, isn't it? They wanted DNA. Right?" A sick sensation crept over me. "Why else would they take such random things?"

Reynel turned to Rhondak. "Scan him. We have to know before we leave tomorrow."

I swallowed nervously. Aneera reached out and grabbed my hand.

Rhondak bobbed in agreement. "Follow me, Quinn."

Aneera kept a tight grip on my hand. "I'm coming, too."

Harnel gave a slight smile. "Well, why don't we all go?"

Great. We all get to see if I'm a spy.

Gulping in a huge breath, I followed Rhondak toward the Information Hall with Aneera close by my side.

CHAPTER 70

A prickling sensation covered my body. What if this scan found something? How would I deal with that?

Every step toward the huge, carved doorways of the Information Hall with their living, winged creatures filled me with dread.

Aneera kept pace with me. She noticed the tension in my face. Squeezing my hand, she whispered, "Even if they do find something, Quinn, I'm sure they can help get it out of you."

I smiled down at her, grateful for her concern.

Once inside the Hall, we walked past myriads of tall bookshelves filled with scrolls, parchments, and books. Ophenim were busy pulling items or re-shelving them after they checked a glowing monitor at a central desk. They bobbed a greeting as we passed by.

Rhondak led the way down a hallway located at the back of the Hall. Bright, glowing stones were placed inside recesses in the wall. The light illuminated our way clearly.

We came to a thick, metal door. I hadn't seen any metal doors on Shargram, only wooden ones, so this was a surprise. It was plain grey with no living stories. I thought it seemed dead compared to all the other surfaces on the planet that hummed with lively action.

Rhondak opened the door and we all followed him inside. It was a large room, brightly lit with the same kind of stones in the hallway. Some of these stones were also suspended from the ceiling with a springy type of wire that could pull the stone closer in order to inspect an object or creature, whichever the case may be.

Eight metal tables lined the left side of the room, while four chairs in varying degrees of recline lined the right side. Wires attached to machines and monitors stood beside each bed or chair.

The clinic was orderly and silent. There were no other patients. Rhondak flicked a limb toward Partak, who quickly left the room. He returned a few moments later with an Ophen who had limbs that were almost entirely red. The solid color was unusual on a planet full of Ophenim who sported undulating, shifting colors constantly moving through their limbs.

"This is Sarnak." Rhondak introduced the red Ophen. "He is the head of our investigatory clinic."

Sarnak bobbed a greeting. "How may I assist you?"

Reynel explained my situation to him, emphasizing our concern that the recent attack on Shargram may have been designed to gather material from me. "We want to know if Quinn has had anything implanted in him that would give off a locational signal."

I remembered several discussions with Trent back at the machine shop in London on nanobots that could be inhaled. It was possible to have digital information placed in them and extracted at a later date. The person carrying them might be completely oblivious to their existence.

Trent's enthusiasm didn't allow for any downsides but,

with nanobots, this was only one of the reasons I had viewed this and other potentially nefarious technologies with suspicion. Being used without your knowledge or consent to carry information that might be harmful made my blood boil. It still had the same effect on me right now.

Sarnak rolled over to me and led me to a chair that stood in a semi-reclined position. "Lie back, please." He pointed to the chair.

I climbed into the chair and lay back. He attached several nodes with wires protruding from them along the right side of my body. "We've never done one of these scans on a human, partly because so few humans have been to Shargram before your Universe Healing Teams. There has never been a need." He checked to see my reaction, pinning me with several of his eyes.

I shrugged nervously. "Nothing like being a guinea pig. I hope this doesn't involve needles."

Sarnak flicked a limb in response. I heard "It doesn't" in my mind as he plugged in the wire harness that held all the wires attached to me into a nearby machine. "I'm not sure what you'll experience when I turn this on. It is our atomic scanner. It scans your atoms for any anomalies."

"It only scans at the atomic level?" I perceived a problem. "Do you have anything that scans the quantum level? I've been traveling through the quantum realm, so I think scanning at those sizes would be best."

"Unfortunately, we have nothing that precise." Sarnak rolled a few of his eyes. "Those pesky photons in this Universe leave their superimposed states in such a way as to make scanning extremely difficult. We're still working on it."

"Hmm... okay." I hoped this scan would at least give us enough information to discover whether or not I was bugged.

Sarnak hovered a limb over the "on" switch. "Are you ready?"

"I think so." My hands gripped the armrests tightly. I had always hated medical procedures.

"Here we go." Sarnak flipped the switch. A high-pitched buzzing started, sounding like an angry bee colony. Within seconds, I was sure there were bees loose in the room.

They must have been attacking me, because I was on fire.

CHAPTER 71

This fire was nothing like the pleasant, invigorating fire from the seven Spirits. Instead, I felt like a billion bees were stinging me with acidic venom. My teeth clenched. I was sure my grip on the armrests was crushing the metal into the shape of my hands. Fireworks exploded behind my closed eyelids.

Abruptly, the buzzing ceased. A gasp escaped my lips, and I unclenched my hands from the armrests. Every muscle in my body continued to burn with waning fire. Spots flitted in and out of my vision when I opened my eyes.

The angels all waited for Sarnak while he reviewed the data from the scan on the monitor beside my chair. Aneera walked over, brushed the hair out of my eyes where it had landed when my head fell forward during the pain of the test, then put a hand gently over mine. Even though her touch was light, it was like sandpaper on my hyper-sensitive nerves.

Sarnak addressed our minds. "The test is inconclusive. There is a curious blip on one cytosine base in Quinn's DNA, but it is impossible to tell exactly what it is because of its small size. It is not affecting the stability of his atomic structure in any way, whatever it may be."

"Can you determine if it is sending out any kind of signal?" Reynel did not appear happy with this news.

"No." Sarnak met all our eyes with many of his. "It is entirely possible that it is a harmless mutation. I'm sorry I can't offer you more information."

I climbed stiffly out of the chair and rolled my shoulders to work out the knots that had formed from tightening all my muscles. The pain from the test was mostly gone.

Reynel looked at me thoughtfully. "I'm still concerned, Quinn. I will ask for an audience with the Holy One about this. Hopefully we can discuss this with your team tonight."

I jerked my head in acknowledgment, then shook out my arms. They were sore. "What else do you use these tests for? That was pretty awful."

Sarnak gestured to the tables lining the wall. "Occasionally, we will have creatures brought in from planets the fallen ones have sought to destroy. Often, the fallen ones will attempt to tamper with and alter the basic structures or DNA of the creatures. We test for these alterations and repair what we can. Unfortunately, there are times when the damage is too extensive, and the creature dies."

"This is why we are all thrilled about the work the Universe Healing Teams will be doing." Rhondak's limbs undulated faster. "We detest the evil done to the Holy One's creation and long for its restoration."

"We're happy to be part of the process." Aneera answered for us. "Healing is what we want to see happen." Joy filled her eyes. I knew she was exactly where she needed to be. A desire to see healing come to all wounded things was one of her primary driving forces in life.

My driving forces were a little murkier. Being one of the Holy One's "Golden Ones" and being part of dealing with the glory involved in my time-splicing missions took a good chunk of my attention. My focus wasn't solely on Universe Healing, as Aneera's was.

"You are free until our team meetings tonight." Reynel moved toward the door, opening it to usher us out. "I hope to have news from the Holy One by then."

Aneera and I followed the Ophenim out, with Harnel trailing along behind us.

—ɷ—

Fraynt deposited the pile of items at Warven's feet. "There should be plenty of usable DNA from Quinn in here." A malicious smirk played on his perfect lips.

Warven picked up the comb and plucked a black hair out of it, then picked up a holey T-shirt. He took a tentative sniff, wrinkling his nose. "Yes, these are sufficient to get what I need for the new tracking module." His golden face was smooth, betraying no emotion.

"Good." Shevril pierced Warven with an intense stare. "This is your top priority. Our intel makes it clear that the Universe Healing Teams will be deployed tomorrow."

Warven gave Shevril a brusque nod, gathered up the items at his feet, and disappeared.

—ɷ—

After strolling through Shargram's garden paths and talking for hours, Aneera and I arrived at the Dining Hall for our last dinner with all the Quadrant Healing Teams.

Reynel was still gone, so Burmel – Misha's angelic trainer from my Healing Team—led us through sharing our favorite memories from our training time.

Listening to everyone, nostalgia swept over me. Three kinds of longing attacked me from different angles.

I wish Aneera and I could bail on this Healing thing. Why can't we just get married and go live on Haven?

That intense longing was blindsided and wrestled to the ground by the next rush of desire.

Or, why can't I focus on only one thing? Why have time-splicing missions and healing duties at the same time? How do I juggle that?

While I was chewing on that thought in order to get it to let go of me, the next thing grabbed me from behind and got me in a headlock.

What I really want, though, is to ditch all of this—well, not Aneera—and go be with the Holy One right now.

Fending off one longing after the other made it difficult to focus on what people were sharing. I jumped when Aneera stood up next to me to share her favorite memory.

"Watching the years melt off our older teammates, Juan Carlos and Jemeem, on our first day of the Spirit of Understanding's training was completely burned into my brain. Seeing the evidence of quantum regeneration in those few seconds changed my life forever." Aneera sat down after she said this and turned her head to me.

I knew I had that deer-in-the-headlights look again as I stood to share.

CHAPTER 72

"Prisms." The picture of the groupings of suspended prisms in our first classroom rose to mind. "Dividing the white fire of the Holy One into the right color to use in our Healing duties is what has captured my imagination the most during my time on Shargram."

I sat down quickly. What I had said was true, but other memories sprang up. Misha's forceful molding of matter during the Spirit of Might's teaching. Baktygul and Nurbek's gentle enfolding of a distraught Fernie in the comforting red fire of the Spirit of the Lord when a wave of grief unexpectedly crashed over her from a memory of her dead husband.

Remembering these encouraged me. My teammates were uniquely gifted and well-grounded in their own relationships with the Holy One. They wanted to serve him well.

As did I, although I hoped I could carve out a useful place on the team where these pernicious longings wouldn't continue trying to derail my focus.

At the end of our time together as a large group, each Quadrant Healing Team went to different areas for a final briefing before bed.

I gave Aneera a lingering kiss before joining my team. I couldn't allow myself to think of our parting tomorrow.

Misha was our team leader. He stood with his trainer, Burmel, as we all waited expectantly.

"We're ready for this." Misha strode in front of us, his powerful muscles contracting and releasing under his skin. "We may face some resistance from what's left of Satan's forces in the Universe, but I am confident they can be overcome with the tools we now possess."

I found myself agreeing along with my other teammates. Misha continued his encouraging pep talk, casting a vision for us of how quickly we would be able to move through the 2.167 trillion star systems in our Quadrant by utilizing multi-presence.

He was a convincing speaker. I hoped he was absolutely right in his assessment of our potential progress.

Seven years for all this Universe Healing never seemed as long as it does right now.

The time in Texas and Petra had flown because I was with people I enjoyed, loved, and trusted. Even though I was learning to trust my teammates and enjoy them the more I got to know them, my heart would be decidedly elsewhere. Focusing on Aneera's picture tattooed on my arm reached down into my core. I knew I would concentrate on it a lot in the days to come.

Reynel appeared when Misha was winding up his speech. He motioned for me to join him as he stood twenty yards away from our team.

I walked over to meet him. "What's up?"

"The Holy One met with me concerning your situation. He heard my thoughts but only said, 'Quinn poses no threat to the Quadrant 4 Healing Team.' He never answered my question about a tracking device, but what he did say gave me no reason to prevent you leaving with your team in the morning."

"Does that seem strange to you?" I was unsettled. "I mean, how there was no definite answer to why the fake Golden Ones wanted my things?"

"I trust the Holy One's assessment." Reynel gave me a solemn stare. "And so should you."

—⚍—

Morning arrived far too soon. Sleep hadn't come easily.

Why hadn't Reynel received a clearer answer? Was I bugged or not?

After a long, nearly-scalding shower, I returned to my room and finished adding the last few items to my pack. I addressed the stories still playing out on all the flat surfaces. "Thank you for your consideration, entertainment and help." I nodded at the mermaid swimming by on the floor. She gave me a wide smile, showing her wicked fangs clearly. "I'll think of you on my journey."

A chorus of "Bye, Quinn" erupted from all the various story characters.

I hoisted my pack on and waved at them as I walked out the door.

—⚍—

Our breakfast was lavish. The Ophenim had gone to great lengths to make dishes from each nationality represented on the Healing teams. We had a great time sampling the smorgasbord.

"I'm stuffed." Aneera patted her stomach. "How am I

going to have the energy to do any star system healing when all I want to do is take a nap?"

I pulled her close. "I'm sure your love for healing things will kick in as soon as you reach your first planet."

She squeezed me tightly. "Hope you're right." Suddenly serious, she leaned back to look at me. "I'm going to miss you something fierce. Know that I'll think of you and pray for you every single day. Probably more than once or twice, actually."

I leaned down to kiss her. "I'll do the same. Multiple times every single day."

Evan, Aneera's team leader, walked up. He waited until we had untangled ourselves, watching us with a quirky grin. "Time to go, Aneera." He pointed his chin in the direction of the Quadrant 3 Team.

A kiss, an "I love you," and she was gone.

The hole I felt inside my chest told me my heart had gone with her.

PART 3
ADVENTURE LIVING

CHAPTER 73

Our Quadrant 4 Healing Team formed a circle in front of the Education Center. Harnel stood beside me, as all the other trainers did with their respective Healers.

"We're really leaving." Dottie wore a bemused expression. "There were days when I never thought we would reach this point."

Roger threw back his head, long dreadlocks flying with the motion. "Yes!" His fist pumped the air. "We *are* leaving. I'm itching to begin the artistic re-crafting of broken systems."

I liked the idea of employing my artistry, although I was still unsure what niche I was to fill in the team.

Ji Woo chuckled, her belly jiggling. "I think I will be re-making all the food producing systems. Ours will be the best fed Quadrant in the Universe."

I liked that idea, too. We could all find new flavors to incorporate into our manna meals. I grinned down appreciatively at our short, plump chef.

Gabriella twirled, her long skirt swishing around her ankles. "You speak of art or food. What we need is move-ment—motion. The movement of every system must be precisely fitted so that the original dance of the Universe moves in sync with all the other Quadrants."

Tulok beamed at her. "That's what I think, too."

Misha clapped his hands to get our attention. "Reynel has already talked with all the Quadrant team leaders. He has observed the giftings of each team member over the course of our training. We held our final consultation last night to determine everyone's focus or assignment." Burmel nodded beside him in confirmation.

We grew silent, waiting.

"Tulok." Misha addressed the Inuit man. "You are well named 'Warrior of the Stars.' You and Gabriella will be in charge of re-formatting each star system." He grinned at Gabriella, which made her blush. "You get your wish to synchronize all our Quadrant's star systems with the larger turning of the Universe."

Gabriella snapped her fingers and flew into a series of unrestrained spins outside our team circle, her skirt whooshing around her.

Spanish dancing with style.

"You'd never guess she's happy," Fernie muttered under her breath, watching this display. She leaned back to observe my face and winked.

"Nurbek and Baktygul." Misha pointed to the Kyrgyz couple. "You are lovers of flowers and animals. These will be your areas of restoration." The couple nodded with satisfied smiles.

Misha moved on to Ji Woo. "You are definitely the best-suited of our team to deal with all other plant systems. Your skill will bring reclamation infused with love and joy." Ji Woo's eyes nearly disappeared in the crinkles of her face as she smiled widely.

"Fernie." Misha indicated our suntanned Australian. "I

know how precious water and all types of moisture have always been to you. Dealing with any form of water will be your focus."

"Excellent, mate." Fernie cracked her knuckles. "I was born for this."

I was next. Misha checked his notes, then pointed at me. "Quinn, you'll be my assistant team manager."

Assistant manager? That's unexpected.

Misha gave no other information before moving on to Dottie. "Dottie, your precision is needed in re-structuring the interiors of every celestial body we encounter. Illithiel," he glanced at Dottie's trainer, "will show you how to navigate the inside of each object."

Dottie appeared perplexed. "You mean I'll be working from the *inside* of planets or stars? How will I survive that?"

Illithiel answered her. "The same way every Universe Healer survives. You are enfolded in the Holy One's love and will not be negatively affected by the forces in the Universe. This is his provision for all of you in order to fulfill your duties."

Dottie twisted her lips and raised her eyebrows, still perplexed. "If you say so."

Finally, Misha waved his hand toward Roger. "Your many talents will have ample opportunity for exercise. You will be dealing with the surfaces of each planet. Reforming the elements will challenge you sufficiently, I believe. You will also be one of our portal sealers, along with Quinn."

Portals? What portals?

Roger asked that very question. "What portals?"

Zimiel, his trainer, said, "These portals link this Universe with the second heaven, or dimension of my fallen brethren. Not every star system has them but, when we find a portal, we will seal it so that it can no longer be used to access this Universe by these evil forces."

Ah-ha! That must be what the fake Golden One meant when he said I had trapped him after collapsing the time-worm's portal during Abram's rescue. He didn't have another portal immediately available to use.

After our assignments were handed out, Misha bent down to pick up his pack. We followed his lead.

"Let's get this party started!" Roger cinched the waist belt from his pack tightly. "Where to?"

"Meet at the Universe's edge." Misha told us the coordinates, then he and Burmel disappeared.

CHAPTER 74

Working in multi-presence was awkward for me in the beginning. Everyone else seemed to adapt quickly as they rushed through star systems in the thousands, or sometimes millions, of "selves." We were literally blazing through our Healing duties, different colors of Spirit fire flying to bring the necessary regeneration. When we started, I felt like I was all thumbs, big toes and elbows. Nothing went smoothly. I suspected Misha made me assistant manager of the team because he knew I would need help.

"Why is this so hard?" Complaining to Harnel, Misha, and Burmel one morning, I thrust my arms wide to encompass the star system we were to work on. Its delicate spiral arms glowed several hundred light years in front of us in the surrounding darkness. The rest of the team was already busy working, hopping through the quantum realm to each new destination in the system.

For a moment, I had a flash of resentment toward Aneera's seamless spacewalking and healing abilities, but I quickly stomped that thought into oblivion. She was probably having a blast on the Quadrant 3 Team. A pang lurched through me as I thought of her.

Stay in the present. You've got work to do.

"You're doing well, Quinn," the Misha standing closest to me said. "Yesterday, you closed that portal in the purple planet's atmosphere perfectly. The blue fire from the Spirit of Might was a good choice." Several other "Misha's" called out, "Yes, you did."

"The multi-presence is coming easier for you now, too." Harnel patted my shoulder. "You're learning how to avoid any of your 'selves' getting hurt after Roger accidentally hit you with that lump of metal the other day while he was terraforming that heavy metal planet."

I touched the bruise on my side, as did all my other "selves" in the vicinity. "Heavy metal. Ha! I prefer the kind of heavy metal that has awesome guitar licks." The bruise wasn't as painful as it had been yesterday. "What you say is true, but I'm not a natural at this. Am I even helping you?" I looked at the Misha next to me.

"You are." Misha grinned at me, his blue Baryshnikov-type eyes lighting up. His other "selves" gave me a thumbs-up. "You are a great manager of interpersonal relationships. The way you handled that spat between Fernie and Gabriella last night was something I had no clue how to do. Did you see them today? Best buds, working in lockstep."

"Okay. Probably comes from learning to manage my sister's moods." I conceded that as a win. "Guess I'll head out for a little portal hunting now and make myself *more* useful."

Burmel chuckled at Harnel. "Humans. Sometimes I still don't get them."

"Yet, they're so entertaining." Harnel grinned at us all.

Shaking all my heads, my "selves" launched into portal hunting mode and spread out over the star system waiting in the distance.

—⚹—

Harnel shook my shoulder to wake me up. I had been soundly asleep. Yawning, I stretched and sat up. "What did you do that for? That's the best sleep I've had in ages." Rubbing my eyes helped me become slightly more alert. "These floating islands here on Denaltan are better than any waterbed I've ever been on." We had camped on a *Waterworld* type of planet which had innumerable floating islands covered in vegetation.

My teammates were spread over the small island, as peacefully asleep as I had been.

"We need to go see Misha." Harnel stood up. "Come on. He's waiting."

"What for? Couldn't this have waited until morning?" Reluctantly, I crawled out of my sleeping bag and reached for my sweatshirt. Cool wind blew off the water surrounding our island and I was grateful for the comforting warmth.

Misha and Burmel were waiting out of earshot of any team members who might wake up. Stumbling blearily in the dark over the island swells underfoot, I managed to follow Harnel's dimly lit white form over to them.

This is like trying to walk on a big water balloon.

I struggled to keep my eyes open and look at Misha. "Hi. What's going on?"

Misha's Russian accent thickened when he was tired. From the sound of it, he was also barely awake. His hands flickered with low orange light to illuminate our surroundings. "Burmel has received a message to give to you." Misha inclined his head toward the angel, squinting through half-closed lids.

Burmel handed me a folded note that gleamed white in the glow of Misha's hands.

Unfolding the note, I leaned closer to the fire. It read, "Meet me in Petra" and was signed with an "S."

How to explain this?

"I've received an urgent summons to return to Earth." I wasn't sure how much I should say. I hadn't been expecting to dash off for any time-splicing missions during my stint as a Universe Healer.

"We talked about how this might occur at some point." Harnel looked at Misha and Burmel. "Do you remember?"

"You could have told me." Lack of sleep made me grumpy.

"Vaguely." Ignoring me, Misha rubbed a hand over his face as he answered Harnel. "That was several billion galaxies ago."

I was distracted. "Have we really gone through that many star systems already?" Our Healing Team had been moving so efficiently through Quadrant 4 that I shouldn't be surprised.

"Yes, we are in the mid-billions now." The shadows playing on Burmel's face were a little spooky, but his voice was upbeat.

"I don't think I'll be gone for long." I stretched again, popping my back. "I'm sure Harnel will think of something clever to tell the team to explain my absence."

"I'm sure I will." Harnel tapped his forehead with a finger. "I'm also sure Roger will stop grousing about you hogging all the portal closing duties."

Laughing softly, I shrugged. "I would have thought he would be pleased that I let him concentrate on matter transformation on all the planets we've been through. Guess he'll get a good taste of portal closing work and see if he likes it."

Waving to my late-night companions, I left to get dressed and grab my pack for my sudden trip to Petra.

CHAPTER 75

Arriving in the golden light that was always present in the time-splicing gateway room in Petra filled me with happiness. I was more at home here than I was at any time out Universe Healing. In some indefinable way, time-splicing fit me better than Universe Healing, even though I knew I was getting better at the healing work.

I didn't have long to ponder this mystery because the Shepherd walked through the wall. He grabbed me in a hug. "Good to see you, Quinn."

I hugged him back. "I'm glad to see you, and to be here. Can you explain to me why I prefer this over Universe Healing, especially with how nervous I've been in the past over time-splicing missions?" I raised my eyebrows, emphasizing my question. Before he could answer, I threw out, "And what was that crazy 'see you in the throne room' incident on Shargram? You could have warned me about how seeing you like that would affect me and what white fire would do."

"Fathers are always glad to see their children." The Shepherd leaned casually on his staff. "Hasn't it been easier for you to get to know me in this form?"

"Definitely. Seeing you 'high and lifted up'[63] like Isaiah talked about and experiencing how mind-blowingly awesome you are was indescribable, but it would have been impossible to talk with you like we are now." I had to glance away, reliving the intensity of the moment. "Since then, I've often thought that dying would be worth it to be with you in that place."

"It will be beyond 'worth it.'" The Shepherd put a hand on my shoulder. "However, you would have unfinished business if you were there now. I want you to be completely satisfied with your life in this Universe before you are with me in eternity."

"I suppose I want that, too, although my feelings get the better of me sometimes."

The Shepherd released my shoulder and moved toward the gateways. "Trust me, you do." The Shepherd smiled knowingly. "Are you ready for the next 'business' that awaits?"

"Am I?" A blue gateway lit up and began pulsing rhythmically. "I guess I'm about to find out."

Blue glory light was sucked into me when I stepped into the gateway. The glory tried to escape when I emerged. I kept having to shove it down, but I was sure I was glowing blue in splotches where it tried to get out. This was confirmed when I saw the slight blue sheen in patches on my arm underneath the translation-orb bracelet.

Yeeks! This glory has a mind of its own.

---

[63] Isaiah 6:1

Even knowing that part of the reason I was on these time-splicing missions was to learn how to contain the glory and release it at the proper time wasn't helping me at the moment.

Blue glory leaked out of my fingernails. Wisps of it seemed to be coming out of my eyes and nose. My skin was morphing into a sizzling blue, although it wasn't painful.

A little help, please.

My silent prayer was sent out at the same time I realized I was on a boat. A boat in a storm.

Harness the glory, Quinn.

A picture of me harnessing our horse on Granny's farm came to mind. Mentally, I gathered up the blue glory and stuck a halter on it, taking firm hold of the imaginary reins. It balked a little, but began to settle down.

I think this might be more glory than I need for this mission.

After recently enjoying the gentle swells and ripples of the floating island on Denaltan, I wasn't prepared to keep my balance on the violently tossing ship I had landed on.

I clung to the side of the boat with my left hand and to a thick rope in my right. My feet were scrambling, trying to keep me upright, while rain blinded me. Shrieking wind hit me on one side, then circled around to hit me on the other side, driving raindrops into my skin like painful projectiles. My knee-length, rough tunic clung to my drenched body.

Blinking to clear my eyes, I saw a group of frantic men in the middle of the ship's deck in a huddle. They were holding on to anything they could while they cried out to their gods.

"Chemosh, save me. I dedicate my first daughter to your service. Calm this storm!" My translation bracelet buzzed before the man's words were snatched away in the gale.

"Baal, forgive your servants! Have mercy on us!" One

man threw coins over the side of the ship. "Accept my offering, my lord!"

The sea grew worse. Dark clouds sent a fresh burst of rain. Lightning struck the water close to the ship, sending a plume of water forty feet high. The falling water crashed down on all of us. I braced myself for the onslaught, barely able to hold onto the rope with both hands now so as not to be washed overboard.

The men were on their knees, sobbing and screaming.

When I could blink the water out of my stinging eyes, I saw a hatch open. One sailor was dragging a man onto the deck. "Call out to your god, wretch! Maybe he will be able to save us." The sailor shook the man. "Don't you know we are a hair's breadth away from death!"

The man saw the terror-stricken men and the crazed sea. He bowed his head. "It's my fault. I'm a Hebrew, fleeing from my God. Don't you remember that I told you this when I came aboard? You have to throw me into the sea. When you do, the storm will stop."[64]

As frightened as the sailors were, they recoiled at the man's words. The sailor who had brought the man up was distraught. "We can't have your blood on our hands."

"You must." The man was resigned. "Throw me into the sea."

Instead, the sailor—who must have been the captain—ordered his men, "To the oars!"

The men moved as quickly as they could below deck. Peering over the side when I was able to, I saw oars straining against the waves. No headway was made and the storm raged on.

---

[64] Jonah 1

Later, an exhausted sailor made his way up onto the main deck. "It's not working. We're getting nowhere."

No one noticed me at the back of the ship. However, the man who had requested to be thrown overboard suddenly raised his head and locked eyes with me. His brow furrowed, but he said nothing because the captain gripped his shoulders, turning the man to face him.

"May your God forgive us for this." He motioned with his head to three other men. They picked the man's arms and legs up, stumbled to the side of the tossing boat, and hurled him overboard.

Immediately, the storm disappeared. Sun broke through the clouds. The water became flat and calm. This terrified the men even more. They fell to their knees on deck, bowing with their faces down.

Quickly, the captain stood. "Bring grain and wine to offer the God of Jonah. Hurry!" A sailor ran below deck at his command.

Jonah? That was Jonah? Of "Jonah and the whale" fame?

I saw Jonah's head bobbing in the water, getting farther and farther away. I also saw ten—no, fifteen—fins approaching him rapidly from all sides.

I don't think those are part of the "great fish to swallow Jonah" plan.[65]

I knew what I had to do.

The sailors were engrossed in offering a sacrifice to the true God. No one noticed me as I climbed up on the railing and dove into the water.

---

[65] Jonah 1 and 2

CHAPTER 76

I had never been the best swimmer. Most bodies of water in Wales were too cold for swimming unless you were a seal with a nice layer of blubber.

Time for some glory action.

I released a little of my hold on the "reins" of the glory in me. Like a stallion given its head to run, it propelled me through the water toward Jonah. I had to fight to keep my head above water, but the distance between us shrank rapidly.

The fins had almost reached Jonah. I was fairly certain they weren't friendly dolphins who intended to help him out. I had to beat them there.

For a brief moment, I let the reins on the glory go completely. The next thing I knew, I was airborne.

"Whoa! Whooooaaaaaa! Ahhhhhh…."

I imagine being shot through the air like out of a cannon would freak anyone out. Regardless, I was glad no one could see me flailing and yelling as I flew through the air.

Splashing down five feet away from Jonah shocked us both. When I was plunged underwater, I opened my eyes. Before the salt water made me close them again, I saw mermaids and mermen goading large sharks with electric-eel whips.

Bobbing to the surface, gasping for breath, I released more glory to surround Jonah and myself. I watched the sharks smash into the glory-barricade and bounce back.

Spitting water out of my mouth, I yelled, "In Jesus' name, I prophesy to your breath that it be taken away!"

Soon afterward, the fins started meandering around with no particular purpose. The sharks drifted away from us after a few minutes, swimming lazily in different directions.

I flinched as an object thudded against the glory-barricade. A merman's face, dead eyes bulging, floated on top of the water briefly before sinking below the surface.

Hybrids, be gone. Good riddance.

Jonah stared at me. "Who are you? Why is your skin blue? You were glowing blue on the ship…." Treading water and turning in a circle before looking back at me, he said, "Tell me what happened here. Who's Jesus? What was that dead thing?"

"You're going to be okay." I wanted to assure him without going into too much detail. "Your God wants you to know that you will be all right and accomplish the task he gave you." I wiped dripping hair out of my eyes while kicking to stay afloat.

Jonah barked out a harsh laugh. "No, I'm not. I ran away from what my God told me to do. Soon, I will die."

"No, you won't." I tried to reach through his despair. "He is a God of second chances. He loves you…." Before I could go on, water churned beneath us. I was bumped out of the way by the huge jaw of a massive fish.

The swirling water around the fish tumbled me around. I flipped over and over underwater until my lungs burned. The glory-barricade had dissolved when my concentration was broken.

Finally surfacing, I drew in greedy lungfuls of air. When I checked the area around me, I found I was alone.

Jonah had made the rendezvous with his ride back to land before his trek to Nineveh to fulfill God's directive.[66]

—m—

"It's working." Tauren skewered Warven with a look. "It's about time."

Warven's face showed no trace of emotion. His smooth, golden skin remained unwrinkled. "Naturally. What did you expect?"

Jaburn glanced pointedly at Warven's twitching fingers. "Your hands give you away."

Warven's eyes flashed darkly, but he moved his hands under the table.

"I noticed," Shevril said, addressing the Council of 13, "that Quinn's signal appeared *after* it was too late to stop his interference with Jonah. Why do you suppose that is?"

Warven shifted uncomfortably in his chair. "This is the first real-time test with the new device...."

Chorne licked his lips slowly, smiling unpleasantly. "Have you, perhaps, put a delay in the tracking device?"

Warven bared his sharp teeth. "I have done what you asked me to do. Stop these insinuations if you want my continued help."

Gruxen laughed. "This is rich." Pointing at Warven, he said, "Do you actually think this device will help us to intercept Quinn if he finds the Book? We have to anticipate

---

[66] Book of Jonah

him—be one step ahead."

Korfal gave a delicate snort. "How do you propose to do that? We don't predict the future. Our timeline access is limited."

"But couldn't we?" Gruxen motioned expressively to Warven. "Isn't there a moment—a tiny moment—where Quinn releases a signal before he travels to any location or time period? Isn't there?"

Warven was thoughtful for several minutes.

"Well, is there or isn't there?" Prynk's bored voice broke the silence.

"There is." Warven nodded slowly. "But it is nearly infinitesimally small."

"So is Quinn's tracking device." Vander rolled his eyes.

"It's smaller than even that," Warven snapped. "However, Gruxen brings up a possibility I hadn't considered." Warven stood abruptly. "I must run some tests."

Hurrying out, he left the other members of the Council of 13 staring after him.

CHAPTER 77

Floating on my back in the ocean swells, I was ready to go back to the time-splicing gateway room in Petra.

"Helllooooooo. I'm done now. Jonah connected with his fishy Uber ride." Singing the words into the air produced no response.

"Time for me to go baaaaaack...," I sang out again. The sun was setting and the blue glory had dwindled to nearly nothing. My skin was almost its normal shade again, with only tiny blue spots in a few places.

Did I use up too much glory when I rescued Jonah? Am I stuck here?

I was starting to get nervous, not to mention being sunburned and waterlogged after floating for several hours. I really wanted that hot pool in the gateway room right now, and then I wanted to be dry. Very, very dry.

Yet, here I was, still floating.

Are you going to leave me here?

My silent prayer received no immediate response. So, I floated some more.

When the top of the sun was nearly swallowed up by the sea, I heard crackling in the air. The color of the sky changed into a glowing, deep purple. I started treading water again to get a better view.

The purple glow coalesced into a ball and hurled toward me.

Is that my ride? Or something else?

The purple ball slammed into my chest, pushing me underwater. When I emerged, I was still in the ocean.

But it wasn't the same ocean.

—⚍—

"Quinn shifted!" Gruxen stood up, shouting, his calm demeanor gone. "He transitioned through the timeline, as well as spatially, with no warning."

Shevril stood up and grabbed the tracking device from Gruxen. "He's done that before."

"Not like this." Gruxen was flustered. "He has always returned to his present time before moving to a different timeline point. This was a lateral time shift as well as movement to a different physical space."

Shevril frowned. "Inform Warven immediately. This should be part of his calculations."

—⚍—

"Oh no. Not again." The ocean I ended up in was dark, with storm swells surrounding me. Rain pelted my head. "Now, where am I?" I could barely see in the dim light.

Debris floated around me. Pieces of wood in varying sizes blew past.

"Grab one! Grab something that floats!" A man thrashed in the water close to me, futilely grabbing at the wood passing by.

A wooden barrel floated past me. I grabbed the rope tied around the middle of it and swam over to the struggling man. He latched on to the barrel, hoisting himself partially out of the water. He reached out a hand to help me better grip the barrel so we could hold on to our mini-lifeboat.

"Jesus sent you at the right time. My strength was giving out." The partially bald, bearded man grinned at me tiredly.

"Yes, he did." Holding on to the barrel, I saw that my tunic had changed. The material was finer, and there was embroidery around the edges of my sleeves.

"That was an awful shipwreck." The man's conversational tone belied the fact that we were clinging to a barrel for dear life in a wildly stormy sea. "You would think that after going through two other shipwrecks, I would be better at them."[67]

"This is your third shipwreck?" I shook my head. "Maybe you should stick to traveling by land from now on."

"I'd prefer it, but sometimes I have no say in the matter." The man grinned again ruefully. "Right now, we've got it pretty good. The only thing we have to be concerned about is the reef ahead of us. It's in the way of getting safely to shore."

"Reef? What reef?" Anxiety churned with the ocean waves.

If I get out of this, I'm not sure I'll ever want to go swimming again.

"That one." The man indicated a dark mass rising before us in the gloom. The waves were pushing us toward it.

Purple glory pulsed under my fingernails. It was humming and thrumming inside me.

I just didn't know how I should release it.

---

[67] 2 Corinthians 11:23-33

CHAPTER 78

Loud cracking to my right made me swing my head around. I saw a silhouette of the back end of a large ship. The mainsail mast creaked and groaned while we watched it collapse into the sea. The waves continued to pulverize the vessel.

"Where is everyone else?" I had to yell to be heard over the wind. "How did they get to shore?"

"There was more open water when the ship got wedged in the reef, but now the tide is going out. They floated over it, but now the reef is completely exposed, from what I can tell." The man rubbed his face on his sleeve. "It's so hard to see anything in this light."

The cold water was numbing my body. I knew neither of us could stay in it for much longer without hypothermia setting in.

Jonah's ocean had one thing going for it—it was a lot warmer.

The man clinging to the barrel with me slipped, nearly falling back into the water. "I'm so tired." His voice was fading. I grabbed his arm and hoisted him higher up on our little life raft. "I don't think I'm going to make it. That's funny...." The man's speech was getting slurred. "I was sure I had to go stand before Caesar in Rome...."

Definitely hypothermia. We have to get out of here now.

Purple glory crackled up my arms. Judging from what the man had said to me, I was guessing this was the Apostle Paul, and the shipwreck had occurred off the coast of the island of Malta.[68] He did need to get to Rome, but first he needed to get to land.

At that moment, a huge spiked head followed by a sinuous, scaly body reared high out of the water, dwarfing the wrecked ship. Lightning flashed, illuminating long, sharp teeth and malevolent eyes. The creature purposely fell flat and hard into the ocean, making a large wave that jettisoned us out into the angry ocean and away from land.

Clinging to the barrel with one hand and to Paul with the other, I knew I had precious little time to get us out of this mess. Paul was unconscious. I had maneuvered his left arm under the rope around the barrel. My left arm was getting fatigued from holding up his right side.

The sea monster was coming after us, its spiky head making quick progress through the water.

Glory time. Multi-pronged attack!

I wrapped deep purple glory around myself, Paul and the barrel. Before I released the glory to get Paul and me to land, I saw questioning hesitation in the sea monster's eyes. He hadn't been expecting this.

Don't worry, buster. I've saved some glory for you.

---

[68] Acts 26-27

As soon as I set the glory free, I directed a spear of the deep purple light toward the sea monster. I watched it pierce the monster's neck. It let out a deep, bone-shaking howl, which I only heard part of as Paul and I disappeared.

—ɱ—

Sand under my knees. Small waves lapping my feet. A fire in the distance. Wood under my torso.

I blinked blearily. Paul, still unconscious, was attached to the barrel at my left. Everything was cold and stiff. Wiggling my toes took effort. I didn't think I could move.

Footsteps pounded toward us. I heard shouts but wasn't able to respond. After several minutes, hands grabbed me under my armpits. Men got on either side of me, half-carrying and half-dragging me across the beach to the fire. They laid me on the sand close to the blaze.

Struggling to speak, something garbled came out of my mouth like, "Pa… l… nee… elp…."

"We know. He's here. Just be still." A kind, tired voice reached through my mental fog.

Knowing Paul was being attended to let me relax. I slipped into an exhausted sleep.

—ɱ—

Rain was drizzling down on me when I woke up to an overcast morning. By some miracle, the fire next to me was still going. I was wet, but finally warm. Grunting to sit up, then stand, I shook my arms and legs to get the circulation flowing. A series of stretches helped banish the stiffness.

Yup. Done with swimming and, possibly, showers. I'm going to begin sprouting moss if I don't get dried out.

Beaming, my companion from the barrel hurried up to me. "Good, you're awake. The people of this island have brought food and shelter. Follow me." He headed up the beach with a bounce in his step, looking none the worse for having nearly died the day before.

Pleased to see his energetic recovery, I walked behind him to a canopy erected inside the tree line off the beach. Smiling men and women were handing out bread and steaming bowls of soup. I accepted them gratefully.

Only a few times previously in my life had food tasted so good.

CHAPTER 79

"How did you get past the reef?" Paul's curiosity lit up his eyes. "Did you somehow carry us across it?" We had finished our meal and were beginning to dry out under the shelter.

"Yes." I didn't dare say more.

"Well, you're a handy fellow to have around." He laughed heartily. "I'm glad you showed up."

I joined his infectious laughter. "Me too. Happy to be of help." Something caught my attention over his shoulder. Purple light blinked in the depth of the forest.

Finally, my ride—I think.

Paul's laughter subsided. He looked at me with an appraising eye. "The thing is, I don't remember seeing you on the ship."

I stood, not answering, and put a hand on Paul's arm. "You'll do well in Rome. Jesus will be pleased."

"Whether I live or die, all to his glory."[69] Paul smiled, but his tone was serious.

"Exactly." I nodded to him, then went to investigate the

---

[69] Philippians 1:21-22

purple light.

—ɯ—

I walked into the forest until I could no longer hear people talking. The purple light stayed a little ahead of me until we reached the mouth of a small cave where it went inside. Stooping over, I followed it. After twenty feet of walking stooped over, I reached a broader opening. When I straightened up, I was surrounded by the golden light of the Petra cave.

Ahhh. That's a welcome sight.

The Shepherd waited for me. He was at ease, leaning on his staff. My jeans and T-shirt replaced my damp, embroidered tunic. I had never been so thrilled to see them, especially since they were dry.

"Boy, it is nice to be back." I walked over to the Shepherd, exhaling in relief. "What was that double-header time-splicing mission all about? That was a first."

"You were already wet." Amusement filled the Shepherd's eyes. "I figured we might as well accelerate your glory holding and releasing training."

"I feel 'accelerated' and quite content to never pursue any career on or near the ocean." I grimaced. "Terra firma from here on out."

"At least for the present." The Shepherd moved toward the back of the cave. I saw that my latest adventures had been carved into the rock walls surrounding each gateway.

Only one gateway remained.

The Shepherd saw me staring at the last gateway. Pointing with his staff, he glanced sideways at me. Lightning flashed in his grey eyes. "That." He paused. "That last mission is what all this preparation has been about."

"When will I go on that one?" Familiar trepidation began inching up from my toes.

"There won't be any question of when it's time. You'll know. Don't dwell on it, but also, don't hesitate when the time comes." There was a hint of sadness in his eyes.

I was afraid to ask why.

—⟋⟍—

"I've got it." Warven strode confidently into the Council of 13's chamber, holding a new tracking device. He set it on the table in front of Shevril.

Shevril observed him, not saying anything. His long, black fingernails clacked repetitively on the tabletop.

Warven wasn't intimidated. "This will do it. We will be able to anticipate where Quinn goes, which should give us enough time to intercept him."

"All right." Shevril stood up. "Try it." He motioned to Korfal. "Quinn is back in Petra now. Intercept him with a time-worm when he leaves in order to see if this works. Don't engage him in any way. This is merely a test."

Korfal rose unhappily to go and get a time-worm.

"Warven, accompany him." Shevril pointed to Warven, who gave a small smile of acknowledgment. Warven picked up the improved tracking device and followed Korfal.

—⟋⟍—

Drying off with the fluffy towel the Shepherd had provided after washing in the hot pool was a small slice of heaven. I buffed myself dry, feeling like a new man.

The Shepherd sat on his favorite rock near the middle of the gateway room. He was quiet, appearing almost pensive.

Walking over after I dressed, I sat on a nearby rock. I waited for several minutes, saying nothing. Eventually, I couldn't stay silent. "Can I ask what's made you so quiet?"

Am I even allowed to ask that?

The Shepherd looked at me, then answered my thought—not the verbal question I had asked. "You are allowed to ask me any question you want to, at any time. However, I reserve the right not to answer."

"Fair enough." I lapsed into silence.

After a few more quiet moments, the Shepherd seemed to make a decision. "You won't see me in this form again, Quinn." He nodded to himself, then turned to me. "But, you won't need to. I am always available when you call, even if it doesn't appear that I answer as quickly as you'd like."

He was holding something back. I could feel it.

The Shepherd tamped his staff on the ground. "Well, you have Universe Healing to get back to. I'm pleased with how you've done during these time-splicing exercises." He smiled over at me. "You've learned to release the glory well."

I was puzzled. "I'm surprised there haven't been more missions. Time has only been messed with by the fallen ones in these few instances?"

"Absolutely not. There have been hundreds of thousands of severed time strands across the ages. Satan has continually tried to derail my plans." The Shepherd blew out a "phhfffttt" sound, as if I couldn't have said anything sillier. "Do you think you're my only time-splicer? I saved the weightier missions for you in preparation for what you'll have the opportunity to do soon."

Wonderful. The "opportunity," he says.

The Shepherd stood, grey eyes twinkling, and waved for me to get going. "Enjoy your Universe Healing. It gives me enormous pleasure to see things restored this way."

"I won't see you again until I'm in eternity?" I had to know.

"Oh, you'll see me. It's impossible to explain exactly how right now." He waved his hand again. "Off with you."

Drawing in and releasing a deep breath, I stood and put my pack on. I did my best to imprint the picture of the Shepherd on my mind as he stood there. "You're a good 'father to the fatherless',[70] you know. I wouldn't have made it without you."

Strong emotion crossed his face. "That's what I'm here for. A good father loves his child and does whatever he can to set him or her up for success in every area of life." He walked over and hugged me.

I wasn't sure how he did it, but I was always stronger and more confident after those hugs.

Releasing me, he grinned and said, "Now, skedaddle."

"Ski—what? What is that?" This was a new term.

"Leave already." He shook his head, sighing.

I laughed. "Oh. Oh, that. Gotcha." Focusing my thoughts on joining my Healing Team, I skedaddled.

---

[70] Psalm 68:5

CHAPTER 80

I landed back with the Quadrant 4 Team while they were in the middle of a dance fest in a wide clearing. We were on a planet with odd-looking, tall hollow trees with holes. They acted like giant, vertical flutes. When the wind blew, it created an orchestra of sound. As I arrived, the wind had been blowing in short bursts, creating a lively rhythm.

The angels tapped their feet. A few were clapping as the entire team danced with abandon. Gabriella and Tulok were the most visually appealing to watch, but the joy of the others was catching. Even quiet Dottie and portly Ji Woo were part of the fun, moving in sync with the wind gusts.

Baktygul and Nurbek stepped out with a traditional Kyrgyz-style dance. Roger was in the throes of a dance that belonged in a mosh pit at a rock concert somewhere. Misha and Fernie gyrated with no particular order to their steps.

What the heck. Might as well join them.

I dropped my pack and went into a loosely-organized form of country line-dancing, complete with a few "yee-haw's."

Welsh country dancing at its finest.

After several more minutes of dancing, the wind—along

with the accompanying music—died down. The dancing came to a halt with everyone flushed and laughing.

"Quinn, you're back!" Noticing me, Misha came over and slapped me on the back. "Welcome. We were celebrating reaching the halfway Healing mark in Quadrant 4."

"Wow. You all have been speeding right along. I didn't think I was gone that long." I nodded hello to everyone.

Fernie came up and gave me a hug. "Missed you, mate. Now, maybe Roger will stop complaining about all the portals he has to seal." She winked at me.

"Now, hang on…." Roger protested.

"And here I thought you *wanted* to be able to have a stint of portal sealing." I chuckled as I walked over and gave him a light punch on the arm.

"Hmmm…." Roger grunted. "I'm all right with you having that particular job back."

"So nice to be appreciated." I raised an eyebrow, grinning wryly.

"Did your… trip… go well?" Baktygul asked, her eyes revealing that she had ideas about what I might have been doing. "Reynel searched for you during a visit he made to us while you were gone. He was checking in on all the teams."

"It was successful." I added nothing more.

Roger sighed dramatically. "Details sealed in the 'Quinn Files,' only to be released at a later date…."

"Heavily redacted, if they are released at all…." I added.

Dottie pointed to the sky. "What's that?"

Everyone turned to look. Black eyes filled with triumph in a golden face peeked out of a rough-edged portal in the sky. I saw a sickly-white time-worm slither back inside the opening.

"We've got you now." The fake Golden One addressed me, smirking wickedly. A hand reached out to pull him back into the portal. Slowly, the face withdrew. As soon as it was gone, the portal snapped shut.

A chill penetrated my bones. I knew what we had all seen didn't bode well for my last glory-absorbing and releasing mission.

"Care to explain?" Misha, shaken, pointed to where the portal had been while pinning me with a stare. "Is this going to be a problem for our team?"

"I don't think so. What you saw—those beings—only seem to want to interfere with a few of the projects I've been given." This explanation rang hollow in my ears.

"I don't like it." Gabriella shuddered dramatically. "How can you be sure?"

"I'm *not* entirely sure." I hated to admit it. "Keeping an eye out for that kind of phenomenon is a good idea."

Harnel added quietly, "Along with keeping an eye out for you in case they come after you."

"I don't think...." I began.

"They've done it before, Quinn." Harnel was serious. "Remember Chloe in Texas? I was keeping tabs on you before you began your Universe Healing training. I know how they have tried to gain access to you."

Exposed, I nodded in agreement. Chloe being a she-cat hybrid had shocked me, scaring me into a deeper awareness of my enemy. As far as I knew, even Harnel wasn't aware of the times I had run into the fake Golden Ones on my time-splicing missions.

I met my team's eyes. "I want to do whatever it takes to get through this Quadrant's healing. At least, to the extent that I'm able to."

Harnel and Misha exchanged glances. "We know." They didn't sound certain, and I didn't know how to reassure them.

CHAPTER 81

Aneera leaned over to give me a kiss. I reached up to play with a few strands of her strawberry-blond hair. I was content, my arm around the girl I loved, relaxing in a bright meadow.

Suddenly, the sunny sky grew dark with ominous clouds. Aneera stared over my shoulder. Fear froze her expression. "Quinn." Her voice quavered. "They're coming."

My shout woke me up. I flailed around in my sleeping bag, frantically seeking the zipper pull. In my panic I couldn't find it, so I crawled out of the bag and stood up in the early dawn light, my shorts and T-shirt soaked with sweat.

Where am I? Where's Aneera? What was that?

Tulok squinted up blearily, startled out of sleep. "What is it, Quinn? What's going on?"

My heart was pounding. I couldn't get a grip on my emotions. I shook my head, not speaking. Fear raged through my mind.

Tulok got out of his sleeping bag and came over to me.

"Are you all right?" I flinched when he touched my shoulder. "Did you have a bad dream or something else?"

"Dream," I mumbled. "Think it was a dream. Not sure." Cool air hitting my sweat-soaked clothing covered me in goosebumps. I shivered.

Tulok bent down, grabbing my water bottle and sweat-shirt. "Here." He thrust them at me.

I slipped the sweatshirt over my head and put it on, then took a sip of water. My heart was returning to a normal rhythm. "Thanks."

The Inuit man kept watching me. "That must have been a doozy of a dream."

I nodded. "It felt like a warning."

"Maybe it was. Talk to Misha and Burmel. They should know." Tulok inclined his head to where Misha was still softly snoring across the clearing.

"I will when they wake up." I headed away from the rest of the sleeping team. "I need to think."

I felt his eyes on my back as I walked away.

Rarely had I ever experienced a dream that left such a visceral reaction. Unlike most of my dreams, this one had clear-cut edges and played out in my mind like a high-definition movie.

The expression in Aneera's eyes when she said, "They're coming," got to me. It terrified me.

Who's coming? The fake Golden Ones or someone else? Why?

Somehow, I was completely certain I was going to find out. Soon. I wanted to go back and finish the dream so I could turn my head and see what she saw. Unfortunately, I was so keyed up that sleeping wasn't an option.

Loneliness engulfed me, emanating out into the cold dawn.

I miss you, Aneera. I wish you were here. You're the only one I want to talk to about this.

A light breeze began blowing, causing the flute-like trees to emit a sweet, haunting melody. It fit my mood.

Eventually, sounds of people stirring in the camp reached me. Mentally shaking myself, I headed back to join them.

—⧓—

"I'm not sure what we can do without more information." Misha pressed his lips together, rubbing his neck with both hands. "Did you have a sense that this involved the team?"

"I don't think it does. Personally, I think it was a warning for me, but Tulok thought I should let you know." I shrugged. "So, I did."

"I'm glad you did." Misha looked at Burmel and Harnel, who stood impassively by. "We'll do our best to stay on the alert for anything strange."

"All right." Assured that I had done what I could to alert everyone, I went to get ready for a full day of galactic Healing.

—⧓—

"It's about time for us to have achieved complete success." Jaburn glanced at Warven, who was seated beside Shevril. "I doubted you could pull it off."

Warven eyed Jaburn coldly. "I know my abilities, whether or not you acknowledge them." His eyes glinted with confidence as he turned back to the members of the Council of 13.

Gruxen laughed. "You have surprised us all, Warven. The proof will still be, however, if we can intercept Quinn when he finds the Book."

Warven stood, his slight stature barely containing his anger at Gruxen's words. "You will. You'll see what I'm capable of." He stalked out without a backward glance, muttering angrily under his breath.

Shevril stood and addressed those left at the Council table. "I am certain now that we will be able to retrieve the Book should Quinn find it, but we need to continue our other attempts to locate it through our network. Keep working on those. I believe, one way or another, we are close to attaining our ultimate prize."

CHAPTER 82

Everything with our Universe Healing proceeded smoothly—even easily—after my troubling dream. The time sped by. We encountered unusual plant and animal species in many of the areas we healed, along with so many different atmospheres I had difficulty keeping track of them all.

Our team often discussed the phenomenon we noticed happening to us. I think Dottie was the first to mention it.

Misha kept track of how long we worked each day. He maintained an even schedule that accomplished a great deal but didn't leave us feeling drained or overly tired. He and Burmel would choose a place for us to stay for a rest of ten to twelve hours. It wasn't always dark, depending on how many suns a planet had or where it was in its rotation. They managed to come up with peaceful places at the right temperatures for us to relax.

There would usually be a form of water where we could get cleaned up. I'd experienced mist baths, sauna caves, huge warm pools, waterfalls, lakes, slippery lava-tube waterslides, and other delightful fare. I had relented on my water-hating stance once I had gotten thoroughly dried out after my two ocean-hopping adventures.

One evening, when we had finished a swim and our manna meal, Dottie brought it up. "Have you noticed that we're expanding?"

Gabriella laughed. "Speak for yourself. My clothes still fit perfectly." She twirled in her gauzy swimsuit cover, long legs flashing in the light. Misha watched appreciatively.

Baktygul chided Gabriella mildly. "I don't think this is what Dottie means."

Gabriella laughed again, asking Dottie, "Please explain what you meant."

"Can't you tell?" Dottie looked at each of us, garnering only quizzical stares. "Every day, we speed through an enormous quantity of star systems in multi-presence, healing them all. Each of us has dealt with the diabolical destruction we've come across at different levels of intensity but still found a way to bring healing. We've healed over 1.5 trillion systems so far, and we remember each individual place we've been and what we've encountered. Our minds have assimilated an amount of information that no humans have probably ever done previously. Our capabilities are expanding."

"Hmmm...." Fernie rubbed an eyebrow contemplatively. "I reckon we are expanding, like you say. I can remember every type of water, sometimes down to each droplet, from all the places we've healed. This isn't normal for me. I used to forget things all the time. It drove my husband batty that I never remembered where I left the truck keys."

"They say humans only use ten percent of their brains." Roger added this tidbit. "Perhaps we are activating the other ninety percent?"

Ji Woo snorted. "I don't think we could deal with all of this information, even with one hundred percent of our brains functioning perfectly. You are forgetting the Spirits' fire."

"That has to be it." Nurbek agreed with Ji Woo. "Maybe the Spirits' fire has not only brought our brains up to one hundred percent for processing information, but it has taken our ability even beyond that so that we can make connections with all the information we get daily. We are diagnosing how to heal places faster."

The debate continued for several hours, with everyone throwing in different ideas, examples, and theories. We would continue coming back to this concept of expansion over and over again, never settling on a definite explanation.

I personally thought it was part of the "enfolding" the Father had given us that let us move through the vastness of space and every system we worked on without harm to our bodies. Why wouldn't this include geopbytes[71] of information?

Whatever the true reason was that made it possible for us to work through this gigantic amount of information, my thoughts always circled back to Aneera.

When Aneera and I are finally together, we won't ever lack for topics of conversation.

—m—

We were a couple of months over the four-year mark of Universe Healing when my world changed.

Our team had bonded to the point where we finally felt like a family of sorts, although not *exactly* like family because I was pretty sure Misha and Gabriella were working into a full-blown romance. I was happy for them but watching

---

[71] Geopbyte – the biggest current measure of digital storage.

them together made me miss Aneera intensely.

Once we had passed the fourth year of our seven-year mission, we had hope that the end was in sight. An undercurrent of excitement permeated our days. We began a countdown of how many systems remained, updating our tally daily.

We hadn't run into any real resistance from Satan's forces still present in the Universe. We continued to seal any portals we came across. Only once had we seen any of the fallen ones, who were trapped once we sealed the portal they had been speeding toward. They fled away from our team when they realized this, and our angelic trainers gave chase. The angels only told us, "You won't have to worry about them anymore" when they came back. We never saw those fallen ones again.

I was following Roger one day, impressed by his terraforming skills on the gooey, thick mud-moss planet we were on when I saw a surprising crystal-blue lake. It was completely out of place in the greyish-greenish landscape around us.

Intrigued, I went to investigate. The water was clear and inviting. I saw rocks on the bottom, the first stones I had observed in this squishy place.

Gazing intently into the water, I watched an object begin to take shape. Inexplicably, my skin began to itch. When I looked at my arms, I saw gold flakes beginning to appear.

A golden book appeared in the water. As it floated there, I heard the same molten-honey voice that was part of my dream at Granny's farm when I was eight years old. "It's time, Quinn, for you to come rescue me."

Without hesitation, I collapsed my multi-presence, reintegrating as I flung myself into the water.

CHAPTER 83

The lake I threw myself into didn't feel like water. It was more like clear glue or pudding. It formed a cocoon around me. As soon as I was fully encased, the clear capsule I was in shot through the bottom of the lake into complete blackness.

—⁂—

"He's on the move!" Tauren held the tracking device up and shouted at the other members of the Council of 13. "This could be what we've been waiting for. It's different this time. He's going through dimensions."

"Warven and Korfal, get ready to go." Shevril nodded at Gruxen. "Gruxen, accompany them. Don't let the tracking device out of your sight." Tauren handed the tracker to Gruxen, who took it and held it tightly.

Shevril stood, pinning each Golden One in turn with his stare. "If this is the Book of Life that Quinn is going after, I want a secondary team to accompany these three. Who will go?"

Jaburn and Draven agreed immediately. Warven cringed

slightly when he saw that Jaburn would be going along. Finally, Chorne agreed to go with the group, although he appeared to have misgivings.

"You know the importance of this Book." Shevril's intensity radiated to each Council member. "We *have* to get it. Our Enemy's plans for eternity—and our eventual judgment—will be completely disrupted when we possess this treasure. All our other avenues to discover it have failed." Shevril's eyes were dark and fathomless. "If you don't retrieve the Book, don't bother coming back."

Chorne and Draven appeared slightly sick at this statement. Gruxen laughed. "Don't worry yourself, Shevril." He oozed confidence. "You'll see that we'll have the Book in our possession soon."

"So you say." Shevril sat back down. "Let's see the results of your words." He nodded for the six Council members to leave.

Korfal left to procure his last two mature time-worms. The other five followed, although Chorne cast a backward glance at the Council's remaining members before slowly trailing the others out the door.

—⚭—

My clear cocoon deposited me with an unusual "blurp." I stood on solid blackness in surrounding blackness. I sensed no movement of time where I stood. I wasn't able to tell if time was moving in slow drips or racing past. Or, if it was moving at all.

A short distance in front of me, a door opened. Honey-golden light poured out of the opening. I was pulled toward it. My nervousness hit proportions I had never experienced the closer I got. When I reached the doorway, I stopped.

What will I find in there, I wonder?

The longer I hesitated, the itchier I became. At first, it felt like an ant crawling on my neck. The sensation of crawling ants increased all over my body until I thought I might go mad.

Lifting a foot, I half-stepped, half-lunged inside the doorway. As soon as I was inside, my itchiness subsided. The door I had passed through snapped shut and seamlessly integrated into the walls.

Pearlescent golden-hued light flowed in waves over the walls. A tall podium stood, sparkling, in the center of the room.

That must have been one huge diamond or crystal to have produced something so large.

When I walked over to the podium, I saw that it came up to the middle of my chest. Taller beings than I was must be the ones who normally stood here.

The Book I had now seen twice sat open on the podium. I hadn't remembered it being so enormous.

What are you... really?

The Book was opened to the last few pages. As my eyes roved over the clear handwriting, I noticed names. Hundreds of names, at a guess, filled one column. Each page held three columns. Judging from the thickness of the Book, it might hold several billion names.

Suddenly, a name was highlighted in gold. I watched as it floated off the page and hovered in front of my eyes.

It said, "Quinn Edward Evans."

My name. Is this truly the Book of Life?[72]

My finger reached out to lightly touch the Book. When

---

[72] Revelation 3:5, 20:15; Luke 10:20; Philippians 4:3

it made tentative contact, the Book exploded into innumerable shards.

Razor-sharp shrapnel pierced my flesh. I had never experienced such vicious pain. I was certain I would bleed to death in moments.

When I checked my chest, expecting to be covered in blood, I saw golden light leaking out of the pinholes punched in me.

I'm like a man-shaped galaxy of stars.

Surmising that I wasn't going to die imminently, I made the mistake of looking up. Millions of needle-sharp pieces of the Book floated in the air. I watched as they turned toward me like heat-seeking missiles.

This can't be good.

There was nowhere to run. I was frozen in terror. In a rush, every piece of the Book sliced into me simultaneously. Golden-white blended fire drenched my body. I was being consumed in the blaze.

All I heard was myself screaming.

CHAPTER 84

I opened my eyes. I was standing before a podium that came halfway up my chest. It had been carved out of some sparkling substance.

A golden book lay open on it, turned to the last few pages. Names filled each page in three neatly-written columns.

I'm experiencing a strange sense of déjà vu. Wasn't I just here?

An urge to pick up the Book filled me. I reached toward it.

Wait! Stop! Didn't this same Book explode all over you a minute ago?

I couldn't stop. The Book had to be in my hands right now. It was only as I picked up the Book that I noticed my skin was golden.

A terrible gnawing sound startled me, causing me to grip the Book tightly to my chest.

This is the Book of Life. I have to rescue it, but how do I get out of here? Where is the glory I'm supposed to release?

Before I managed to formulate a plan, a large hole appeared in the wall opposite the podium. Two medium-sized time-worms slithered out, followed by six tall golden beings. I knew these were the fake Golden Ones who had been hunting for me.

One of the taller beings walked over to me, grinning. If I didn't know what these creatures were, it would have been easy to be taken in by this one's beautiful appearance. "Nice to finally meet you, Quinn. You've led us on a few merry chases."

I squeezed the Book to my chest, desperately trying to focus on somewhere I could spacewalk.

"Gruxen, not here." A thinner, less confident being urged the one in front of me. "We're on the Enemy's ground. Surely his guard will be here at any moment. Let's go to the 5th dimension. It's neutral territory."

"Fine." The tall being gripped my arm. "Surround him. Quickly, so there's no opportunity for escape." The six beings linked arms and encircled me. They emitted a force field that left me immobilized.

"Come on, boys." A golden being with waist-length golden hair motioned to the time-worms. They speedily slid inside the circle. One wrapped around my feet, oozing slime onto my ankles.

I shuddered in revulsion.

The light-filled room that had held the Book vanished. We were in an open plain with large, blue-colored mountains in the distance.

"Perfect." The being who commanded the time-worms pointed at them. "Wait over there, my pets." The time-worms slithered away from us to wait several yards away.

Gruxen grabbed the Book with no prior warning and wrenched it out of my grasp. Pain exploded in my right shoulder and something popped. The other beings chortled in glee.

"You're a poor protector, Quinn." Gruxen laughed. All the other beings joined him. "And the eternity you thought you had to look forward to has just been ripped away from you."

"It's time for the real Golden Ones to order things properly," another being said.

"Well spoken, Jaburn." Gruxen nodded, holding the Book casually under his arm.

"We shouldn't linger." The thin, nervous being kept scanning the horizon. "The sooner we get back with this Book, the better."

"What will we do with him?" One of the beings who hadn't spoken yet came over and gripped my face with his hand, black curved nails digging into my flesh.

"Leave him." Gruxen's voice dripped with disdain. "He's worthless. If our Enemy has any power, he'll probably dispatch him for being such a miserable failure."

"Let's go." The thin one spoke urgently. "I want to get this over with."

"Fine." Gruxen pointed to the others. "We go back as a group."

I watched them gather together. The time-worms congregated around their master. Powerless to do anything but watch, I was blinded by the flash when they left.

Falling to my knees, in physical and emotional agony, I wept great gulping sobs. "Forgive me. I'm so sorry I failed you. So sorry." I wailed into the air, not expecting a reply. I deserved to be abandoned. An eternity was lost because I didn't protect what had been entrusted to me.

All those names. All those people. What would happen to us now?

Falling to the ground, unable to see, I remained weeping in my despair.

CHAPTER 85

"Quinn?" A hand touched my arm. I got on my knees, violently flailing at whatever was near me.

"Get away, you filthy thieves." I swung the arm I could use. The other hung limply at my side. "Did you change your mind and come back to put me out of my misery? I curse you to the pit of hell!"

"Quinn!" Whoever was there yelled at me. "It's Aneera. Your fiancée!"

Aneera's voice finally penetrated my pain. "Is it truly you, Aneera?" I stopped punching the air and, instead, groped for her.

Her hands were warm on my arm, and then she caressed my hair and face. "What happened to you? Can you see me?"

I was completely blind, but that wasn't what bothered me. "I held it in my hands, Aneera. I was going to escape with it...."

"Escape with what?" Aneera gripped my hand tightly. "What are you talking about, love?"

"The Book of Life." I suppressed a sob. "Those evil angels ripped it away from me. They nearly tore my arm off as well."

She ran her hands expertly over my shoulder and upper arm. "Fortunately, they didn't, but your shoulder is dislocated. We have to put it back into place. Lie down for me."

I lay down. She grasped my limp arm with both hands and put a foot gently on my collarbone area. "This is going to hurt." Her voice was full of sympathy.

Nodding, I gritted my teeth. Aneera pulled on my arm with great strength for such a petite woman. There was a soft "pop" and I could feel my arm go back into the socket. I was happy I only let a muffled cry escape instead of the yell I had wanted to release.

Aneera knelt beside me. I sensed her nearness. Wind flowed over my face. She must have been waving a hand in front of me. "Can you see anything? Tell me about your eyes."

Confused images swarmed my brain. The golden Book. A supernova-type explosion. Tall beings. A blinding light. Incredible pain.

What did I see? What did I only hear?

Something unusual was stirring inside me. I had never experienced it before. I faintly heard voices. Thousands of voices, or maybe more.

"The Book was so bright. It was beautiful beyond words." The last hours were a jumble. "It went supernova when I touched it and exploded. I think that's what hurt my eyes." The concept of linear time was fracturing. "Or, the bright light that flashed when the evil Golden Ones left. I'm not sure...."

"How did you even find the Book of Life? Why were you searching for it?" Aneera sounded puzzled.

I explained my dream of the Book of Life as a kid and how, recently, it had called to me from a lake.

"You saw the Book of Life when you were younger?" Her voice held reproach. "Why didn't you tell me?"

I shrugged my shoulders, thankful that they worked. "I thought it was a dream."

"Hmmm… Well, let me pray for your eyes." Her hands covered my eyes as she prayed for my vision to be restored.

When she removed her hands, I could see. Only, I had never seen anything like this.

Aneera was a transparent being of light, shining and so lovely I almost couldn't breathe. I could see her thoughts and emotions. In fact, I could see everything about her. Love, so intense I thought I might die, filled me.

"Thanks." I forced the words out through my overwhelming emotions. "I can see everything clearly now."

—⚶—

Aneera let out a squeak of shock. She was staring at me like she had never seen me before. "You can see me now?"

"Yes. You're luminous, more beautiful than I can possibly describe." I searched for words. "You're glowing in a way I never noticed before."

"Your eyes have changed, Quinn. They're gold. *All* gold—like you swallowed a molten treasure chest full of gold and it filled you up to your eyes." She looked me up and down. "Now that I mention it, *you* are gold. It's a little freaky."

I couldn't understand what she meant. "I can't picture this." I noticed my arm, which was indeed glistening gold.

Aneera was wearing armor, a fact that I only now realized. I remembered Jarl talking about having the armor of

God[73] available in the 5th dimension. She pulled her sword out and held it up. "Here. The reflection from the blade will help you see what I mean."

I peered into the shiny blade, holding back my eyelids and turning my head in different directions. "Sure enough. Golden eyes. That is a little freaky."

When I glanced around, I was astounded. I could see our surroundings. The plains and mountains were obvious. What was amazing was the overlapping layers on top of them. Everywhere I turned, there was another layer—a road into another dimension. They were all over the sky, the air, and the ground.

"Can you see them, Aneera?" I spun in a circle. "They're everywhere. Can you see the lines and read the directions?" Every layer had directions on how to access it. I wanted to go explore them. "There's no end to them." I started moving toward the layer closest to me. "The dimensions. They each have a name and a map to get to them...."

Aneera's hand grabbed mine. "Hold on, handsome. Where do you think you're going?"

I blinked several times. I still saw all the layers, but it wasn't so overwhelming. "This new vision—or whatever it is—will take some getting used to."

---

[73] Ephesians 6:10-18

CHAPTER 86

Aneera was giggling. "I can picture you throwing yourself in the lake. It's rather funny."

The voices inside were getting louder. They were unifying into a single cry.

What's happening to me?

"I feel a life force growing in me, Aneera." My organs began to vibrate. My heart quivered, jumping in my chest. "I think I'm going to have to go."

"Go where? But I just found you! Please don't leave." Aneera's voice carried a tinge of desperation, alarm in her eyes.

The internal voices were reaching a crescendo. "Before time! Before time!" was all I could hear thrumming through my body.

"I don't think I have a choice." The air around me began to liquefy. I ran my hand through it, creating whorls and waves. Light began shooting out of my pores.

Fear and distress filled Aneera's face. "Quinn, what's happening?"

I was dissolving. All I was able to say was, "Never forget that I love you, Aneera."

Then, I was gone.

—⟊—

I was one with the golden light. It had no distinctions or variations. It was only pure, living gold. Somehow, I was still myself even though I was entirely integrated in the light.

An organic knowing presented itself, arriving with no fanfare.

I'm in the 'Before Time,' when time didn't yet exist. This is quite the time-splicing adventure. How can I splice what doesn't exist?

I was saturated with peace, having no concerns. I wasn't waiting for anything to happen. I was happy to simply "be" wherever I was forever.

"I've known you since before the foundation of the world."[74] A voice met me in my contentment. "And now you've finally remembered entirely who you are."

"Shepherd? Is that you?" My question was a combination of emoting and knowing. I was already fully known and was discovering that I knew everything I needed to.

"Yes, Quinn. You are in me, and I am in you."[75]

I knew that.

Humor surrounded and filled me. "You catch on quickly." Silence reigned for a while.

"What were the voices? Where did they go?" I didn't hear them anymore.

"Ah, so you don't know everything." More humor infused me. "The voices are all those I have known before the

---

[74] Ephesians 1:3-8
[75] John 17:22-23

foundation of the world. You, Quinn, became the Book of Life. You hold everyone in the timeless medium of your spirit since the Book of Life exploded."

Wow. That's a lot to process.

Except that I already understood what the Shepherd meant. He, as creator God, had always known how he would keep the Book of Life safe. I had only needed to cooperate.

"I will never lose any who belong to me. You are all eternally mine."[76] His voice again, yet it was a part of me.

"What was the Book the fake Golden Ones took? It appeared exactly the same as the real Book of Life." I was curious, but not troubled. I couldn't feel fearful even if I wanted to.

"A decoy. The Council of 13 will be sorely disappointed when those rebels return with their 'prize.'" I understood his sadness. He grieved over the fake Golden Ones' rebellion but would allow them their choice, as he also did for every human being.

"Shall I be the Book of Life forever?" It was a fascinating idea. I was able to hold all those who belonged to the Shepherd. I was holding them *right now*. Untold billions of souls in worlds upon worlds inside me.

"No, my boy. You still have years' worth of individual life to live in the Universe before all things are made new."[77] I was immersed in love and filled to overflowing. "Now, you will release the glory and the treasure you contain. The Book of Life will be secure with me, and you will return to take your place in a grand party."

---

[76] John 10:27-30
[77] Revelation 21:1-8

A party? Sounds great.

"Couldn't you have kept the Book with you all along? Why did you want me involved?" I thought I should already know this, but I didn't.

"Of course I could have, but you would have missed all the understanding you've gained that will be a part of your eternity. You would also have missed knowing me as Father. Your reluctance to step out in life would have affected how you operate in the eventual 'After Time.' There are some things that can only be learned during a human life before death. You can know me now in ways you will never be able to experience in the perfection you live in after you die."

What he said swirled around inside me, sinking into my comprehension. "Well, thank you then. I wouldn't have traded this for anything."

"Are you ready to release the glory?" He waited patiently.

I opened up my spirit, feeling bright yellow-golden glory rush out of me. Innumerable voices—lives—flowed out. The atmosphere around me grew brighter as each one exited my spirit.

Stationed in light so bright I was surprised it didn't kill me, I saw the Book of Life coalesce into its former shape. Then, it winked out of my vision, no doubt safely stored until it was needed at the Great White Throne judgment[78] when the destinies of all people would be revealed.

---

[78] Revelation 20:11-15

CHAPTER 87

Gruxen strutted into the Council of 13's chamber, holding the stolen Book aloft. "We've returned. Wresting the Book of Life from Quinn was ridiculously easy." The five other Golden Ones following him appeared extremely relieved to be back. Korfal left to return the time-worms to their holding pens.

Shevril rose and went to meet Gruxen. "Let me see the Book." Gruxen handed it to him, smirking. Shevril held the weighty tome carefully, checking the cover before turning it over to examine the back. The intricate, interlocking geometric designs seemed to please him.

"This matches the few pictures we've been able to procure through the ages." Shevril began to smile. "You may have truly succeeded." Chorne and Draven puffed their chests out in pride. Gruxen gave a confident wave of his hand while Jaburn leaned toward the book eagerly. Only Warven seemed uncertain.

"Don't you think it may have been *too* easy?" Warven nervously fidgeted with his fingers. "Quinn put up no real resistance. Did you notice the color of his skin…?"

"Of course it was easy once we found him." Gruxen

looked down his long nose at Warven. "Did you really think a human would be a match for us?"

Warven fell silent but worry continued to crease his brow.

All the other Council members hurried to where Shevril held the Book. Quovern peered at it. "Open it, Shevril. I want to see those who have lost the eternity they thought was secure."

Tauren, Prynk, Gomert, Fraynt, and Vander stood close to Quovern. Korfal came back into the room and stood with the others.

Shevril slid a long, black fingernail under the Book's cover, flipping it open. Each Council member leaned in, jostling each other for the best view.

The first page had three columns of names, starting with Adam.[79] Shevril began to run his finger down the first column, reading out the names. As soon as he touched the page, wisps of smoke began to arise. Everywhere his finger touched blackened and began to spread over the page.

"What is this?" Shevril growled in alarm, pulling his hand back. "What's going on?"

Gruxen tried to slam the Book's cover. "Quick! Close it. Make it stop!"

Shevril jerked away from him. Smoke began to rise faster. Each page began to crinkle and curl, sending up more ribbons of smoke. Shevril took the corner of his golden robe, attempting to smother the Book and stop the burning. His robe and the Book burst into flames.

The Book began sending out shafts of light, skewering each member of the Council of 13. Warven dropped to the

---

[79] Genesis 1-2

floor, scurrying under the table to avoid the light, to no avail. A beam of light speared him through the chest.

Unearthly screams ricocheted through the Council chamber as the light immolated the Council of 13, obliterating them. In moments, silence reigned over the piles of ash on the floor while wisps of smoke continued to rise to the ceiling.

—ᴍ—

A dusky twilight sky and warm air met me when my feet hit the gravel path. The stars were beginning to show in the sky. A sense of peace rested on me, even though I didn't know where I was.

In the distance, I saw what appeared to be a grouping of white tents. Moving toward them, I noticed that everything I saw gave off a level of luminescence, even the gravel crunching under my feet. Some things glowed more brightly than others, but all hummed with a frequency that gave off light in varying colors.

This must be my new sight in action.

I was wearing my jeans and a dress shirt. I had no idea where my pack had disappeared to. Holding my arms in front of me, I could see that my skin was back to its normal shade, although it had a slight sparkle to it in the waning light.

Laughter escaped from the large tent I was walking toward, followed by applause. The tent glowed brightly inside, and had lanterns on both sides of the path leading up to the doorway.

To my surprise, when I reached the glow of the lanterns on the path, the tent flap moved slightly and Harnel slipped out. He came toward me, smiling. He glowed exactly as he had when he kept me from walking into the Father's throne room when I had combined all seven of the Spirits' fire into white fire on Shargram. His wings were tucked neatly behind his back.

"You're right on time, Quinn. Your entrance cue is about to come up." Harnel beckoned me forward.

From 'Before Time' to right on time. Will wonders never cease?

"Right on time for what? Where am I?" I didn't recognize my surroundings.

"Aneera is ready to give her speech. You figure into it." Harnel clapped me on the back. "Come on."

I was thrilled to be able to see Aneera, but I still wanted to know where I was and said so.

"You're in Jerusalem, in Israel, on Earth." Harnel urged me on. "Jesus is presiding over the banquet to celebrate the successful completion of the Universe Healing. All the Quadrant Teams are here. You're the last to arrive."

My stint with the Book of Life took three years in this Universe's time? Certainly didn't seem that long.

I heard Aneera giving a speech when I reached the tent. I hesitated outside the door to listen. She was recalling favorite memories from Universe Healing, then thanked Jesus and her teammates. Aneera ended by saying, "This has been an almost perfect evening. The only thing I find missing is our Quadrant 4 teammate, Quinn."

That must be my cue.

Sure enough, Harnel gave me a push. I lifted the tent flap and went inside. "Did I hear someone say my name?"

Aneera turned. She glowed from within, her stunning beauty taking my breath away. "Quinn!" She ran toward me, her burgundy gown flowing around her. "You're really here!" Tears ran down her face.

I met her, picking her up and twirling her around. The air was filled by a combination of gold dust sparkles falling off me and the healing joy-snow that I had heard Aneera was famous for during the years of Universe Healing. Soon, the interior of the tent was covered in a layer of cool, white fluff with a sprinkling of sparkles.

Jesus was laughing at the head table and—I was later told—started a snowball fight. I was oblivious to it all because I was too busy kissing Aneera.

Our moment was eventually wrecked when we got whapped with a snowball. We joined the fun for a little while, but soon left the gathering to stroll outside under the stars.

We talked for hours, watching the sunrise from a bench that overlooked part of Jerusalem. I was sure happiness was leaking out of my pores along with the gold dust that continuously formed on my skin.

Aneera yawned while looking at me. "I don't want to let you out of my sight." She yawned again. "You're not going to disappear again, are you?" Her eyelids drooped and she laid her head on my shoulder.

Tightening my arm around her, I leaned my head on top of hers. "Nope. I made a promise. You and I have some Universe exploring to do."

"I never forgot, Quinn."

"Never forgot what?" I breathed in the fragrance of her hair, sighing in delight.

She chuckled tiredly, followed by another yawn. "I never forgot that you love me."

With that, my joy was complete.

CHAPTER 88

I met with my Quadrant 4 teammates the day after I crashed the wrap-up banquet. I wanted to apologize for disappearing on them for nearly half of the Universe Healing time.

Misha spoke for the group. "We were upset with you, but then we were concerned that some of the fallen ones had finally captured you." Misha nodded to Roger. "Roger felt especially bad for giving you a hard time when you had to be gone for the first short time you were away before you disappeared entirely."

Roger hung his head. "I thought I had done something or missed someone kidnapping you, especially since you disappeared on the planet I had been working on."

Tulok patted Roger's shoulder kindly. "We were all upset until Reynel came to give us a status report."

"Reynel was quite mysterious." Fernie entered the conversation. "He cryptically said that Aneera had seen you in the 5th dimension, that you were all right, but wouldn't be rejoining the team."

"That's all he told you?" I was shocked. "You had no idea at all of what was going on?"

This was worse than I thought.

They all shook their heads.

"Oh, man." I ran a hand though my hair, sending gold sparkles flying. When I delivered the Book of Life to the Father, he finally released me to talk about my time-splicing adventures. "I am so sorry you weren't given more information. I wasn't allowed to talk about the missions I was being sent on at the time."

"Can you talk about them now?" Ji Woo moved forward, eagerness in her countenance.

"Yes, I can." I grinned at her enthusiasm. "Can you give me a few minutes to go get Aneera? She should hear this, too."

"An hour." Ji Woo smiled excitedly. "Give me an hour. We will have the feast I have been preparing for you all, as I promised when we first began our training. You can tell us then."

Everyone agreed. When we met an hour later, we feasted on the indescribably delicious food Ji Woo had made for us, and I regaled the group with the tales of my adventures.

"All the time we were in Petra and on Shargram, you were flitting off on time-splicing missions?" Aneera accosted me after Ji Woo's feast. "And, you never told me *anything*? I admit, I suspected something unusual was going on when I saw your sketches, but nothing like this...."

I started to speak, but was cut off.

"And another thing." Aneera was on a roll. "If you kept these secrets so well, are you hiding anything else? Are there other things you need to tell me?" She waited, hands on hips, for me to answer.

*That reddish-blond hair **does** indicate a bit of fire under-*

neath.

I grinned at her, even though it was probably the wrong thing to do. "I realize my eyes are a little more normal since my pupils have been restored, but they have been permanently changed." The whites of my eyes were now gold colored, but my pupils were brown again. "Did you know you're all sparkly-colored when you're mad? It's really intriguing."

Aneera huffed and threw up her hands, but I saw a glimmer of a smile. "Are you going to answer the question?"

"You bet. I was commanded not to tell anyone, even you, about my missions. I almost slipped up several times, but managed to bite my tongue." I remembered the intense frustration from those days. "Concerning any other deep, dark secrets—I don't have any. No former girlfriends. No love children. No diabolical deeds—unless you count the time I roped and hog-tied all my neighbor's dairy cows…"

Aneera was laughing. "All right, all right." She reached up to kiss me. "I wanted to make sure before we get married."

Hugging her tightly, I chuckled. "Well, maybe I should ask you the same question." I could feel her shake her head, her hair brushing my chin.

"No secrets on my part. Just a normal, boring girl who has traveled the Universe, helped destroy Satan's kingdom under the sea on Earth, battled mermaids… you know, regular stuff." I heard the humor in her voice.

"Mmmhmmm…. I think we'll have plenty to talk about. One lifetime might not be enough."

She leaned back to look into my eyes. "Probably not. We'll simply have to do our best."

I kissed her long and hard. "We should begin our honeymoon by going to Petra, where I can show you the time-splicing gateway room."

"Wonderful." The glow surrounding her increased, light shining out from her. "That's exactly what I wanted to see."

CHAPTER 89

Romance had blossomed with several Universe Healing Team members. Misha and Gabriella from my Quadrant 4 Team along with Todd and Charis from Aneera's Quadrant 3 Team, wasted no time in getting married after the banquet that concluded the seven years of Universe Healing. They, along with three other couples from the Quadrant 1 and 2 teams, celebrated their nuptials the following week.

Not to be outdone, Aneera and I organized a simple, meaningful ceremony for ourselves. Darion, Aneera's angelic trainer, presided over our wedding. All the attendees from the Universe Healing Teams had to bundle up against the joy-snow blizzard that Aneera produced when Darion declared, "You may now kiss the bride."

Aneera and I wanted a honeymoon with amenities, so after our stopover in Petra, where she "ooohed" and "ahhhed" over the time-splicing stories the Shepherd had etched into the rock walls over the gateways, we spacewalked to a spa planet named Sarntaya in Quadrant 3 that Aneera had helped to heal.

We relaxed under the attentive care we received. Fortunately, I was reunited with my pack in the Petra gateway room and was able to go through my sketchbook with Aneera and explain each mission in greater detail. I also had time to sketch in the final mission of rescuing the Book of Life.

"Look at you." Aneera lounged back against a pile of pillows in our luxurious bed. "I'm going to have to start calling you 'my golden boy.' You've been on quite the journey from ordinary to extraordinary."

"You're a cheeky girl." I stuck my nose snobbishly in the air. "I was always *extraordinary*."

Aneera snorted, then laughed. "Naturally, naturally. However, you weren't golden."

"This is true. I'm a bit of a nightmare for the cleaning staff, spreading gold dust everywhere." I watched a gold flake slide off my arm and flutter to the floor, where it joined numerous others.

"It's a good thing I never cared about dusting." Aneera lifted an eyebrow. "Hope you're not a stickler for a spotless house."

"Nah. Speaking of houses, I was thinking of where we should live. After all, we have a whole Universe out there...." I was gearing myself up to present my "Top 3" list of places to consider living when Aneera stopped me.

"Did you read the note Darion dropped off yesterday?" She pointed at a note in Tessa's handwriting lying on the bedside table. I had completely forgotten about it in all the activities we had been involved in.

Walking over to pick it up, I flipped it open. Apparently, news of our wedding had reached Haven. Tessa chided me for not sending an invitation—or, more accurately—raked me over the proverbial coals. She insisted we come to Haven immediately after our honeymoon to celebrate with everyone there. The last part of the note was the best, however.

Tessa said Ted and Geneva were growing us a house like hers and Jarl's. She described the wonders of Haven and said it would be an ideal "home base" from which to explore.

"They want us to move to Haven." I lifted surprised eyes to Aneera. Haven was at the top of my "Top 3" list. Did this get any better?

From Aneera's expression, it was obvious that this was what she wanted to do. With no further comment, I pulled the "Top 3" list out of my pocket and handed it to her. She unfolded it and burst out laughing, then reached up to pull me down beside her on the bed.

"Haven it is, then." She ruffled my hair.

I ruffled her hair back, which led to wrestling over my "Top 3" list. I finally grabbed it and threw it on the floor.

"But I want to save that for posterity." Aneera tried to crawl after it.

I pulled her back to kiss her. "Posterity can wait."

And it did.

Arriving on the path going up to Ted and Geneva's lodge on Haven, Aneera and I clasped hands and breathed in the cool, scented air. The rainbow waterfalls in the distance sent up plumes of colored mist, which refracted beautifully in the sunlight.

If I was any happier, I knew I would burst.

We walked slowly up the path, taking our time to exclaim over all the birds and flowers. When we got closer to the lodge, we were spotted by a sandy-haired girl who was around six years of age.

"Momma, they're here!" She ran into the open doorway.

Ted and Geneva bustled out onto the porch, looking exactly the same as when I had seen them seven years ago.

I guess you don't age quickly on Haven.

Jarl and Tessa followed. Tessa was holding a dark-haired toddler who was chewing on a finger and holding a stuffed lion in his other hand. He looked exactly like Tessa. The little girl peering around Jarl's legs had more of his features.

A niece and a nephew. Those are good surprises.

Aneera and I walked close to them but stopped a few feet away. Buster, the dog, and a golden retriever sauntered out the door of the lodge, followed by four yipping, playful puppies.

Joy welled up in me. I squeezed Aneera's hand and smiled down into her eyes. "We're home."

She didn't say a word. Her eyes showed me everything I needed to know. Joy-snow began to fall. The pathway and porch were soon covered.

The puppies thought this was the best thing ever. They rolled and tumbled in the unfamiliar white stuff. The little girl ventured out onto the path, spinning around and trying to catch the falling flakes.

Tessa handed the boy to Jarl and flew down the steps to hug us. She flicked a finger over my arm, scattering gold dust, then peered up at the lazily drifting snow. Jarl joined her, giving us one-armed hugs while introducing us to the kids.

"This is Jachin," Jarl said, pointing to the little boy, "and this is Esther." He inclined his head at the little girl dancing in the snow.

Ted and Geneva then rushed to hug us. Geneva began pulling Aneera into the lodge, chattering and wiping away happy tears. Ted pounded my back, bellowing, "It's about time you got here. Geneva's been cooking for two days!

Come on in."

Aneera and I smiled wordlessly at each other and let ourselves be pulled into the warmth of the Great Room in the lodge and our new lives.

ACKNOWLEDGEMENTS

Some books pour out of you in a rush, demanding to be written and plowing over anything that would dare to take precedence over getting the words on paper. Other books have to coaxed into existence, yielding the next few pages only after intense effort. Quantum Spacewalker: Quinn's Quest was one of the latter books. Its existence is beholden to a number of people.

My husband, Tucker, provided time, meals, healthy non-book-obsessive distractions, along with hugs and smooches, to keep me going. I truly couldn't have done this without him.

Several friends kept the writing process going by asking about how Quinn's Quest was progressing. Joye Brenner, Marilyn Stokes, John Stokes, Judi Calhoun and Nancy Huber provided encouragement, beta reading, corrections and suggestions. I appreciate you all!

I also am thankful for the hard work of my editors, Imogen Grace and Belle Manuel. They helped shape this story into a more polished version of the draft they originally received.

And, finally, to you – the reader. You are ultimately what this is all about. Enjoy!

ABOUT THE AUTHOR

Grace S. Grose began learning to read at four years of age and writing not long thereafter. Granted, the writing involved large block letters, some of which were occasionally backward, but the satisfaction of putting pen to paper only increased with time.

Writing throughout her college career played a large part in her becoming Woman of the Year at her graduation from Colorado Christian College, and helped her along in her jobs as a business manager for a small oilfield corporation and a purchaser for a hotel renovation firm. Her life-long love of science fiction wove its way through all aspects of her life, fueling her interest in astronomy, space constructs and quantum physics.

Following people's journeys from "ordinary" to "extraordinary" and breaking down the steps along those paths fascinates her. She is convinced that there are no *regular* human beings; only ones with the seeds of greatness ready to sprout *if* they take the first step on the path to "extraordinary" and keep going.

You can find her at:
Gracesgrose.com
www.facebook.com/gracesgrose or
on Instagram at @quantum_spacewalker

A Sword meant for only One. Will he lose everything he holds dear to deliver it?

Jarl Henderson had a normal, active life until The Disaster. His family, save for his sister, Aneera, was wiped out. As the world moves inexorably toward the revealing of Satan's messiah and the end of the age, Jarl – at Jesus' request – is launched into the quantum realm to travel its pathways and retrieve items vital for Jesus' followers still on Earth.

During his travels he meets shapeshifters, angels, hybrids and demons and has to determine friend from foe. And he meets Tessa, the most beautiful woman he has ever seen. His final task is the most shocking – the retrieval of the Revelation 19 sword that Jesus will use at his return. Will he recover this item necessary for the ending of the age at the risk of ultimate loss for himself and those he loves?

Discover more at tinyurl.com/Jarl-S-Journey